WORST CASE

BECK ANDERSON

Margot + Burke Press
4255 South Eagleson Road
Boise, Idaho 83705

Design by Lindsey Gray
Cover design by Caroline Tse

Library of Congress Cataloging-in-Publication Data is available

ISBN ISBN-13: 978-0-9996851-0-5
ISBN (ebook) ISBN-13: 978-0-9996851-1-2

Dedication

TO THE MOMS.

TABLE OF CONTENTS

CHAPTER ONE
UNDONE

When my mom goes to sleep, she leaves her tennis shoes by the bed—on the floor, with the laces undone. She positions her shoes with the toes facing the bedroom door, and the tongues are pulled out so she can slip her feet in quickly. Lately, she's been trying to buy slides or mules or loafers, which she can slip on without even bending over.

When I was younger, I liked to crawl in under the covers with her at night when it was damp and cold. Mom was usually awake when I got there. Some nights I'd wake up, and she'd be dozing next to my bed in the armchair upholstered with yellow and pink roses, fully dressed, car keys in her hand.

Many mornings when she'd come to the breakfast table in her nightgown, I would spy her jeans poking out from underneath.

At some point after I started going to school with other kids, I realized Mom was different. Other kids' parents didn't sleep in their clothes. They didn't keep watch over their kids in the middle of the night.

I'd love to tell you I didn't care what other people thought of us, but that would be a lie.

I'd also love to tell you I don't care now that I'm older, but that's not particularly true either.

CHAPTER TWO
APRIL FOOL

At first, the ride to Coeur d'Alene didn't seem to be helping Mom. She gripped the steering wheel so tight her hands kept cramping up, and she had to have me hang on to the wheel while she let go, one at a time, to shake them out.

The white Toyota is partly to blame. I don't have a driver's license, but I can tell when the tires are out of alignment. As we drive east from Washington, the whole car shudders, trying to follow the crooked wheels' lead and lunge into the barrow pit.

And the weather isn't cooperating, either. So far we've had snow, rain so hard the wipers on high didn't help, and gusts of wind that almost pushed our car into the eighteen wheelers in the lane next to us.

So it's no surprise that we're both exhausted from the whole ordeal.

But the farther Mom gets from the Pacific Ocean, the farther we drive away from everything I've known for my seventeen years (at least the ones I can remember—I was born in California, but I don't remember living there—I was too young), the more I can see Mom's face softening. Her shoulders relax a bit with each hour.

Now, as we drive across the bridge coming up from the south of town, she smiles. I'm barely awake, but I see the smile start in her eyes.

"Welcome to Coeur d'Alene," she whispers, and to me it seems like a prayer, or a thank you. I don't know why exactly, or who she might be thanking. Maybe it's from her lips to the universe.

It's late on the night of April 15th, and we drive up to a little gray house with the porch light on. I stumble from the car with my backpack and my toothbrush.

"I'll come back for a load of stuff," I tell her over my shoulder. "I just need to go to the bathroom and brush my teeth."

"It'll be fine overnight. This is a safe town."

"How do you know that?"

"Everybody tells me." She goes to the front door and unlocks it with a key that's still attached to a large plastic tag with the address on it.

"You don't know anyone here." I push past her to get to the bathroom.

She calls after me. "Jeanne, the property manager. She said so."

I feel bad for calling her on her choice of words: *everybody*. I turn the light on in the bathroom. It's probably the only bathroom, since the tiny front room has only one hall coming off of it, and I can see the kitchen at the back of the house, and the back door, and I just walked in the front of the house.

It smells clean, though, like bleach, and the mirror in which I'm watching myself brush my teeth has a little hand-painted bird at the top of its white frame. It's a homey kind of touch to me, and maybe, maybe we're here for a while. Maybe this will be our home.

"We'll get something bigger after I save up a bit," Mom says.

She comes in behind me, watches my face in the mirror, rubs my back in between my shoulder blades the way she's always done since I can remember. Nothing feels more like love than a warm palm making lazy circles on your back, smoothing out your T-shirt, counting the knobs of your backbone.

She's still a tiny bit taller than me, her eyes big and blue in a thin face. I'm darker skinned, with thick eyebrows, chocolate brown eyes, and apples of my cheeks that always seem to be blushed. My face is soft and round in browns and pinks, and she's tall and narrow in blues and blonds. I can look at her temples and see the veins there, and sometimes, I can see the beat of her heart, right in the hollows next to her wide eyes and long nose.

I spit in the sink, rinse the toothbrush, and turn around to give my mom a hug.

"Mom, it's great. Let's go to sleep."

She points back to the front room. "I just dragged in the sleeping bags and pillows for now."

I nod, and my head feels heavy on my neck. I have one day, tomorrow, before I start at a new school. In April. As a senior. I try to shake away the dread that sinks its teeth into my spine where my neck meets the top of my back.

The advantage I have is exhaustion. I crawl into the sleeping bag Mom has spread out on the carpeting in the front room. I worry for a moment about bugs or strange smells in the carpet left by some other person who lived here. I hope I can't smell anything.

I reach into the front of my backpack and find my rollerball tube of lavender oil. I glide it over the insides of my wrists and slip it back into the bag.

"I could find the teakettle and teacups in the back of the car and make some chamomile if you want." Mom comes in from the bathroom and sits down on the sleeping bag next to me.

I shake my head. "I'm fine. I'm too tired to wait for the water to boil."

She brushes my bangs out of my eyes and blows me a kiss. "Okay, kiddo. Love you." She gets up and snaps off the light, checks that the front door is locked. She comes back, creeping slowly in the dark, and kneels next to me. She folds her sleeping bag down and crawls inside, rolls over so she's facing away from me.

I close my eyes, feel sleep settling on my tired legs and arms.

"Thank you, Vivi." Mom's voice is soft.

"For what?"

"For coming with me. For doing this."

"Wouldn't want it any other way, Mom. I love you."

She reaches behind her and takes my hand, holds it close to her and kisses the top of it. "I love you up and down, forward—"

"And backward, and always." I finish the sentence, and Mom releases my hand.

"Try to sleep," she says. "When we get up we'll see what we need to get you ready for school."

I try to breathe in deeply and let go of the worry. I think back to rain on the roof of our old house. I breathe in again, and finally, after counting at least twenty deep breaths, I fall asleep.

The light slips between the curtains, and when I open my eyes, I panic for a minute—first lost as to where I am, and then convinced that it's Monday, convinced I need to get up to get to the new school I know nothing about.

Mom offered to homeschool me, since there are literally twenty-six days of school left, but I worry about graduation, and I definitely don't want it to look weird or like I couldn't hack senior year and withdrew at the end, so close to being done.

Plus, I can't stay at home with her all day. I need to be out in the world. We're alike in some ways, but I get claustrophobic. I can't stay in. I have to be out, and I have to be connected to something bigger than myself.

Finally, I remember it's not Monday, it's Sunday. I get up, get dressed, brush my teeth, and put deodorant on.

"I want to be completely unpacked, so you really feel like it's a good start tomorrow morning," Mom says as I come into the kitchen. "No looking for your favorite socks at the crack of dawn, you know? I want it all ready to go."

She's been up a while, I can tell. The coffee pot burbles, and it seems like she's had a pot already.

I don't mention that I don't really have a favorite pair of socks. I'm not opposed to the concept—I'm no killjoy—but I've got no time and no money to spend on goofy footwear.

I shake off what already feels like a bad mood and give Mom a kiss on the cheek. "Morning."

"It shouldn't take too much time, right?" she asks.

I'm not sure why she's trying to convince me.

"There's not much," I respond. "Maybe we can accumulate some more stuff here."

I leave off the part about wishing we were packrats. Just once I wish I could be the kid complaining that my mom and dad have way too much crammed in the garage.

But she's not paying attention to any subtle wishes or slams on my part anyway. She gets up and dumps the rest of her coffee in the sink.

"You ready to unload?"

I'm ready to unload on her for dragging me across a state because she got spooked, and I could tell her I'm pretty sure nothing's coming after us. But I don't. I'm chalking up this souring attitude to a lack of sleep and a change of venue.

Mom stands, looking for her keys, and I watch her smooth the front of her T-shirt. Suddenly I'm so, so sorry that I picked on her, even if it was just in my own mind. She tucks a loose strand of hair behind her ear, and I can see just how tired she is, especially around her eyes. She's worked so hard for so long to keep us safe and clothed and fed and warm.

The least I can do is help her unpack the car.

"Mom, it's not much." I pluck her keys from the

counter by the coffee pot. "Why don't you have another cup of coffee? I'll bring in the first load."

"You don't have to do that, lamb."

"I want to. You drove all night." I tuck the keys in my back pocket and go to get the first pile of things.

I go outside and look at our little car. I wonder how it's going to be this time.

I wish for a time that is long. Longer than the others.

Monday rears its ugly head in the form of my freaky phone alarm: fake birds, who start chirping quietly about five seconds before they get loud, *so* loud.

I sit up with a jerk, try to find where it was I put my phone last night.

I'm still on the floor, though now with an air mattress between me and the hardwood in the bedroom. I hope for a minute that we stay long enough for me to actually have a bed frame. A real mattress. Maybe I'll get a job and earn the money myself.

But when I go away to school, like I want to, then I can stay in a dorm. So maybe I can put up with an air mattress for the end of school and summer.

If I think about it too much, though, I don't want to go away to school. I feel like I'm a traitor. I chicken out, punish myself for thinking of leaving, hyperventilate on really bad days.

I plan to go on a run tomorrow morning. It's late enough in the year that it's light when I wake up, so a run will be good for my brain. My anxious brain.

Today, though, I need to get ready.

Mom offered, when she decided to come here, to give me a ride every morning. But there's a city bus stop not far from the house, and I've already Googled it, so I know I can get to it, get on a city bus, and get to Coeur d'Alene High, home of the Vikings.

I'm sure there's a school bus, but we didn't give the school system enough notice to get themselves organized to pick up a new kid with five weeks left of school.

And Mom doesn't need an extra task in the morning. She's already started to fret about the job she's lined up, as a cashier in the gift shop at the Coeur d'Alene Resort.

Mom has a bachelor's in kinesiology. She has a teaching certificate, too, and she taught PE in an elementary school when I was really little. It's been a long time since she was a PE teacher. A lot of stuff happened before I was old enough to be aware that there was something going on. But she doesn't teach anymore, and she doesn't talk about it.

I finish getting dressed and find Mom at the stove. She's making me eggs.

"You found a pan. Well done." I give her a kiss on the cheek.

"Today only. Tomorrow you have toast like the rest of the peons." She hums a bit. Her mood is light, airy, and her shoulders seem straighter than I've seen them in a while.

"Tomorrow I'm going to try to run."

She turns from the stove to face me. "Good, Vivi, I think you should. It does a body good."

"I'm glad you approve." I plunk my backpack on the ground next to the folding chair and sit at the card table. She sets the eggs in front of me.

I eat and brush off the growing worry. *Reframe it, Vivi,* I tell myself. I think about this house, about the bluebird on the mirror's frame in the bathroom, about the sun shining in the windows.

Fresh starts might be a good thing. Maybe this is ours.

I eat, Mom leaves the kitchen to go get ready for work, and I call a goodbye to her as I walk out the door, reaching for my phone.

"Be careful. Have fun. Meet people!" she yells from the bathroom.

When I get out in the street it's sunny, and the air is fresh, almost a little chilly. But the sun, oh, it's so nice. I love Washington State, but after living there I feel like I've forgotten there's a big ball of gas up in the sky that warms our planet. Spring in Seattle is wet and windy and gray, and it's nice to know that maybe April brings more than showers.

My phone navigates, and I look at the little houses on my street before turning the corner to go up the hill.

I pass the library. That's a place I could apply for work. I like books. I love books. Books love me. I fancy that they do, at least, since every new girl deserves some friends, even if they are made of pulp.

I don't have my earbuds in, because I'm trying to be all smart in a new place and not get jumped my first day out in the world. I become aware of footfalls behind me.

I turn around. Listen, I could spend many minutes imagining terrible serial killers with hooks for hands wielding chainsaws behind me, but part of keeping myself under control is ripping my imagined serial killer Band-Aids off summarily. Cutting to the chase, so to speak, helps to keep me in check.

The person behind me stops short. He looks up, Beats over his ears, big plaid shirt with the collar popped up, like it's really cold out. But his tan legs stick out of khaki shorts and are stuffed into socks and Birkenstocks.

Interesting.

"What?" He flips a Beats over, off of his ear.

I didn't say anything, I don't think. *Geez, maybe I did.* I do that sometimes. "I didn't say anything."

"Oh. I couldn't hear." He grins, points to his ears. "What do you listen to?"

"I couldn't say." I don't want to reveal my musical tastes to a random person. It's the window into the soul.

"Well, I'm currently all over James Blake. With Bon Iver, especially. It's not the newest album, but man, in the morning, it's the perfect start. Definitely." He walks up to my side and points ahead. "Walk to the stop together?"

"The bus stop?" I step a little to one side. He stands next to me as though we're besties.

"Yeah. You're headed to school, right?" He pulls his headphones all the way down, around his neck. I've been upgraded to full attention. "Unless you're an NIC girl. My apologies for insulting you, then."

"No. I'm in high school."

"Sophomore?"

I raise an eyebrow. "You've gone from thinking I might be at the community college to assuming I'm a sophomore?"

"Well, you're new, and I've never seen you before, so

I figure you're just not in the halls when I am. I'm a senior, so you're a sophomore."

"Or, I'm a senior who just moved here from Issaquah."

"Where's that?"

"East of Seattle. Inland a bit."

"Cool. You want to sit together on the bus? I can check your schedule and give you the lowdown. Maybe we have a class together. I could find you at lunch, save you a spot at my table."

I can't help it. I laugh. It's one of my weird, high, kind of snorty, nervous laughs. Not attractive.

"What's the laugh for?" He's kind to call it a laugh and not a pig snort.

"I thought for sure I'd have a tortuous first day—the weird girl moving here at the last minute of senior year."

"There'll probably be tortuous moments. I haven't seen your schedule yet, remember. Plus, I give you no guarantees on the women in my school. I've found most of the senior girls to be pretty insufferable."

"Is that so?"

"Well, you strike me as my type of person, and you and I, we don't gel with a lot of the preppy types."

"Maybe I'm a preppy."

"You'd be preparing to try out for the cheerleading squad—actually, I guess you wouldn't because we're almost out of school—but you'd definitely have a whole lot more makeup on, and I suspect nothing you're currently wearing came from Urban Outfitters or Anthropologie, so you're not a prep."

"Do you really give everybody a label? I don't want a label."

"How about a 'like me' label?"

He smiles at me, and his smile is white, so white in his amber face. He has a golden brown face kind of like mine, and I'm almost startled at the realization. Maybe not the browns and pinks I get from my dad, maybe brown from somewhere else, a different, honey kind of shade, but brown nonetheless. And deepened by time in the sun, I think.

A "like me" label. He doesn't mean because of our skin, does he?

He shakes his head, reading my expression. "I don't mean because of your skin. I'm a little Japanese, a little Canadian, a little Cuban. I don't care what you are."

"My dad's Mexican."

"I wasn't talking about that. I'm talking about the fact that I'm wearing socks from my dad's top drawer that have a hole in the heel, and I don't care. You're wearing a men's belt, and you have a spoon as a bracelet."

He touches me then, right above Great Aunt Agnes's silver spoon that I bent into a bracelet, and that's it. I'm done for. A good-looking guy speaks to me and makes physical contact? In my desperate little brain that's tantamount to a marriage proposal. I know it's time for me to put the brakes on my reaction before I really embarrass myself.

I take a step back. "What's your name, please?"

"Why? Am I in trouble?"

"If we are to wear the same 'like me' label, I should know your name. And I consider you my friend already, so let's just be clear that I'll be clinging to you for the whole of my first day at school, and if you ditch me at lunch, I'll find out where you live and tell your dad you're wearing his socks."

He puts out a hand to shake. "Win. Win Kemper."

"Win?"

"Winchester. Long story."

"Vivi. Vivi Lewis."

"Nice to meet you, Vivi. Now get on the bus. Your brief adventure in the CDA public school system is about to begin. After the bus ride, of course."

My insides feel like warm maple syrup. I don't even know how to react, except to suspect that at any moment I'll wake up and realize I've been knocked cold by the guy on the street I turned around to face.

Win is easy, funny, relaxed, and honestly, he acts like we've been best friends since our moms took us to Hopalong Friends Daycare when we were two.

My mom never took me to daycare. It made her too worried.

On the bus he chats, puts his number in my phone, and looks at my schedule. And he sits close enough to touch elbows.

I feel lightheaded.

"Okay, let's see. Mr. Grazer. He's pretty cool, for a math teacher. Calc, huh?"

"Yeah. Not AP, though."

"So?" He plucks a pack of gum from the pocket of his flannel, offers me a piece.

"I don't know. I just didn't like the stress. No more MIT for me."

"Did you want to go there?"

"Nah. I don't know where I'm going."

"Next year? For college, you don't know where you're going, you mean?"

"Well, yeah." I think about it for a second, and I can't help it. "I don't know where I'm going, at all, in general. I have no direction."

Win smiles again, and he looks up at the ceiling of the school bus, breathes in really deeply. "You and me, sister."

"Another rudderless soul?" That's another reason to be like him. I like adding things to the "like me" list. Already.

"Yeah. Another long story. Except the college part, I'm not so rudderless there." He pulls me up from the seat, as the bus has bumped up against the curb at the high school.

"What do you mean?"

"It's the one thing I do know. I'm headed to UNR. Wolfpack all the way for this guy." He points at himself and blows a bubble with his gum at the same time. He's the opposite of me on this one. I can't walk and chew gum at the same time, much less blow bubbles and point. As I walk down the steps of the bus, I keep my eyes fixed on the yellow line on each black rubber step. I will fall down them if I don't focus.

"Where's that?"

"University Nevada Reno."

"Any reason?"

"Major in atmospheric science. It's a done deal. It's my thing."

"What?" This guy. What a puzzle. How'd we run into each other in this big universe?

"Yeah. I like storms, weather, any kind of natural event. Kind of a master of disaster. Probably a geophysics minor, if O-chem doesn't ruin me in college."

He's walked me to the door of the school and swings it open. Then he steps to one side so I can go in first.

"Thanks."

"For what?"

"You let me go in first."

"My dad would beat me if I went ahead of you. He's kind of a Neanderthal that way, but what can you do? My mom puts up with it."

"They still together?"

"They're insufferably together. I'd never let them know, but I like them 90% of the time."

"Okay. I've got to go find the first class of the rest of my life, or what's left of my high school life. You keep on being unreal."

"I'll meet you in the main hall at lunch time so you can sit with me. I have a couple friends you'll probably be able to stand."

"What about the rest?"

"No, I have, like, two friends. You might think I'm all that, but *weird* tends to be the consensus around here."

"See you."

"Text me if you get lost."

"In a school?"

"You never know."

I hurry through four classes before lunch, head down, eyes averted. My teachers are decent. They don't humiliate me by introducing me to the whole class, but the art teacher pulls a couple girls aside and introduces me. They tolerate me sitting at their table, but one stays on her phone the entire time, even while she works on a pencil drawing of an iguana with the other hand. The other girl stares at me.

"Do you use eyebrow pencil, or are your eyebrows just like that?" she finally asks, when I estimate she's stared at me for about twenty-seven minutes.

"I don't have to fill them in, if that's what you're asking." I feel one of the referenced eyebrows raise up in question, and I try hard to stay expressionless.

"Cool. I kind of pulled out all my eyelashes and eyebrows when I was in eighth grade. I was bored. But they haven't grown back very great."

"That happens. A friend of my mom's lost her eyebrows after she was really sick in the hospital."

"Whoa, really?" She looks impressed. She picks something out of her teeth.

"What's your name again?"

"Phoebe. And you're Vivi? They rhyme."

"Kinda."

The bell rings.

"See you tomorrow, Phoebe."

"Yeah." She's still looking at my eyebrows. She doesn't even make a move to pick up her backpack until I'm almost all the way out of the room.

And Win stands at the door.

"Hey. Vivi."

As if I'm going to walk right by him. As if I'd be able to miss him. He leans a little against the doorframe, and his hair looks like he just ruffled it. The front of it falls a little into his eyes. And the muscles in his neck disappear down into the collar of his sweatshirt, and those muscles are tan and ropy. I look back at his eyes, brown with bits of gold at the rims. I avoid his eyebrows, because no one else should suffer the eyebrow scrutiny I've just experienced.

"Hey."

Phoebe and the girl with the phone molded into her hand walk by, and they stare—not at my eyebrows, but at Win. Win standing with me.

So that part where he said he wasn't liked, or popular, and only had two friends? I think he has no clue. Or he's lying. Because those girls are looking at him like he is as ultra as it gets. They'd eat him for breakfast and lunch and come back for thirds.

We walk to the cafeteria, and I confirm he truly has no clue. Some kids say hi to him, and he says hi back. The big beefy football guys don't, but he takes up just as much space as they do.

The space thing, I've always been fascinated by it. Grown-ups take up a lot of space, most of them. Men. They spread out on bus seats. They take their half of the hallway out of the middle. They stand in a line and take up a doublewide worth of space.

Win does this, but not in a man-spread, irritating way. In a "clear the way, here he comes" kind of way. He is noticed, and people move for him. He doesn't move people. For a while my mom went through a musical phase, and she rented a lot of old musicals from the library on VHS. In musicals, the main character can walk all through town, and everyone clears a path for her. Judy Garland in *Meet Me in Saint Louis*. That girl, she commanded space.

A path clears for Win. And here I am, riding in his wake. What an intoxicating feeling.

Boy, I hope he doesn't get tired of me in my twenty-odd days of Viking glory. This could be quite a pleasant way to round out an unpleasant high school career.

We move through the cafeteria to a round table, and I sit right next to him. Listen, there's no playing it cool with me. It's a miracle I'm keeping it together the way I am, and if I have one friend? I will cling to him with every shred of my being.

"Are you eating?" He's pulled out a brown bag. It has his name on it in Sharpie.

"I brought a protein bar and a water. Trying to keep from vomiting on my surroundings today."

He looks at me for a minute. "You get nervous. No big deal."

I look at him. "Big deal. It cripples me sometimes."

He shrugs. "I get it. What I'm saying is, I'm cool with it. My cousin Nate has anxiety to the point that he's homeschooling right now."

I nod. "I could see that. But I need to get away from my mom."

"Is she not nice?"

"Super nice. Also super anxious. But it seems like with good reason, so…" I can't finish that sentence.

He digs out a banana and waves off the lost end of the sentence. "Enough. I want to know about you."

"I'm a girl, sitting next to a boy, trying not to puke on him. That about sums it up."

"I'm a boy who writes his own name on his lunch bag. Explain that."

"You're thorough?"

"Or odd."

A big guy, really tall with wide shoulders and no neck, comes and sits across from us, thumps down a gigantic cooler. He points at Win. "He's odd. Don't let him tell you any different."

"Orion."

"Win."

They stare at each other for a second.

"How'd it go?"

"I did not ask her, actually. Thanks for bringing it up."

I sit quiet. I want to ask who Orion neglected to ask and what the question was, but I feel odd interjecting myself into the conversation.

Orion eats a bologna sandwich with pickles and too much mustard, which leaks out of the sides and lands in big plops on the cafeteria table. It makes me look around for a napkin.

"Who's this?" He nods at me.

"I'm Vivi."

"Like Vivienne Leigh? I like that actress. Man, she was perfect as Scarlett O'Hara."

Orion the man-mountain likes *Gone with the Wind*.

Win interrupts. "It's short for…what's it short for?"

I look at him before I answer. "Genevieve. You thought you knew what it was short for?"

"I don't know. I guess yes."

"Maybe you are very thorough."

"Or psychic. I'm psychic."

Orion breaks in. "If you're psychic, then tell me what Lulu'll say when I ask her to prom. Spare me the agony."

"Just ask her. You're wearing me out."

A long, lanky girl walks up to the table. She has white-blond-dyed hair with big blue streaks in it and black eyes, as dark as the winged eyeliner she sports. "Gentlemen. Who's the new girl?"

"Lulu, this is Vivi."

Orion looks at me and narrows his eyes to slits. I'm pretty sure he's threatening my life in a nonverbal but still quite threatening way.

"Hi." I wave at Lulu.

Orion stands up. "Joining us?"

"I don't eat. You know that."

Win points at her. "The undead have no appetite. You could sit with us. Chat with Vivi. She's a girl, you're a girl, you can tell her if there are any nice girls she can be friends with in this school."

"I can tell her no without even sitting down." Lulu turns to face Orion straight on. "Are you going to prom?"

Orion spits out bologna. "What?"

Lulu sneers at him. "That's a no. Do you want to go?"

"Yeah."

"Good. I'll give you the details later."

I look around, pull out my water, and take a sip. This place is not what I expected. I'm not sure what I was expecting, but a girl with white and blue hair just asked a human locomotive out on a date, I have a friend already (and I'm not even done with day one), and I feel fine.

I feel fine.

Orion stuffs what's left of his sandwich into a grocery

bag. "You two are going to have to figure all this out. I'm going to make up my Government quiz." He strides off.

Win laughs. "You've met my two friends. What do you think?"

"They like each other?"

"They tolerate each other more than they tolerate most people. I wouldn't go any further than that."

"When's prom?"

"The 12th. About a month."

"You going?" I instantly regret this. *Why, why did I ask?*

"No." Win looks into his lunch sack and pulls out a coconut water. "Long story."

"No worries. You have a lot of long stories. You don't have to share them all right now."

He smiles. "I like you. You're going to be hard to not get to know well enough. We need more time to hang out."

"Twenty-six school days isn't even long enough to wear another hole in those socks of your dad's."

"Exactly."

Then I stand up, and it hits. Inexplicably. My palms go sweaty, and the whole cafeteria spins. I think it might be because I can suddenly see over everyone, or because everything's gone so well, and heck, why not have an anxiety attack right now in front of the whole school? That's the best and most embarrassing way for it to happen.

Or maybe it's because I've met the perfect person, and he's going to slip through my fingers in less time than it takes to use up a tube of toothpaste.

Mom gets a call from the school nurse, and I hear them talking about medications, coping skills, history, all while I lay on a squeaky brown pleather cot in the other room, a damp washcloth over my eyes.

It wasn't the worst attack I've had. I did not throw up, mercifully. I did, however, hyperventilate and cry and sit down on possibly the grossest floor a person could ever sit down on. I was at least not wearing a skirt.

Win, I think, stayed with me until I could get up and get down the hall. Someone held my hand. But I get in an awful zone. It's narrow and dark, and I can usually only hear my pounding heart in my ears, and I can usually see only a pinpoint of light at the end of a tunnel.

So the first day of my fresh start didn't quite end up being a whole day of success. There was a tortuous part.

There's a knock at the door of the nurse's office.

She covers the phone. "Win, honey, come on in."

No. I swear. I don't want the one friend I've made have to be my caretaker. It's the worst.

"I'm fine." I sit up and toss the washcloth behind me.

Win walks into the darkened room. "You want to walk home with me? It's not super long, and I figure the bus might be a bit much."

"My mom's probably coming to get me." I feel shame creep into my cheeks, clamp up my throat, and brim my eyes with tears.

"Oh, okay." He looks at me for a second. "Was it Lulu and Orion and me? Were we too much?"

"Too much what?"

"We're kind of weird. And we talk fast, and a lot, and I just thought we didn't give you time to process, maybe."

"No. It's definitely not you. You're lovely."

"Lovely?"

"Really. The loveliest person I've met in ages." I start to cry.

"I'm still lovely, and I'll still be lovely to you, I promise. You're 'like me', remember?"

"I'm *so* not like you. I wish."

He points at me. "You. You and me, we're more alike than you think. And I'll see you on the walk to the bus stop tomorrow, and then we'll eat in the art room with Lulu and Orion where it's quieter, and I swear you can't ditch me just because you're embarrassed. Orion threw up on me on the first day of school in fourth grade, and I still pester him, so you're stuck with me for the next twenty-six days."

"Okay."

"Excellent. See you tomorrow." He pushes his hands into the pockets of his khaki shorts and turns on his heels and leaves.

The nurse doesn't get why I'm crying. But it gets really old—being less, being the freak, being ashamed. It just does. So I cry some more, until my mom comes to get me, and we drive to our new home in silence.

CHAPTER THREE
PALINDROMES

When I get home, Mom gives me time to myself. It's been a long time since we didn't have a roommate, and so before this, she and I always had to share a room. Here I have my own room, and even though it currently has only an air mattress, I already love the private space.

After a while, I decide to go walk.

It sucks, anxiety. I had a psychologist once who told me it's best to try to think of anxiety like it's like the flu. When you have the flu, you don't get owned by it. It doesn't dominate you, it doesn't define you. It's just something you have, and you deal with it.

I am trying to just have it. But when it strikes out of the blue—when I'm feeling fine—I think that really, anxiety has me. In its clutches. In its jaws, ready to crush the life out of me.

And the monstrous personification, or monster-ification, if you will, isn't helpful.

Mom cracks the old, white door. "Can I come in?"

"If you come bearing insight or context or a way to re-evaluate the day, no. I'm not ready for the logic and the softening just yet."

"I'm not even allowed to say we should have expected at least one attack, given the huge change we're going through?"

"Not even that. We're still in calamity mode. Let me wallow in Calamityville."

"I prefer Calamityburg."

"I'm going on a walk."

I get up. I don't need to walk, but it feels like what a person would do if she were trying to be sensible and manage her anxiety. I'm a new person for twenty-six days, so this new Vivi is a sensible manager who has a handle on her anxiety.

Maybe if I say it a million more times, it'll be true.

"You still going to run in the morning?"

"Yeah, I think so."

"You're doing this whole upheaval thing like a boss."

"No one says boss anymore, Mom."

"I do. I'm an influencer. Ask anyone."

"You have a vintage Blackberry and an old iPad. You're not an influencer."

"I know how to use the desktop PCs at the public library, by golly."

"Influencers don't ever say 'by golly'. Proven fact."

"Fine. Go on a walk. I'll stay here and influence some meatloaf for dinner."

"Fine." I give her a kiss and leave.

On the street, I venture down the sidewalk in the opposite direction of the city bus stop. I haven't been down to the lake yet, and we're close. It's one reason why Mom picked the rental she did. Everybody told her it was the place to live—a stone's throw from Sanders Beach.

Again, I take issue with the *everybody*, and no one I know can throw a stone this far.

On the way down to the lake, there are pines and a huge, looming hill on my right, and the houses seem to be getting bigger on my left. I spot a glimmer of water.

And then a turkey barks at me.

I see the turkey, sprinting across the street from the yard of the old, white Craftsman home on my left and up the forested hill on my right.

I don't think the turkey actually barked. One of the dogs that turn the corner in front of me probably barked at the turkey.

Or their owner. The owner of the dogs might have barked.

Because it's Win. He seems unpredictable like that.

Granted, I knew he must live somewhere in my neighborhood since we crossed paths on the way to the bus stop, but to see him now, here, with dogs? It's like a unicorn wrapped up in a bow made of chocolate on Christmas.

"Win! Dogs!" I forget my embarrassment, my tears, my fear of vomiting on him.

"Yes! I have dogs! You're enthusiastic! You feeling

better?"

I nod, and as I get close, I kneel to greet the two leashed dogs in front of him. "What are their names?"

"The gray one's Tacocat. This one's Racecar." He reaches down to give Racecar a scratch behind the ear. Racecar is a little sandy-colored Corgi.

"Palindromes. I like it. You know my middle name's Hannah," I say.

Tacocat leans his whole hairy body into me, plastering my black yoga pants with gray dog hair. He's some kind of mutt—lean body like a Border Collie, but with big, stand-up ears like a Husky.

"No way. That's your middle name?"

"Nope, not really. It's Meriwether. But I had you for a second. You disappointed I'm not a palindrome?"

"I could call you Vivviv."

"That rolls off the tongue."

He clucks to the dogs and turns to walk down toward the lakefront.

"Where you headed?" I say, surprising myself. I'm not ready to let him go yet.

"Taking the dogs down to the beach. You want to come?"

Yes. "Sure. If it's okay."

He smiles. "I think it's okay. Do you?"

"I think so. Do you need some time alone? I get that. But I feel better, if that's what you're asking."

He waves at me to come with him. "C'mon. It's all good. You're fine, I'm fine, let's walk."

The dogs seem a little reluctant to leave the scene of the turkey sighting, but the turkey's long gone into the woods on the hill next to us.

"I can't believe the turkey."

"Tubbs Hill has all kinds of critters." Win points at the hill. "Someone said they saw a moose once, but I doubt it. They're too private. It's surrounded on all sides by the city, except for where there's lake."

We come to the bottom of the street, halting just before a house with a copper roof, and before the street makes a hard left to run parallel to the shore. Just past the copper-topped house is a postage stamp-sized beach. The lake is out in front of us. It's steel blue and shimmering. The sun is edging down to the tops of the hills across the lake, sinking in the late afternoon sky.

"Let's walk to the end of the road." Win gestures with one of the dog leashes, but the dogs are already pulling that direction.

On the lake side of the road, there are lawns, terraced gardens, and sandy volleyball courts. And there are fences between us and the lake.

"This is private?"

Win shrugs. "Kind of. To the high water line. But we can walk on the water's edge." He points to the dead end. "There's another access spot down there."

I look at the houses across the road from the lake. They rise up from green, manicured lawns. They spread wide, with pools and pool houses, but they clearly also own the matching lawns across the street next to the water. "Lake hogs."

He laughs. "Yeah. They suck. Trying to keep the whole lake to themselves."

As we are almost to the end of the lane, I look at the

house in front of us. It's a white colonial, wide, with at least twelve windows across the second story. "That's a beast of a house. Holy cow."

"Yep."

"I wonder what kind of family lives in that?"

Win shrugs. "Probably super dysfunctional."

The dogs dance around Win's legs, impatient.

I hold out my hand. "Can I walk one of them?"

He hands me Racecar's leash. "By all means. They're a pain in the butt. Monumental."

I skip down the road. "I've never had a pet," I call behind me. I watch Racecar's little Corgi legs scramble as fast as they can, now that I've given him a slack leash.

Win calls after me. "No pets? You're a monster. Not even a fish?"

Tacocat can't bear to fall behind the other dog, and he pulls Win after us. They break into a run just as I come to the end of the road and a high fence with a narrow, slotted opening.

"Nope," I yell.

They reach us at the end of the line. Win points to the opening. "That's our 'public access' on this end of the street."

"Well, that's dumb." I follow him to the lake's edge.

"You're from the coast, right? Lots of public beaches there. Oregon is all public coastline. I'd like to live there, I think. Washington would be cool, too. How come you and your mom moved?"

I wince a bit, but my voice stays neutral. "Long story."

Win nods. "You and me, we're going to have an extremely late night when we decide to spill on all these long stories."

The dogs pull hard on the leashes, swerve into each other and swing wide, correcting themselves. I bounce into Win, and the collision sends shivers up through my rib cage and stands the hair on the back of my neck on end.

"They want off their leashes." Win gives a short whistle, and they sit.

"Won't they run off?" I watch as he lets them both go.

"Racecar can't get very far before he has to lie down and rest—Corgi stamina and all that. And Tacocat would never leave him. They're friends to the end."

He walks to the water's edge, picks up a stone to skip across the lake's surface. As the sun dips behind the hills, I can feel a breeze pick up off the lake and push by us.

"I better get home. I don't know how fast it gets dark. I don't want to get lost." I feel my pulse pick up a bit. Mom would worry. A lot. Just me being out after dark would make her worry.

"I'll walk you back to your house."

"You don't have to do that."

"The dogs don't want to go home yet, and this way, I'll know where you live."

"And you need to know that because?"

"Because we're friends. Friends hang out and pick each other up at their houses and stuff."

"Oh."

I don't tell him that I've never had many friends, and when I did we usually didn't hang out much outside of school. Mom and I are, I don't know, private? Shy? Introverted? Happy to just have each other? I admit the answer to myself: *reluctant to let anyone know too much about us.* I leave the train of thought there.

Win whistles to me, a soft little "hello," a sweet note. "Vivi? You in there?"

"Yep. Walk me home, then. I'm up on Bancroft."

"Close to 8ᵗʰ? You're right by the dog park. How convenient."

"I told you I don't have a dog. I want one like crazy, though."

"But I have two, and we can take them over there, and you can live vicariously through me, dog owner that I am."

"Excellent." I wonder what it is that compels him to make plans with me. Or want to make plans with me. I'm quiet, thinking. I may be chewing on a fingernail.

Win taps me on the shoulder. "Hey. Relax."

If it were only that easy.

We walk home, and I feel the muscles in my back tensing up, the closer we get. I just don't want Mom to start.

"You're quiet." Win looks at me in the fading light. His features soften as dusk falls around us.

"Are we the kind of friends who tell each other the truth a lot?" I ask.

"Except for our assorted long stories, I think yes."

"Well, you meeting my mom makes me nervous. I want you to like her, and I want her not to scare you away, and I especially want her not to overthink the fact that I have a friend already."

Win smiles. "I feel like that's the mom code. They're all potentially a disaster when you're trying to accomplish stuff."

I think, then get brave. "I'm thinking my mom takes it all a little farther than usual."

"Is she going to answer the door with a gun?"

I shake my head, determined not to ruin this new friendship. "No, we don't have guns. I don't know. Maybe the details are best left to another one of our long stories."

"Fine. Let me be the judge of your mom. Plus, you didn't get to choose her, so I wouldn't worry too much. I still like you."

"It's been what, not even twelve hours? That's no record."

The dogs hop around our feet. Win points at them. "We need to get you home. The dogs are going a little nutty. They like to be fed on a schedule. It's a good motivator."

I resign myself to the fact that my new friend will meet my mom, and who knows what's going to happen.

The little gray house is pretty friendly from the front, actually. It's tidy, and the front yard is well kept. There are a couple of tall trees that rise around the front room window. The lights are all on, and now it's officially dark out. I worry.

The door swings open. "Viv?" Mom stands behind the door, her head poked around it.

"Yeah, Mom." I hand Racecar's leash to Win.

Win walks ahead of me. "I'm Win. I go to Coeur d'Alene High with Vivi."

He walks right up the sidewalk, tall and confident and cool, and I wish I could bottle that up. Never once in my life have I been that calm and self-assured.

Mom steps out on the front porch, pulls the door a little

closed behind her.

I hate that—that move of hiding the inside of the house from him, of closing the door on our front room so people can't see it, like we're wrong to have no furniture, or to live by ourselves, or to have dishes in the sink at the end of the night. I can feel my ears flush from the embarrassment.

I *really* hate that. Plenty of people have stuff like that inside of their houses. People have liquor bottles in the sink. Or twenty people staying with them, or nine hundred pizza boxes stacked up in the laundry room. Or bruises on their faces. Or scars on their arms. Plenty of people have plenty to hide. I know that's true; I just wish I knew more people who have lives a little more like mine and my mom's. I'm sure I've met them at one point or another, but they do a better job of hiding it than we do.

I'm tired of hiding. I'm tired of the door pulled closed behind Mom's back. I wish it were different.

"Nice to meet you. I'm Vivi's mom, Samantha Stone." She steps forward and shakes his hand, which has two leashes around it.

The dogs want in the house, and they try to push past Mom to get in, eager to explore and learn the inside.

Next time I have Win over, I'm going to let him in, and I'm going to make sure Mom's off at work, and we'll hang out like normal people do. I don't know what that involves, but I can make pizza rolls and sit on the couch and pretend the rest of it.

Win probably can feel how twitchy I've become, standing next to him in front of Mom. He points back down the street. "I better get the dogs home. Nice to meet you, Mrs. Stone."

"It's Ms. Stone. And it's nice to meet you, Win," Mom says.

Win looks at me. "See you at the bus stop."

"Definitely." I give Racecar one more pat on the head. "Text me so I know you got home okay."

He laughs. "Happy to, but I'm trying to guess what worst-case scenario you're imagining that keeps me from making it the approximately four blocks to my house. This is Idaho."

I smile. "Guy with a hook for a hand?"

"Fair enough. Racecar'll tear him apart."

"The Corgi. Quite the vicious breed," I agree.

Win shrugs. "Tacocat will have to knock the guy over, but once he's at Racecar's level, he's a goner. I'll be sure to text that we made it home with the hook, torn from the murderer's bloody stump."

My mom even laughs. "Ew, you two."

"Goodnight." I squeeze by my mom and swing the door wide, so wide that I hope Win gets a good look into our house, into our life.

I want him to know me, not a closed door.

I worry I was too much for him to bear for a full seven minutes and twenty-two seconds until he texts me:

Next time we Snapchat. That way I can send pics of the hook, but they won't be admissible for evidence in court.

I laugh and send a text with my username. He sends back a picture of a hand turkey he seems to have hurriedly drawn, covered in ketchup. He's captioned it: *Didn't stand a chance.*

The next picture is an extreme close up of Corgi tongue and a couple teeth, smooshed up against the lens.

I reply, *What is that?*

Pure viciousness. See you in the morning.

I plug in my phone and crawl onto my air mattress, pull the covers up over my head, and wish for a world where I have more hand turkeys and walks with dogs and fewer tears and tunnels of dread. Then Mom calls me for dinner.

The next morning is rainy—I flash back to Seattle—so I bag the idea of running and promise myself I'll do it tomorrow. I get to the bus stop alone. No Win. It sucks. Suddenly the whole idea of living here in Coeur d'Alene sucks, and I hate my mom for moving us, and I want to go home to Issaquah and return to my desolate little existence.

The day is bleak, and I drag through my classes with my head down and hood up, until art.

I come into the room and head to the table from yesterday.

Phoebe, the eyebrow-starer, is waiting for me. "You and Win."

I sit and wait for her to finish her sentence. Girl with phone-hand is, surprise, surprise, on her phone. Phoebe doesn't say anything else.

"Me and Win what?"

Phoebe throws her hands up. "C'mon. You've got him already. How'd that happen?"

"I've got him? What do you mean?"

She seems to have changed gears, and she reaches out

and pats my fingers. "Sorry about the cafeteria freak-out. No worries, though. Something always happens."

"What are we talking about now?"

Phoebe shrugs. "You don't want to talk about Win. That's fine. And you're not the only one to lose it in the cafeteria. I thought it'd make you feel better. Freak-outs are regular time around here. We have one at least once a month. No one likes that honkin' big cafeteria. You're still cool."

Phone-hand chimes in. "Legit. You're fine."

"Thanks?" I'm so confused. I wish Win were here to rescue me. On a chance, I point to Phoebe. "Where is he today? He wasn't on the bus with me."

I don't want to tell her we walked to the bus stop together yesterday. She doesn't get to know that detail.

"Today through prom kind of sucks for Win. Long story."

I laugh. "There are so many long stories around that guy. What?"

Phoebe leans in close, points at my eyebrows. "You may be the girl with the gorgeous eyebrows, Bébé, but that's his story to tell."

"My name's Vivi."

"Sure, Bébé, you can count on us to be your friends. I don't care that you freaked out in the cafeteria."

Phone-hand agrees. "Sure. We've got your back, Bébé."

I have to do meditation techniques through the rest of class to keep from screaming in these girls' ears. Honestly.

I leave class and wander down the hall for a bit, then circle back. Win said he'd eat lunch with me in the art room. *There isn't another art room, is there?*

He's not waiting for me, and he's not in the art room, but his large friend is, and so is the girl who's apparently taking him to prom. I stand at the doorway and consider being brave and going in to sit with them.

My phone vibrates in my bag. I pull it out.

It's a text.

Sorry I left you hanging.

I want to ask. But I don't. He's not pushed me on my long stories.

People don't remember my name already.

What's your new name?

Bébé.

Who did that to you?

Phoebe in art. She REALLY wants us to have rhyming names. And phone-hand girl.

I'm not asking how she got that nickname.

If Racecar were to tear her hand off, it'd be a Galaxy S8 Edge.

I think about taking a big, courageous step forward into the art room when there's someone behind me.

"Two attacks in two days could land him in the pound." Win stands behind me.

I whirl around. "You're here!"

"We're eating lunch in the art room. I said so yesterday."

"You just getting here?"

"Yeah."

I hold a hand up. "We need a code word for long

story."

"LS?"

"No, that's dumb."

"Tough crowd." He shakes his head. "What if we keep track of how many we've promised to divulge later?"

"I've already lost count. It's that many."

"Well, we're complicated people. We're intense. The Beat poets got nothing on us."

"Code word," I suggest. "How about *palindrome*?"

Win puts a hand on my shoulder, guides me to the table where his friends sit. "Yes. Genius and inside joke-y, which I love."

Lulu points a chopstick at Win. "You two have an inside joke already? You're trying too hard. Just let the serendipity happen."

Orion eats more bologna. "I want in on the joke. I'm always on the outside. I'll be scarred by this, and you'll get a short reference in my biography. You'll be Peggy in *Hamilton*. Lulu and I will be Eliza and Angelica."

Win jumps to our defense. "Peggy saved a baby from raiders with tomahawks. I can live with that. And it's not really an inside joke—we're not making fun of anyone. We're not mean."

I nod as I sit next to, but at a safe distance from, Lulu. I'm pretty sure she could destroy me, and I'm not very sure she likes me yet. Her white-and-blue hair and heavy eye makeup conjures up women in movies who know how to wield baseball bats. My general appearance brings to mind America Ferrera in *Sisterhood of the Traveling Pants*— before she got all politically empowered and self-aware and red hot. I do not destroy anything, unless I can count chocolate chip cookies.

"Nice doesn't get you very far in this life, girl who just met Win yesterday. You and Win need people like me and Orion. We arm-bar the other mean people for you. We're the sergeants-at-arms of your lives," Lulu says.

Win pats Lulu on the shoulder. "Yes, you are. But we're your moral compasses."

Orion seems to take issue with this, but his mouth is full of a huge bite of white bread and bologna and too much mustard, so he says nothing.

Win turns himself a little away from the two of them and faces me head on. "How'd the morning go?" he asks, looking me over.

"Fine. It was bleak but fine."

Phone-hand and Phoebe stroll in with lunch trays. "Hey, look, it's Bébé and Win."

Lulu almost spits. "That's not her name. Come on."

Phone-hand's eyes narrow. "What's her name, then?"

Lulu looks at Win. "Tell them."

"It's Vivi."

Phoebe nods. "That's what I said. Bébé."

Win nods at the other girl. "What's *your* name, actually?"

"Fiona. It's French, like Bébé. You gonna give me a hard time about my name, Winchester?"

"No. Are you both going to sit and eat in here?"

"We've got Bébé's back. We're her friends, even though she freaked out in the cafeteria." Fiona Phone-hand sits at the table with us, and Orion looks very confused.

Lulu gets up. "The world's so backward. And Fiona's a Gaelic name anyway. Is Mercury in retrograde or something?"

"I think it's actually a Scorpio moon," Orion reports. "That's supposed to screw with everything."

He sounds up on the whole astrological situation, perhaps for obvious reasons.

I smile. Win looks at me and laughs, his glorious smile wide. His eyes crinkle, and it's like pure joy shot straight into my veins. I could get very used to watching him smile.

"I'm going to go buy prom tickets. Y'all can sit here and bond or whatever." Lulu shoots Orion a death stare, and he responds obediently, hopping off his work stool and grabbing the remnants of his enormous lunch.

"Later." Win pulls out another brown bag with his name on it. He hands me a sandwich.

"What's this?"

"I made an extra sandwich. Well-fed people have good blood sugar. Blood sugar helps you feel mellow. I know these things."

"How?"

Fiona snorts. "The Google, Bébé."

"My mom's a nutritionist," Win says.

Fiona Phone-hand gets back to her Snapping or texting or Googling or what have you.

I take a bite of the sandwich. "Thanks."

Seriously. My mom can't even manage to make me a lunch. I was a hot-lunch kid all through elementary. Win's taken better care of me in the span of two days.

I walk through the front door after school, and I can tell we're at Defcon 5. Maybe because I'm a person with anxiety, when Mom's wound up, I can feel the house vibrate.

"That didn't take long," I say out loud, and I immediately feel guilty.

I beat her to it, after all. I already had my meltdown, and all I did was stand up in the middle of a cafeteria.

Here's the deal with my mom, though. There's a pretty specific set of things that wind her up, and I'm usually pretty good at maneuvering our lives to avoid what I know will send her off the deep end.

The things that wake her up in the middle of the night often lead to my mom sleeping in the chair next to my bed. Of course, right now there is neither a bed nor a chair in my bedroom, so maybe we can avoid that particular scenario for a few weeks.

However, today I'm a pot calling a kettle black. I take a deep breath, in through my nose and blow it out through my mouth, thinking about Corgis and my new name and my friend who makes me sandwiches.

"Mom?"

"Oh, Vivi!" She calls to me from the bathroom.

So of course, I immediately take it straight to visions of bad, bad things that involve people in crisis in a bathroom, and I hurry my steps and push the door open.

She's fine. She sits on the closed lid of the toilet.

"You okay?" I ask, putting out a hand.

She takes it and stands up, following me out of the bathroom and to the futon in the main room. I sit with her.

"How's it going?" I hold her hand.

She wipes at her eyes. "Fine. What do you want for dinner?"

"Something happen at work?"

She shakes her head. "No, work is fine. I just…" She leaves the sentence hanging in the air between us. It's another wave that trembles and makes the space in our little house feel taut, like a string of fishing line pulled between two nails.

"Just what?"

"I wondered how you'd do today at school. I felt really bad for sending you off to that huge new school after what happened yesterday, and I knew that because I was working I wouldn't be able to come get you if you had another attack, and then I couldn't really leave my phone on during my shift because I'm trying to make a good impression, and the two managers at the shop are super nice. I kind of feel like I held my breath for seven consecutive hours."

"But you didn't actually, because you have to breathe to live, so thanks for that."

"And I did talk to customers, which also takes some basic breath, since you have to vibrate your vocal cords and all that."

Mom smiles, and it seems like the muscles in her jaw are relaxing. Maybe I can divert her attention long enough that we avoid a full-blown panic attack on her part.

The weird thing is, when she's amped up, I actually don't feel panicky. I like having purpose, and when it's my job to keep my mom from spinning out, I have purpose.

She stands up. "I'm going to make you a nice dinner. Salad and spaghetti, and maybe even some garlic bread under the broiler. Would you like that?"

"I'd like that a lot."

"You didn't even take a lunch today. Or lunch money.

I can put some on your account with a credit card."

"It's not worth it, Mom. There aren't even enough days." I leave out the part about the boy who seems to be making my lunches from here on out.

I just want to go shut myself in my room and write bad, syrupy poetry dedicated to this new magical person, but my mom needs me.

"We should go on a walk after dinner." I also leave out the part where I hope to run into Win.

"What's the name of your new friend again?" Mom's psychic powers are on point tonight. I hate it when she guesses what I'm thinking.

"Win. Or maybe you mean Phoebe and Fiona, who think my name is Bébé. They sit with me in art."

"No, I mean the boy. He seems nice. Good manners."

"He has dogs. I'm just using him for his canines."

She looks sad for a minute. "You always did want pets. It's just too hard when you rent."

"It's fine, Mom. I get it. No big deal."

"What's he into?"

"Mom, I've known him two days. I don't really know. He wears socks with holes in them."

We eat, and it's not dark out yet after. I wash the dishes and put everything away, but I'm in a hurry to get outside.

I grab my sweatshirt and my phone. "Want to take a little walk? Clear the head, calm the brain?" I know it'd be good for her to go out and walk with me, get her mind off of things.

"If you'll make it back before it gets dark, you can go without me. I think I'll take a hot shower and have a cup of tea."

I give her a big kiss and get out the door.

I walk straight down to the lake's shore in the falling light. The wind is calm tonight, and the lake is paler blue than when I walked down here with Win and his dogs. It looks like a wide, delicate plate, with deep green pines edging its porcelain.

I pass down the narrow lake-access path and look up and down the shoreline. Far down the crescent of the beach is someone sitting on a rock, knees drawn up to his chest, staring out at the lake.

Win.

Maybe it's because I spend a big part of my life reading my mom for signs of trouble, but I can read a person's mood, even from a hundred feet or more.

This is a person in despair.

As this realization hits, it knocks the wind out of me. He's in some kind of pain, to the point that as I watch, he buries his face in his arms, folded on his knees.

And today I could only think of how he should be there at school for me, be there for me at lunch, and I could only crow and preen at the fact that he brought me lunch.

Maybe he needs me more than I need him.

Because really? I am here. I am healthy. I am in one piece. Sure, Mom and I left a lot of baggage behind in Washington, and yeah, it could certainly catch up with us with a vengeance. But I'm seventeen, and I've made it this far.

What are Win's long stories? I don't know. Maybe they are really, really long.

I stand for a long time. I don't know if I should

approach him.

I hear him cry out.

It's a short sob, like he's struggling to keep a lid on the pain. I know I shouldn't approach. That pain is from deep inside him, and he doesn't know how to trust me well enough yet to share his story with me.

Maybe he's protecting me from that long story. I know my mom protects me from parts of her story, and I feel like there are parts of it that left actual physical scars. Parts of her story would frighten me, I think.

I turn around and walk back down the beach, hugging the snobby lake owners' high water mark and sticking close to the fences to keep out of sight.

He doesn't pick his head up, even when I turn around to check on him.

Sometimes sadness is company enough.

CHAPTER FOUR
DRIVING THE GREEN

The next morning, I wake up early to run. In all honesty, I'm not that into fitness. But it is calming sometimes, and now I have new reasons why I want to run. I run this morning because I might run into Tacocat and Racecar and Win. But I also run this morning because I've decided I really like Lakeshore Drive. I love looking at all the houses. I love the tall trees, the big white house, and the crazy medieval castle house at the end of the road. I love pretending I live in one of these houses, even though those houses monopolize all the great lake frontage.

This morning I look for the turkeys. Win said there's actually a whole flock of wild turkeys that wander the area. He told me they come into the neighborhood to eat birdseed from under feeders and hassle the neighborhood cats.

When I come down the hill, coming to the corner by

the marina, I see a guy.

He's old. He's maybe sixty? I don't know. He has white, wavy hair, combed back from his forehead.

He's standing on the corner in his bathrobe.

I'm going to have to run right by him. I'm not going anywhere else—there isn't anywhere else to go. It would be weird to turn around and run back up the hill. It would imply that I was afraid of him or embarrassed for him, and I think if I were standing in my bathrobe on the corner of Lakeshore Drive, I'd be embarrassed enough. I wouldn't need some dumb girl to rub it in by turning tail and running away from me.

I'm going for it. I keep running, slowing a bit, give him a nod. "Morning."

He points at me with his newspaper. "You gonna run by every morning? Is this your new thing?"

I stop. "My new thing?"

"I get the paper same time every morning. Have for twenty years. Just wanting to know if I should make the investment in knowing your name, or if this is some lame resolution and you'll be giving up on it before the end of the school year."

"I just moved here, so…"

He nods, takes a sip of his coffee. "Okay. What's your name then?"

"What's yours?"

"Jack. Jack McCann."

"Nice to meet you, Jack."

"You can call me Mr. McCann."

I like him. He's old, and potentially crazy, but he feels like a warm version of my ceramics teacher from

Washington—more friendly and less tortured by his poor life choices. Happier about his lot in life.

"I'll call you Jack," I tell him. "You're too late to pull rank by authority of age. Shouldn't have given me your first name. Or worn your bathrobe to get your paper."

"This is my house. I can wear a bathrobe to get the paper on my driveway if I want." He waves the paper over his head in the direction of the house behind him.

It's massive.

There's the huge driveway that leads to a three-car garage, a long paved and lighted path to the front door. The roofs of the garage and the house are a shiny, polished copper. Pricey looking.

The front of the house doesn't reveal much, but I can get a peek around to the back, where all the action is. There's a monster dock and a wide, sandy private beach. It's the only house on the whole street that's on the same side of the road as the lake. Coordinated red Adirondack chairs dot the beach and the manicured lawn, lining the trimmed grass of the badminton court. A series of barstools line an outdoor bar, which seems to be equipped with a full outdoor kitchen. Deluxe. All waterfront access, with a large rock outcropping separating it from the marina property next door.

And the man in his boxer shorts, T-shirt, and robe in front of me owns it.

"Vivi," I tell him.

He squints at me. He's not even trying to leave now. He stands, weight on one foot, sipping coffee, paper tucked under the other arm. "What?"

"My name's Vivi."

"Short for Vivienne?"

"Short for Genevieve."

"Nice. Well, finish your run. Saturdays you can stop back by and have a cup of coffee or a doughnut if your mom says it's okay. She can come by. Is she single?"

"Yeah."

"Figured. I'm not, but if I ever am, you tell your mom I'm a nice guy."

"That remains to be seen."

"Go get your run done—you've got to get to school. Those attendance ladies at the high school are stingy. No excuse meets their muster."

"How do you know so much about it?"

"A million years ago I worked there as a counselor."

"That didn't buy this house."

"Nope. Running the family lumber business did. Second job. Always working, that was me." He takes a big swig of coffee. "I could use a housesitter once in a while. If you don't bail on the routine, maybe you'll get the job. Do you golf?"

"Not well."

"My wife doesn't either. I need a ringer. Ask around at school—one of the guys there has to be decent."

"I just moved here. I don't really know."

"Figure it out and report back. You have three runs to get me the name of a guy to golf with me."

I take a couple big steps down the street, ready to leave. "You can't be serious. I don't know you, and some high school senior is certainly not going to randomly come play golf with you."

"You tell them my name, they will."

"Why?"

"Vivi, everybody knows me in this town. I'm the Rockefeller of Coeur d'Alene. The Bill Gates, without the computer sense. Steve Jobs without the pretentious turtlenecks."

"Okay. I'll ask around. See you."

He turns and walks back up his driveway. "Vivi, make it a great day or not. The choice is yours."

Now I know he was a counselor. That's such a high-school-affiliated-adult thing to say.

But today, I kind of agree with him. It is my choice today—and it's going to be a great day because I say so.

Getting to see Win again might have something to do with it, too.

I get ready and get out the door. Mom gives me a kiss as I leave, and she also seems chipper this morning.

As I walk to meet Win (I hope), I think about fresh starts. A new place feels good, if you've never made a move before. But Mom and I have moved more than the average family. And after the first couple moves, it just starts to feel wobbly.

The first time we moved (that I can remember), I cried a lot, because I was six, and the new school and teacher smelled different. Teachers give you hugs and pat you on the back when you're crying the first day at a new school, but if—like me—your tears drip into the next couple days, and then the whole first week, the kind smiles eventually freeze into impatient, firm grimaces.

But I was ready the next time. When we moved again,

I left behind the embarrassing story of running into Chad Cameron in the hall at a full gallop and giving him a black eye with my head. I'd had my head down because I'd realized I'd left my library book in the library, and Mrs. Welch was going to put me at the back table (she called it "Siberia") for forgetting again.

Leaving history like that behind is kind of liberating.

Or the time I got my period and wore a skirt with a stain on it the whole day because I had no friend to tell me I'd spotted on my skirt.

That was move number eight. That's history I wish I could not only leave behind but obliterate from my mind.

Not that any of these moves had anything to do with my sad story of shame and embarrassment in the halls of public education in America.

The reason for the moves? That's Mom's long story.

When it's someone else deciding or being forced or whatever it might be that makes them decide to move, it's wobbly. That's the only word I can think of for it. It spins me like a merry-go-round and leaves me wondering if we're going to stay long enough in the new place to get a bed frame. Or make real friends. Or fall in love.

When that last thought pops into my head, I stop walking.

I can't.

I've never been in love. Talk about wobbly.

If I got pulled away from something like that, if I had to move away... I don't know if there'd be any coming back from that. I don't know.

But I also don't know if I can help it, whether I fall in love or not.

The realization melts from my mind to rest on the back of my tongue, and I swear it feels like I can't swallow or get a deep breath.

"Quit it," I say out loud.

I refuse to have a stupid panic attack at the thought of falling for Win. I have the tendency to be pathetic, but for the love of nacho cheese, I'm stronger than that.

"Quit what?" Win stands in front of me.

I put a hand out. "I swear, I'm going to have a heart attack. You're like a stealth ninja."

"You just walk with your head down. And you talk to yourself. You make it too easy."

"I like to charge around. Leftover toddler habit, I guess."

"What's today going to be like at school?" Win looks at me and smiles, but it doesn't reach his eyes.

"I've decided to make today great. I was persuaded by an old guy in a bathrobe."

"When was this?"

"Down on Lakeshore Drive this morning."

"What were you doing down there?"

"I went for an early run. I can do that when it's light out. I can't wake up and run when it's dark. I hate dark mornings."

"Which house?"

"The one right next to the marina. The only one actually on the lake."

Win shakes his head, smiling at something he knows that I don't. "Typical."

"Typical what?"

"Pretty sure that's Jack McCann."

"Yeah, it was. He told me people know who he is."

"His family owns a huge lumber company. And he's just a loud guy. If he's out downtown, you'll hear him. He's hard to miss."

"He's looking for somebody good to golf with."

"He already asked you to go find him a golf partner?"

"Yes."

"Well, I golf, but he's ridiculous. Maybe I'll run with you the next time and tell him so."

"He seems pretty persuasive. You'll probably end up golfing with him."

"Seems like it'd be good for you to have a running buddy anyway. Old men in bathrobes coming after you? You need a wingman."

"I can hold my own."

"Okay, but do you want me to run with you?"

"Sure. I'm not going every morning. I like sleep too much."

Win's face settles into thought, his eyebrows knitted together and his eyes down, focused on the sidewalk in front of us.

He lifts his head and looks at me. "You know what?"

"What?"

"We run together next time you go, and I'll get us both a golf date with him. It's probably a trip to go golfing with him."

"He did say he was the Steve Jobs of Coeur d'Alene without the turtlenecks."

"If he knows how to turn on a computer, I'd be surprised."

"I'm not very much of a golfer."

"You can drive the cart. We go together." He points to the city bus pulling up to our stop. "Right now we go suffer through another day of senior year."

I think about what he'd do if I reached out and took his hand, but I can't risk it. Instead, I just sputter, "I'm glad, really glad you made it to the bus stop today. I like this a lot more with you here."

I can feel my cheeks getting hot with the admission.

Win smiles. "I like this more with you, too."

I wonder if he knows how much more I like this than usual.

And then I think about him on Sanders Beach last night, in the twilight. Maybe I need to be more of a giver than a taker. Maybe I need to tell him I like him here in general; I like him in the world.

And I set to worrying about my new friend Win and his long stories as we ride on the bus together. But I also enjoy the fact that our elbows are touching.

Win is a man of his word. On Friday he goes on my morning run with me. He meets me at my house, and we jog straight down to Lakeshore. He chats and whistles a bit.

Then we see a guy standing with a cup of coffee, pretty much waiting for us on the corner.

"There he is," I announce.

"Seems like he's expecting us, doesn't it?"

"Kinda seems that way," I agree.

"Howdy, neighbors." Jack waves the paper at us. I wonder if he ever opens it up and reads it.

"Hi, Jack. I brought my friend Win."

Win stops jogging and shakes Jack's hand.

"Morning, Win."

It feels like Jack already knows Win. A *lot* like that. I start to wonder if I'm missing something.

"Mr. McCann."

I elbow Win. "No, he goes by Jack. Trust me."

Jack looks at me and squints in retaliation. "Your friend here, she's new, but she seems like she's a little too much."

Win nods. "You're kind of the definition of too much yourself, Jack. Or so I've been told."

"Is that so?"

"And Vivi says you need a golf partner."

"Someone good. You any good?"

"Not particularly. But I can drive the green when I need to show off."

"You'll do."

"Take me and Vivi golfing tomorrow. Then I'll play whatever tournament you need to win."

"Seems fair. Meet me here. Wear something decent."

I worry right away. I don't know what decent golf attire means. Jack must notice my worried face.

"You don't have to worry. Just no denim. Wear capris. You own any of those? It's all my wife wears when we go out. She considers it dressing up from yoga pants. I miss skirts."

I nod. "I can wear something decent. I don't have clubs, though. And Win probably doesn't either."

Win jumps in, waves me off. "I'm good. I can find a set of clubs for me."

Jack smirks. "I bet." He looks at me. "Don't you

worry. I've got the last clubs my wife rejected sitting in the garage. You can have those."

"I just need to borrow them."

"Whatever. You don't care if there's pink writing on the shafts, do you?"

"No."

"My wife did." He puts a hand through his hair. "Why did I marry her again?"

Win turns and begins to jog back up the street. "You don't want to die alone?"

I swear there's a line of this conversation I've missed. That's pretty snarky.

Jack points me up the road, in Win's direction. "Go catch up to him and trip him. He deserves it."

"What time tomorrow?"

"Eight on the nose. Right here. No yoga pants. And make that boy run a comb through his hair."

I nod and take off after Win.

Jack calls after me. "Trip him! Body check him! He has it coming!"

I'm definitely missing something.

I catch up to Win. "You two know each other?"

Win smiles. "My parents. Mom and Jack worked on a fundraising campaign for the library."

"I wondered why he was so cheeky," I say.

"Well, I'm pretty sure it takes him about eight minutes to get that cheeky with anyone."

"I'm supposed to knock you over now. Jack's orders," I tease.

Win takes off sprinting. "You have to catch me first!"

The next morning, I meet Win on the sidewalk at Jack's house. He's arrived before me, and he stands with three sets of golf clubs piled around him.

"Mornin'," I call to him. "You carrying all of that?"

Jack comes out the front door and slams it behind him. "We need to hurry out of here before the wife decides she needs me for honey-dos more than I need to golf." He picks up a set of all-black clubs from the pile next to Win. He points to the others and then to me. "You're not too embarrassed to carry the clubs with the pink writing down to the boat, are you?"

I'm not sure why I need to put them in his boat, but I shake my head. "I can carry them. I'm not embarrassed."

Jack lugs his clubs down to the beach behind his house. I follow, and Win follows me.

"We should take the car, Jack," he says.

"Driving's boring." Jack tosses the clubs into the back of a ski boat. It's a Chris-Craft, with a mahogany body and white inlay on the nose. It looks expensive and old.

Win and I put our clubs in the boat, and Jack claps his hands, full of efficiency this morning. He gets in and starts the engine, then motions to the lines tying the boat to the dock.

"Cast those off and hop in."

Win comes up alongside of me, helps me release the line at the stern, and points to the backseat. "Get in. I'll push us off." He goes to release the bowline as I climb aboard.

With a shove, Win hops in, and Jack wheels the boat

out into the lake. I sit low on the back bench of the boat, trying to stay out of the way.

"This is how you golf?" Win shouts over the roar of the engine as Jack pushes the boat out into the lake, throwing up a wide, white wake behind us.

I shiver in the early morning air, feeling the spray kicking up all around us.

"There's a lake in between me and the golf course. This is the logical solution."

I turn around and look at the lake spread out behind us. The sun dazzles on the water, casting thousands of little jewels into my eyes.

My mom would freak. But for a moment I'm sad she's not here to feel the spray in her face, to enjoy the sun and the two people here with me who seem a lot less worried about everything than Mom and I are.

I think of her almost every minute, worried that she's worrying.

I turn back around, and Jack lets Win take the wheel.

Win drives the boat, looking out over the windshield. His dark hair whips around his golden face, his eyes and smile bright. He concentrates on his task, and the effortless ease, his posture—it's so irresistible. His shoulders are wide, and I can see the contours of his strong torso under the polo he wears.

I have to take a big breath. He literally makes me forget to breathe. How ridiculous is that?

I start plotting. Where did he say he wanted to go to college? Where was it? That's where I want to go.

I've got decent grades. I'm smart, and my first go-around on the SAT was good. We're supposed to get our spring SAT day scores back any day. I bet it's not too late to apply, and it's definitely a possibility I'd get a big, juicy financial aid package. Mom and I go to McDonald's to get wi-fi, for crying out loud.

He said UNR. Wolfpack.

I make a note to find out more about that. At the high school, where the wi-fi is free.

Win slows the boat now, and I see a retaining wall looming in the distance.

I make my way to sit in the seat next to Win at the wheel.

"What's that?"

Jack pulls himself up and stands next to Win. "That's where we're starting our round of golf this morning."

Win shakes his head as he kills the engine. The boat stills, dipping forward and back with our wake as it catches up to us. "You're storming the floating green?" He pauses for a moment and answers his own question. "Of course you are."

Jack raises a golf club, what looks to be a nine-iron, over his head. "Avast ye, me hearties. Prepare to be boarded, floating green!"

I look at Win. "What's happening?"

"That thing in front of us is the world's only floating green. We're about to land on it, which, if it's not obvious, isn't really the way it's supposed to work."

I look at Jack, who grins and twirls the golf club over his head.

"He's crazy," I laugh.

"He's an old guy who's stopped caring what other people think of him. And he has a lot of money, so he does what he wants."

Jack encourages me to stand next to him. I pull myself up, and Win puts a hand out to steady me. His stable grip on my elbow sends a wave of chills through my body.

There's one poor caddy sitting in a folding chair on the surface of the floating green, under a little orange and green striped umbrella. There's a boat tethered to the other side of the floating green at a dock. I figure out that most people probably approach the green from the other side, and the caddy ferries them out to play their shots and then drives them back.

Not us.

"You can't park there." He points at us.

Jack scoffs. "You don't park a boat. I'm moored. And we're playing through." He tosses a putter and three balls onto the green before lashing the boat to the ladder that hangs over the side.

"I'll get in trouble." The skinny guy stands up and comes to the side of the green, offers Jack a hand up at the top of the ladder.

"I've got a hundred bucks that says you don't." Jack stands tall now and waves me and Win up the ladder.

As I follow Win up, I see Jack peel a hundred-dollar bill off a wad of cash and hand it to the caddy.

"You weren't kidding," the caddy murmurs. He shrugs and walks back to his post, sits in his folding chair.

"Is this how it's going to be today, Jack?" Win asks. "You just bulldoze your way through the whole course, and we follow in your wake?"

Jack's head is down, and he's randomly dropped a ball. "Hush," he says as he taps the ball, "or you'll force me to take a mulligan."

The ball rolls obediently into the hole, about twenty feet across the floating green.

I speak up. "We didn't even drive the green. Something tells me mulligans are really not a factor."

Jack picks his ball out of the hole and pulls the pin. "Listen. We could all die—Earth struck by a meteorite and vaporized—at any moment. Really, if we're being honest, I could just drop dead. I'm an old guy, after all, and I have a tendency to get wound up about just about everything. So if I know I'm going to die any minute, I'll play the floating green first. It's the best part."

Win rolls his eyes. "Fine. But you're just impulsive. Don't pretend to be some great philosopher."

Jack ambles over and hands me his putter. "Try it. And relax. There's not a meteorite headed our way. Just try to enjoy being here, right now."

I smile and take the putter.

I take a really deep breath and look up. The sky is bright, crisp blue. The air smells clean and fresh, with the breath of lake water carried in its breeze.

If I get vaporized, so be it. Hopefully I won't notice the meteorite barreling down on me before I'm done for.

I drop the golf ball Jack's given me and line up my shot with the hole. Jack stands next to it with the flag.

Win whispers to me, right before I hit the ball. "You're smiling. I like it."

I send the ball into the water.

We use the floating green for personal putting practice for

about fifteen more minutes, until our attendant spots a foursome of legitimate, rule-following golfers approaching from the correct direction. We make our escape, getting back on the boat and making our way to the actual dock just to the left of the floating green.

Jack slides the boat smoothly up to the side of the dock, and Win hops up to lash the boat's ropes to the dock tie-downs.

There's another skinny guy waiting in a golf cart for us. He has a radio in his free hand. "Mr. McCann, you golfing with two guests today?"

"Help us with the clubs."

"Very good, Mr. McCann." He pulls the golf cart up and loads Win's and Jack's and Jack's wife's clubs. "Toby's coming with the other cart. He'll be your caddy for the day." He gives us a wave and walks back down the dock.

I start thinking this through. "I shouldn't golf. I can just drive the cart. I'll slow us down too much."

Win smiles. "We'll play best ball. We take the best hit off the tee and play from that. It makes it fun. You won't slow us down. You and I can ride in the other cart. Jack's stuck with the caddy."

"I just want to see how this guy can play," Jack says, nodding to Win.

"Uh-huh." Win shoots him a look.

The caddy, Toby, shows up. He's the first person on staff here who weighs more than a buck twenty-five, and he's tan, tall, and wearing plaid golf pants with a crisp white Polo and spotless white golf shoes.

I sit at the wheel of the cart the last skinny employee

abandoned to us. Win sits next to me. I lean over to him. "This guy is definitely not 'like us'."

Win sighs and whispers, so close I can feel the breath on my neck. "Toby's my older brother."

Embarrassment washes over me. "Um, sorry," I mumble. If I weren't on a dock, sitting shoulder to shoulder with him in a golf cart, I'd be looking for a place to hide.

He nudges me. "He's definitely not like us, though. It's okay."

Except here's the thing. Toby's smooth stride to us, it matches Win's. And Toby's dressed head to toe like money.

Which means the way Win dresses? It's by choice.

Which is fine. Most of what I wear is by choice, too.

But what if I decided suddenly I wanted to wear Anthropologie, not Saver's?

Well, I'd be out of luck. I don't have the option to change labels. I am this way because it's comfortable, and I like the spoon wrapped around my wrist, and I'm not much of a flowy, bohemian-vibe kind of girl, but I also can't go on a spending spree and change who I am.

Turns out Win's got the option.

Toby walks up to us, and Win's out of the cart to meet him. I get out on the other side and follow him.

"Toby."

"Brother of mine. What's up? You're golfing?"

Win points to Jack. "Jack needed us. He's looking for a ringer. And I wanted to show Vivi the course."

Toby puts out a hand to me. "Nice to meet you, Vivi. Win mentioned there was someone cool at school now."

"Nice to meet you." I shake his hand, try to think and

communicate my all-around coolness with a powerful, confident grip. Mom had me practice handshakes when I was little, probably about seven. It was a time when I wouldn't speak to strangers, even the people behind the counter at McDonald's. She decided I needed "social graces," so she took me down to the YMCA and we got a tour so I could practice shaking new people's hands and looking them in the eye. It was pretty much the worst. But, as Mom says, because of it I've got a great handshake, "by golly."

Jack's impatient. "Let's get to it, people."

Jack and Toby get in the other cart, and Win and I follow them. I drive, pushing the rattling cart to stay close behind them.

"You drive like Dale Earnhardt. Don't roll us." Win smiles at me.

"I don't drive for real yet. But I really do like this. Someday maybe I'll live on an island where all they drive is Vespas and golf carts. That's my kind of living."

"There's a place like that in North Carolina. Or there's Hydra, in Greece. They only have donkeys."

"I'll stick with golf carts." I think for a second. "So Toby. He's a sharp dresser."

I don't know if Win knows what I'm getting at.

He seems to. "Yeah, he's a prep."

"So when you said the 'like me' label, that label, it's—"

He stops me. "It's really important to Toby to fit in. As I think I've discovered, you and me, we don't try to fit in."

"Or we fundamentally can't fit in because we are way, way, way off target in knowing how to fit in. We are a dodecahedron who would love to contemplate fitting into a square peg, but it's never going to happen." I stop myself before I start ticking off examples of how ridiculously awkward I am.

I pull in behind Jack and Toby's cart at the first hole. Win puts his hand on my arm before I can climb out.

"When I was three, I spoke in a tiny voice like a munchkin in *Wizard of Oz* and told everyone my name was Bullion."

"So? You were three. I bet you were really cute."

"I didn't stop until the teacher in kindergarten wanted my parents' permission to have me see the school psychologist." He looks me straight in the eye. "The label stands. Stop trying to find ways we don't fit. We fit."

And then I start to wonder if we fit like how I might want us to fit, or if Win's idea of fitting just means as really swell friends.

And then I freak out about admitting I'd like to fit in some different way.

This all happens as Jack drives off the tee, straight down the fairway.

Toby takes the driver from him. "You up, Win?"

"You gonna play or just caddy?" Win asks him.

Jack calls from the other cart, "Toby can play if he wants; that's fine."

Toby shakes his head. "Caddies don't play. The club would fire me. Unless I'm instructing, I don't play. Even then I usually don't. Only the pro ever really does that."

I try to join the conversation. "You want to be a golf pro someday?"

Win looks at his brother. "He wants on the PGA tour

someday. And he's good enough, too, to do it."

Toby puts an arm around his brother's shoulder. "Always the optimistic one. Thanks for the vote of confidence."

We play eight more holes. I hit off the tee each time, and each time my ball either falls off the tee because I've only grazed it, or shanks hard to the right, landing in the rough no more than twenty or thirty feet from the tee. Needless to say, mine is never the best ball.

Toby doesn't have much to say. Jack is chapped. I don't know if he envisioned all of us riding in the same cart or what, but I think he wants in on the conversation Win and I have in between shots.

But Win makes Jack happy in one way for sure. He is a ringer. He drives to the green on two of the three-par holes in the first nine.

I get a couple putts in that count for something on our scorecard, but on the whole, driving the cart goes much more smoothly for me.

We're about to make the turn to the back nine when Jack makes an abrupt about face toward the dock.

"We're done for the day, lady and gents," he declares. "We played the floating green, and I haven't thrown out my back. Let's quit while we're ahead."

After struggling through the first nine, I'm happy to be done. "It's time to put me out of my misery, anyway. You all were way too patient. Next time I'm just driving the cart."

Jack won't have any of it. "All you need are some

lessons. Maybe Toby can teach you."

Toby looks right at his brother. "I think Win might be the better teacher."

Mystified, Jack presses. "Why wouldn't she work with someone who's on his way to the pros?"

I hope someone changes the subject. I don't want to push Win to define what I am to him. Not yet. Just in case, you know, it might be something interesting later, and if asked now, that interesting would never get to be a possibility.

Sometimes that's how that goes. Under the heat lamp of scrutiny and definition, new things wilt and don't get past being new.

Toby pats Jack on the back. "There's more to golf than golf. Leave it at that, Mr. McCann."

"You know you call me Jack."

"When I'm in the employ of the Coeur d'Alene Resort Golf Club, you're Mr. McCann." Toby salutes the three of us and walks back toward the pro shop. "It's been a pleasure. See you at home, Win. Nice to meet you, Vivi."

He leaves, and I can't help but notice that Win seems to relax, letting his shoulders slacken just a bit with Toby gone.

I get that. Just hearing Toby mention the resort reminds me that Mom's an employee, too, and I immediately hope there'll be no occasion for the golf staff to cross paths with the gift shop employees. Family's so complicated.

The three of us walk back to the dock. The boat bobs up and down on the gentle waves of the lake. It'd be uncomfortably hot without the breeze from the water. The sun is high over the lake, and I squint to find my footing getting back into the boat. I find a spot to sit behind the driver, at the stern.

Jack takes the wheel, and Win comes to sit with me, two bottles of water in his hands.

"For crying out loud, did I leave my phone in the cart?" Jack stands up and checks all of his pockets. Win hops up and checks the zippered pocket on Jack's golf bag.

"No luck here. Sorry, Jack." Win points to the clubhouse. "Do you want me to run up and check if Toby's found it?"

Jack's already out of the boat. He played great golf today, and now he springs down the dock at a jog, seemingly no worse for the wear. I'm not as fit as he is, and I have to be at least forty years younger.

"I got it," he says. "You two stay put."

Win sits back down, cracks open the water bottle in his hand.

Suddenly I feel self-conscious. I sip a little from mine and blurt out the first topic I can think of.

"So, you want to go to University of Nevada Reno, huh?" I'm such a total loser. *Gee, Vivi, we just played golf all day. What to talk about, what to talk about? I don't know, maybe golf?*

No, instead I lead with the college thing.

I hadn't thought much about college before because Mom and I have been in survival mode. Me, get through school. Mom, keep a job. Then move and start the process all over. Survive. Pay bills so we can stay in the place we've rented. Stay safe, keep our truths to ourselves.

That kind of stuff takes up a lot of real estate in a

brain. It doesn't leave a lot of room for dreams, or plans. Or hopes.

But hanging out with Win, it just seems like maybe, maybe it's safe to think ahead.

Just a bit.

The only thing I've really liked in school has been art. But it seems pretty out there to study art—it's hard to imagine making a living as an artist.

Every once in a while, before I fall asleep, I do think about living somewhere abroad—like a study-abroad program—and going to amazing museums and maybe wearing sunglasses and a scarf like Audrey Hepburn in *Roman Holiday*. My mom had a friend she sometimes talks about who went to Barcelona and would tell her stories about staying up all night, eating wonderful midnight meals of tapas and olives in sidewalk cafes, and taking siestas in the hot Spanish afternoons. Mom made it sound like the entire nation operated that way. I'd love a whole country that revolved around not being stressed out. I could support a place like that.

At some point, Win realizes I'm not listening to his answer. I was planning on listening to it, I really was.

"What are you thinking about?"

"How I'd like to live in a country so blissed out that I couldn't be anxious. It'd be against the rules. You know, like citizenship depended upon your ability to nap."

"I'd like that, too." He smiles. "Not sure how your question about my college led you into that territory, but I'll go with it."

Maybe because we're alone, or maybe because the sun has cooked my brain, I disclose. "I'm thinking about college. Going away to college. Don't know about that. But then I thought, what about just running really far away from everything, all of it?"

"Your mom makes you anxious by being anxious? Is that it?"

"No. Maybe, but I don't know. It might be in our blood, but we each have our own worries. And like I said, I think Mom's are with good reason. There's a difference between real threats and imagined anxieties, in my book at least."

"Anxiety's not about an overactive imagination. I hope someone's told you that. Your anxiousness isn't made up. Don't diminish it." Win says this in a way that seems as though he's said something really, really similar to someone else. Or someone's said it to him.

Turning away from me, he takes a look up the dock back toward the clubhouse. I wonder if he has a reason to hide his face from me. Is this topic too close to something else? To the reason the girls in art say he struggles this time of year, maybe?

I can see Jack coming back down the dock, phone in hand, so I wrap up this conversation.

"I want to do a better job just soaking everything in, and take good care of myself. But I do want to know what so's great about University of Nevada Reno."

"Like I said, atmospheric science. I like weather. The gnarlier, the better."

That makes me worried. I try to sound mellow. "You're a storm chaser?"

"I haven't had a chance to chase any storms. But I like weather systems. I really like fire."

"That doesn't count as weather."

"I could be a fire meteorologist. Fire has a mind of its own, makes its own weather systems. But geology, too. Earthquakes."

"Tsunamis?"

"Yep. Hurricanes, tornadoes. All of it. Data and weather and disaster prediction. I'd love to have a job that could save people's lives. How amazing would that be?"

"Super amazing. A golf pro and an earth science guy in the same family."

I can't help but feel a little worried and maybe a little depressed. I don't think I'm very "like me" in this moment, and I'm trying to imagine how I would fit in with that kind of family. My mom can't know about these career aspirations Win has. He's so enthusiastic about disaster, and he's so positive his college career will be a wild success. She's not a positive thinker like that. She's a mom who doesn't even know I want to go away. Not only have I not crossed that bridge, I haven't even built that bridge.

"But what about the summer? You have any plans for that yet?" Win asks.

"Not a clue. I thought I might work at the library. I like books."

"Okay, a job. What kind of adventures do you want to have? That's the good stuff."

"Um. No clue. You have a list or something?"

"I don't, really. But you just moved here. There's lots of cool stuff to do here in the summer. Have you ever jumped off a cliff?"

"No. Seems like a bucket list item that would actually bring about the bucket kicking."

"No, it's awesome. Off the cliffs on Tubbs Hill."

"You say the word *cliff*, and I'm out. Sorry."

"We'll work our way up to that. Ever had a late-night picnic?"

"Nope."

"Watched a full solar eclipse?"

"Not that either. But I don't think either of us saw that—last time it was visible in this part of the US was 1979."

"I was there." Jack's back.

I give him a look as he climbs down into the boat. "I wasn't talking to you."

"I figured. That eclipse was kind of lame, anyway. It was February, and the weather was sub-arctic. This one is the one for the ages."

Win stands up to cast the lines off the boat. "First item on the list, then, is the eclipse. Last part of the summer, but top of the epic-things-to-happen list."

When Jack gets the boat out on the lake, I sit in the back and watch Win, sitting in front of me, talking to Jack.

This could be a big problem. Win's my friend, and every minute I watch him, I think of him less and less that way.

He's just sitting there, talking, and I keep thinking of how I've never wanted to be adventurous before. But his dark eyes sparkle with possibility, and his smile transmits this infectious happiness.

I didn't know I could feel this happy.

And that feels dangerous.

The next day I go out on a run. It's a Sunday, and though no one knows this yet, it's going to be the last day we get rain in Coeur d'Alene for the rest of the summer.

The drizzle turns to mist as I get closer to the lake. Everything is damp, and the streets are empty, cars all still huddled next to the curb in the early morning gray.

I make the turn on to Lakeshore Drive at the bottom of the hill, and Jack's not out. His paper is still at the end of the drive, still wrapped in plastic to protect it from the wet. I consider picking it up and taking it to his front door when I see movement two blocks down the road.

Someone, a guy about my age dressed in a black suit, stands on the sidewalk in front of the big white Colonial house. From where I am, I can't recognize him, but it could be Win. Or Toby, or any other deeply tanned, tall, lithe young man in a black suit. It really could be anyone.

The only reason I stop, that I don't run any farther down the street, is what the person is doing.

He has two bunches of roses in his arms, each more than a dozen apiece. The roses are white, bright and clean against the dark arms of his jacket.

Paired with the black suit and the black sunglasses the guy wears, even in the rainy gloom of this morning, the roses feel like one thing to me: funereal.

It's Sunday, yes, but it's too early for a funeral service. It's even too early for just a standard church service.

Then the guy starts walking.

He doesn't get into a car; he turns and begins to walk down the sidewalk with the two huge bouquets in his arms.

Am I going to follow him? Of course I am.

It might be Win. It might be Toby. It might be some

random guy, but my curiosity's piqued. And I have the best cover. I'm out on a run, and I was going to run in that direction anyway.

Here's hoping he walks somewhat quickly, because I will give him as much of a head start as I can, but I'm running, and he's in a suit, so at some point I could overtake him. I might not be much of a private detective, but something tells me that's a no-no in tailing a suspect.

I concoct a plan to double back on blocks, too, as discreetly as I can. He'll walk a block, and I'll stay behind and run up and down the block one street over as a way to maintain my distance.

As I slowly jog behind the mystery guy, I size him up as best I can. Definitely a confident gait. Long-legged, tall and thin, and walking with his head up. The person doesn't look distressed. Instead, he's purposeful.

I jog on the trail past the dog park as he walks a block to the north of me. I feel confident that I'm totally inconspicuous except for the one time I trip over my own shoelace because I'm watching him out of my peripheral vision and not paying attention to where I'm going.

I tail him for twenty minutes. He turns onto a wide boulevard with trees down the middle of the road: Government Way.

I'm not sure how to follow him here and still keep up the charade that I'm just out on a run. I duck down a side street and start to think about giving up and going home when I realize what I'm looking at down the street about four blocks: a cemetery.

That's what the roses are for.

But why walk? Why not just drive? And why so early

in the morning? And alone?

I pick up the pace and get down the side street a little ahead of the mystery man. I want to be in the cemetery ahead of him, try to get a bead on where he goes, what grave he visits. I come to the end of the lane I'm on and have the luck to come to face to face with a padlocked gate that dangles from its hinges. I'm able to squeeze through and get into the cemetery ahead of the man in black.

The cemetery drive is wide, and the trees are tall. Shrubs are neatly trimmed, and most of the headstones are small and modest. The trouble is, the whole area is open. He'll see me in the cemetery from a distance, and my cover will be blown.

So I run at a breakneck pace into the cemetery, trying to get far ahead of him, and I hide behind the biggest tree trunk I can find. To my left is a large statue of a Union soldier from the Civil War. I hope the guy comes in the cemetery along the main drive, and I hope no one else drives by and wonders what a teenage girl in running tights and a pink "Rose Tyler, Run" T-shirt is doing hiding behind a ponderosa pine.

The black suit guy comes walking down the cemetery lane in less than a minute. I thank my lucky stars that I panicked and ran as quickly as I did, or he would've seen me picking my hiding spot.

He still has his arms full of roses. Suddenly, my heart thumps in anticipation: I'll recognize him if I know him. He's coming close enough.

Then I worry. If he finds me out, and he's someone I know, how will I explain following him more than a mile through town on foot?

I hold my breath.

Silently, he walks past me, past the statue of the Union soldier. From my position behind the wide trunk of the pine tree, I can lean out a bit to get a good look at him in profile.

He keeps walking, toward the back corner of the cemetery.

I keep my eye on him and run to another tree trunk, then another. If there's someone behind me in the cemetery, I look like a raving lunatic.

Finally, he's almost in the far corner of the sprawling grounds, but I see where he's going.

Surrounded by a black wrought-iron fence is a tall, white, marble angel, wings in rest, eyes cast downward, arms full of flowers.

I take a chance and peek around another tree trunk just as he kneels and leaves the two large bunches of roses at the angel's bare feet.

It's Toby. There's no mistaking. It is exactly the guy who caddied for Jack just yesterday.

He stands, looks around for a moment, and walks back the way he came.

I'm terrified to move. I lean against the wet trunk of the tree, staying still and breathing as quietly as I can. Now would be a terrible time to be caught, and I can run home by a totally different route, so I try to calm myself down before I make any sudden moves.

Toby walked to a cemetery, left two huge arrangements of roses, and walked back the way he came.

What is going on?

I sit down and breathe in the vanilla-and-pine aroma of the ponderosa. The ground is covered with pine needles, a soft, damp bed under the trees. Some little finch chirps and tweets and sings high in the branches above me as a soft rain begins to fall.

Really, everything else aside, this is quite a lovely place, and if I were certain I could hang out in my beyond-the-veil ethereal form in a place like this, I think I'd be more ready to meet my maker.

After a while, I realize it's probably safe to leave.

I walk home in the mist. The clouds hang low, and the evergreens are black with moisture and dripping with rain. Birds perch under the thick cover of their branches and call to one another. I feel the raindrops gathering between my shoulder blades, at the nape of my neck. The streets shine with pools of water, and the town is quiet. When I get home, Mom is in the shower, so I make myself a cup of tea and curl up under a blanket on the futon in the front room.

And I commence to think.

I wonder if what Toby did today has something to do with why Phoebe and Fiona said this time of year is tough on Win.

What was Toby doing down on Lakeshore Drive? Why does he deliver white roses to an angel statue in a cemetery?

Though I thought it would, I don't know if it makes me feel any better to know Win is a person who probably pulls the door shut when he stands on the porch, just like my mom does.

We all have secrets to hide.

CHAPTER FIVE
LOVELY, DARK, & DEEP

The next Saturday smells like summer. Our new neighbor cuts the grass in his backyard. I haven't met him yet. As a teenager, going next door and making random conversation with someone adult makes my neck itch. Mom's not much better, usually, but she's trying really, really hard here in Coeur d'Alene to reinvent herself. Or let go of stuff.

Actually I don't really know what her plan is, but it feels like she's trying.

It's been only the one time so far that I came home and she was in the bathroom as her typical wound-up, super-anxious self.

So far.

It's not that I don't believe in fresh starts. I want to, enthusiastically so. But Mom has a pattern.

I grew up with her. I've been living the pattern since I

was small.

There were nervous days, after nights of watchfulness. Days of Mom in bed as I got up, pulled clothes from the hamper, and wore them dirty to school.

But this morning I brush away all the old starts, all the old patterns, because David next door has cut his grass, and it smells like summer, and Mom was brave enough, new enough, fresh-start enough to go next door and bring him muffins (from the Jiffy blueberry mix, but hey, she made them) and introduce herself.

I know his name because Mom was brave and introduced herself and tried.

So I can try this Saturday morning, too.

I get out of bed before nine and take a shower before next-door-neighbor David's even had a chance to finish weed-eating.

I dry my hair, pull it up into a thick ponytail, and find a baseball hat to pull the ponytail through.

Mom comes into the bathroom as I weigh whether or not to put on mascara.

"What's the plan today?" she asks as I decide against it.

"I thought I might go hike." I leave out the part where I hope to run into Win.

"Sounds good—nowhere obscure, okay? I don't have a search-and-rescue team or Saint Bernard to locate you."

"Though the idea of a Saint Bernard finding me sounds kind of fun, I had a trail on Tubbs Hill picked out. There may be a few trees, but not much wilderness past that."

This seems to satisfy Mom's built-in fret-o-meter. She waves a hand in the direction of the backyard. "I'm thinking about pulling weeds. Maybe it's not too late to plant some tomatoes out back." She braids a tiny strand of my hair as I put on eyeliner. She points to what I'm doing. "Eyeliner for a hike? You're going to sweat it off anyway."

I know she's prying in her own subtle way.

I've never had a boyfriend. I mean, I don't have one now, either, but in the past it was pretty rare for me to even have a friend who was a boy. Okay, it was rare for me to have a friend who was a friend. Who was a human. Not an imaginary friend.

Listen. I'm fine. I like being alone. I've had friends along the way. But you get a little cavalier about them when you leave so often. I had to get nonchalant before my heart got broken for good. Survival is a basic human instinct, after all.

"I'm a teen. Why do we do what we do? Who can know why we like the winged eyeliner, anyway? The heart wants what it wants." I finish what I'm doing and turn around to give her a kiss on the cheek. "Love you up and down," I begin.

"Forward and backward," she continues. She gives me a little kiss on the tips of my fingers in return.

"And always," I finish.

I walk out the door, smell David's cut grass, and head to the base of the Tubbs Hill trail.

On the first part of the trail, there's a lot of sunlight that filters through the trees. The pine trees have wide, smooth trunks, and the earth below them is dusty and thick with pine needles. Not much undergrowth crowds around them, and I can see up the slope and out across the marina to Jack McCann's house, with its glorious backyard. No one sits at the outdoor bar, or uses the outdoor grill, or plays croquet right now, though. Weirdly, in the early morning, all that equipment guaranteed to entertain any average person seems like it's trying too hard. And all the red chairs and red umbrellas and red bar cushions, it's just a little matchy-matchy.

Is Jack lonely? I don't know. He did recruit me and Win to play golf with him.

I turn my attention to the trail as it ascends, winding up the hill and away from the shore of the lake.

As I hike farther up, the trees begin to crowd. The light must fight through more and more dense pine boughs, and the air cools around me.

I whistle a bit. It's early, and I haven't run into anyone yet, but I hear the jangle of a dog tag against a dog collar and get excited.

A black lab rounds the corner of a huge gray-granite outcropping, followed by an affable couple, the guy toting an adorable black-haired little boy in a backpack kid carrier.

"Hi." I wave to the little boy.

"Hat!" The little boy greets my headgear.

The mom pulls the black lab by the collar and keeps him from licking me as I go by. "Sorry," she says. "They like everybody."

"It's a good trait," I call. They've moved along.

I hear the little boy greeting the next object in sight: "Plant!"

I make one more turn around another large pillar of

rock, and I must be on the north side of the hill. Not only is the air cooler, now it feels damp, and the woods are dark and green. The trail isn't dusty here at all.

It's suddenly quiet.

I hear the snap of twigs above me, up a draw between thick trees and the large slabs of rock piled on one another.

Win.

He stands and waves with one hand, a large notebook in the other.

I wave back. Something tells me not to be loud, not to yell.

He motions to me. "Come up this way. It's cool."

I look up the slope. Remember when I worried about chewing gum and getting down the steps of a bus at the same time? This is steep, and the dirt is loose, and there are rocks and slippery pine needles.

"I don't know."

"You can do it." He stands still. "You've got this," he calls, but it's in such a gentle, calm way, I feel like this must be how the horse who's whispered to feels.

I put my head down and pick my first footings, then my next, as I climb up the little gully. I don't look up until there's a strong hand in front of me, extended.

"Almost there."

I lift my head and take his hand. He pulls me even with him. I'm right next to him, close enough that the brim of my baseball hat brushes his shoulder as I steady myself.

"Here I am." I look around. "What's up? What're you doing up here?"

He holds up his notebook. "Communing with nature. Thinking of brilliant Thoreau things to say."

"Thorough or Thoreau?" I ask.

"Whichever. I'm punny like that." He smiles.

I brush off the flat slab of rock and sit. "You're too young for dad jokes, really," I tease.

"Only humor I know. My dad's brainwashed me, I suspect. It's a little of the Canadian heritage. We're kind of a nation of bad dad jokes waiting to happen."

"I thought you were part Canadian."

"My dad's Canadian and Cuban. My mom's Japanese. I'm multi-national. You should be impressed."

"It might balance out the dad jokes, but I'm noncommittal on that." I tuck my knees up under me, trying to decide if I'm brave enough to ask more about the tattered notebook in his hands.

He must notice me eyeing it, and he holds it up so I can see the cover. It's plastered with stickers from NOAA, Schweitzer Mountain ski area, and Sierra Club, and he's doodled a big pine tree and a mountain goat in the center. "I just like to write down observational stuff, research."

"Research?" I wonder about that. "On what?"

"I like weather and the Earth, right? I'm trying to observe with a scientist's eye, or if I just want to know about something, I look it up and jot notes on that. I can spend hours taking notes on stuff like tectonic plates and subduction zones. It's kind of meditational."

"Mom tries to tell me pulling weeds is meditation. I'm thinking it's a way to trick me into dull kinds of work."

He looks hurt. "I'm dull?"

Lord, why do I even bother trying to be normal? It's no use—it's inevitable that I say dumb stuff that runs off normal people.

"Not in the slightest. You're lovely, remember?"

He sits on the rough outcropping with me. "So you're out on a hike. Pretty adventurous."

"Can I read some of what you wrote?"

He smiles, but it's a straight-across, teeth-set-on-edge kind of smile. "Eh, I think no. You've got the general impression that I'm mostly normal. The journal pretty much shoots that theory full of holes."

I nudge him a bit, proud of myself for thinking of an opportunity to make physical contact without appearing like a total stalker. "You know I'm totally abnormal. Why not make me feel better about myself by joining the ranks of the lonely and weird?"

His face gets very solemn. It puts me right back to following on Toby's heels, and I feel like I've ventured onto tender ground. Bursts of bright white roses bloom in my mind's eye, and I instantly regret my jokey tone.

He looks me straight in the eye, his dark eyes black in the dim light of the forest. "Lonely and weird, right here." He puts his hand on his chest, owning it.

"It's okay, you know," I whisper.

"What?" He leans into my shoulder, but his head is down, his eyes cast on the ground.

"It's okay that we don't fit. We fit with each other. We already figured that part out. It's okay now." Saying it makes me breathless with the honesty. I can feel tears crawl up my throat and well in my eyes.

He's quiet. He pulls open the notebook, to a page with a corner folded over.

It's my name, Vivi.

Actually, it's my palindromic name, Viviviv, in a

cursive hand, and traced over and curlicued and shaded out and starred. The embellishments grow from the center of the page to the edges, bleeding over and through to the other side.

"Here." I turn my hand over and open my palm. Written on my heart line, curved around the thick pad of my thumb, is his name. Win.

He laughs, tilting his head up to the trees above our heads. "We are a pair."

"A pair of what, I don't know." I feel a broad smile on my lips, and it feels like home.

"A pair of long stories," he suggests. We look at each other. We let the long stories hang in the air, unspoken, like smoke from a smothered campfire.

"Something like that." I touch him on the hand. He takes mine, opens my hand again to his name drawn on my palm in Sharpie.

"That's a better place for it than on my lunch bag. It looks good there." He looks at me, leans forward, but he doesn't cross the distance between us. I wonder if he was considering kissing me, but the moment doesn't feel like that. It's bigger, more.

"It belongs there," I say, but that's as much honesty as I can do in one sitting. "But now I'm thinking my legs are cramping up, and I should probably hike more before I'm stuck up here."

He nods. He's done, too. There's only so much soul-searching two people can manage in a day.

"I've got an adventure for you," he says. "You up for it?"

"By all means, if I make it down this hill without

splitting my head open." I turn and start making an awkward mess of myself, sliding and shuffling down the leaves and needles and pebbles, back the way I came.

Win chats and jokes and puts as much conversational distance between us and our hilltop confessional as he can.

We make our way around Tubbs Hill, emerging by the statue of Millie and Mudgy, the children's story mascots and unlikely moose-and-mouse friends.

He points over to the floating boardwalk, an invitation in his voice. "So, you said you're down for an adventure today?"

I nod. Who knows what I've gotten myself into with him, but it's not a worry, and that's something I take note of.

I follow him past the tour barges, party pontoons, and the sleek chrome-and-white yachts moored in the resort marina.

"These look like someone over on Lakeshore Drive might own them."

"Probably a good bet. We're just taking the scenic route." He leads me around the outside of the marina, on the wide wooden planks of the boardwalk. We pause at the top of the bridge over the marina entrance to watch a Malibu speedboat with bright, gecko-green sparkling paint glide under us, the passengers all tan and hidden behind sunglasses.

City Beach bustles in the noontime sun, under the blue Saturday sky. Warm weather like this feels luxurious. Maybe Idahoans are used to more sunshine than I am, but I try to soak it up in the event that the Seattle gloom catches up with me and clouds the sky.

"Is it fair of me to ask if this is a wild goose chase yet?" I let just an inch of worry seep under the door in my brain where I've kept it shut all morning. Mom hasn't texted me, so hopefully she's busy pulling weeds and hasn't thought that it's much too long for me to be gone on a hike around the hill by our house.

Win's adamant. "No way. I've got all of this planned out."

"Even though we just ran into each other out on a hike."

"Well, you know, serendipity makes plans for me when I'm out on hikes."

"Serendipity is what happens when you're busy making other plans?" I wonder.

"That's just goofy. You're verging into my Canadian-dad-joke territory." He points to a tiki hut-style shed on the edge of the sandy beach. "This is our grand plan, Viv."

I follow him to the shed. Coeur d'Alene's a far, far trail from Hawaii, but that fact hasn't slowed down the owners of this establishment. Tiki statues, palm fronds, hula girls—pretty much every Hawaiian stereotype is plastered all over the front of the little hut.

Inside are piles and piles of paddle boards. And a very pale person with vivid orange hair.

"Audrey." Win calls out to her. "How's it going?"

Audrey lets out a little shriek. "Win! You scared me."

I look sideways at Win. He shrugs and waves to her. "We're your first customers this morning?"

"Naw." She comes out of the little hut and squints,

surprised by the sun. "Just busy thinking about stuff. It's almost noon. Wind'll come up later and paddle boarding won't be any fun."

"Good thing we caught you now." Win approaches the shed. "Can I sneak in and grab my two?"

I look at Audrey's face under the visor of her pale hand, all her fingers decorated with henna tattoos and little silver rings. She closes her eyes. "You know where they are."

He steps out of the sunlight and into the depths of the shed. I nod to Audrey. "He has two boards?"

She doesn't look surprised. "He likes to come out whenever he gets a minute, so he just stashes his boards here. I don't mind, and Charlie doesn't care."

"Charlie?"

"My manager. He knows Win's dad. Whatever." Audrey's grown tired of me—she turns her back and walks away around the side of the shed.

"Okay." I'm left holding both ends of the conversation.

The noses of two paddle boards emerge from the shed first. One is gray and rubber, and the other is red, white, and blue. Win's got one under each arm, even though they look cumbersome, heavy, and large. I can't help but notice that he's stripped his long-sleeve shirt off, and his arms are muscled and tan, the tank top he wears bright white against his amber skin.

I swallow hard.

"We're in business." He drops the gray one on the sand, turns the other one to stand tall next to him. "My paddles are right around on the back side of the shed. Can you hang onto this one for me?"

I come to steady the red, white, and blue paddleboard, surprised by how much it wants to swivel on me. It takes a good deal of my concentration to keep it vertical and still.

Win's back in a minute with a wooden paddle and a black one, shorter than the other.

"Okay." He takes hold of the paddleboard and hands me the paddles.

"You always stash a paddleboard or two at the lake?" I wonder why two, specifically, and there's a tiny knot of fear in that wondering. Like, is this his standard play with girls? This is a typical date?

But his face clouds over. "I used to have a buddy I paddled with a lot, but that doesn't happen anymore."

"Toby?" I ask. Then it occurs to me. Someone else. Someone remembered with roses. And I wish I hadn't asked.

"No. Toby's busy with golf. He sticks to what he's good at."

I'm determined to take some of that load from his shoulders. I don't like the heavy worry in his knit brows. "Lucky for you I don't stick to what I'm good at, which is mainly eating Ritz crackers and making up nicknames for the cats I see in videos on the interwebz," I say, maybe a little too brightly. "I like to get in way over my head and make a severe fool of myself."

Which isn't really true, but I'm trying here. I don't like to make a fool of myself, but it seems to happen over and over whether I plan it or not.

His chin lifts a little, taking the bait I've tossed his way. "Way over my head is my style, too. But give yourself some credit. You tried golf the other day and lived to tell the tale."

"There seems to be a real possibility I could actually drown on this adventure, though."

He lifts the red, white, and blue board and carries it to the water's edge. "You could've fallen overboard when we were storming the floating green." He tosses me a lifejacket. "And this time you've got a PFD. You were unprotected while golfing."

"Floatation device. Brilliant." I try to push away all sorts of *Mom's going to stroke out* pesky thoughts that occur to me as I drag the gray paddleboard down to the lake.

"So the gray one is wide and stable. You don't even have to stand up the first time. You can sit on your knees. And it's all about the touring, so at the very least I can tow you around while you take in the sights."

He's out in the water, up to the waist, and when I put a toe in, it's really, really cold. But he doesn't even seem to notice.

"It feels hypothermic. Like, Jack-and-Rose cold," I offer.

He raises an eyebrow. "It's not *Titanic* cold. Lake Tahoe, that's cold. Or Big Trinity Lake. I got an ice cream headache just wetting my hair there. That's iceberg cold."

He pushes through the waist-deep water and emerges close to me, dripping. I look at my board intently now, embarrassed to be caught staring at him. Him, soaking wet. Yikes.

Standing next to me, he takes my gray board and pulls it deeper into the water. "The tail can't catch in the sand— it'll get warped or snap. So I'll hold it while you pull up on it, then just tuck your knees under you."

I do as I'm told. The board doesn't feel wobbly, but I look down and realize he's holding it steady. "Let go. I want to see how I can balance."

He pulls his hands away, and on my knees, it's not bad.

He hands me a paddle and comes close to me. I'm face to face with him, close enough to feel his breath on my face. He stands in the water next to my board and reaches out to zip up my life jacket. "Now you're ready for anything."

I start to sweat. It's nerves, sure, but it's also hot with the life jacket on, and I'm putting forth a lot of effort trying to stay steady.

I watch as he pulls himself out of the water onto his board. "Try to raise your head and watch me. It'll help you balance," he calls, then pushes through the water with a smooth sweep of his paddle. In one deft move, he puts the paddle down in front of him and stands on the board.

Watching him isn't a problem. He's tall, and his feet are planted on the board, strong and sure. He pulls the board through the water with a solid stroke of the paddle on one side of the board, then the other.

And at about that moment I realize he's leaving me in the proverbial dust. I lean a little forward, worried about being abandoned. The movement wobbles the board, and then my arms go up and the whole board dips hard to the left.

"Whoa!" I cry out. But the board is wide and forgiving and pushes back up to the surface. I don't go in, and I can feel that the water doesn't seem so freezing anymore.

He's suddenly by my side on his paddle board. "Nice recovery."

"How'd you get back here?"

"I've been doing this for a while. I can get around. Don't worry about where I am. Where do you want to explore?"

I look around. The whole lake is spread out in front of us. We could paddle out into the middle. I don't even know how long that might take, but then I immediately imagine a boat bearing down on me. "I don't know. Maybe follow the shore over toward the community college?"

He nods. "Sure enough."

We paddle together, Win standing tall. I get a little more comfortable, but I can't think about trying to stand up. It just doesn't feel like I'm ready to swim yet. All sorts of possibilities worry me right now, including that I left my phone in Win's backpack in the shed on shore, and boy, I hope Mom doesn't try to call. She doesn't do well when a cell phone isn't answered. I joke about imagining murderers with hooks for hands, but there was a 911 call when I didn't answer a text once, even though I just misjudged how long the battery would last, and I was only in 6th grade, and I was too afraid to have it at my desk in class because Mr. Deakins didn't like kids to have cell phones, since when he was a kid they could paddle backsides and the classroom didn't even have a phone, and here he was, doing just fine.

Anyway. I watch Win smile, pointing out the bird diving in front of us and popping back up behind our boards. We watch little kids having a splash fight on the beach by the levy road. We watch a float plane take off while I match the rhythm of Win's paddle strokes.

The sun bakes into the life jacket on my back, and I feel the muscles in my arms and shoulders stretch and loosen with the warmth of paddling. My thighs hurt a bit from sitting on my knees, and it occurs to me that it might be easier or more comfortable if I were standing up.

"I'm going to stand up," I announce, and I set my paddle on the board crosswise in front of me, like I saw Win do. Then I put one foot up, and then the other, and all of a sudden I am standing tall. Standing tall like Win.

"Take a stroke. The motion will keep you balanced. It's like pedaling a bike—if you don't, it's easier to fall over." He sweeps his paddle to show me, pulling himself and his board through the water, the dark lake parting for him.

I wobble for a second and resist the urge to overcorrect. My paddle goes in the water, and I pull back on it, feel the traction I get with the wide side of the paddle.

It strikes me then—how weird that the paddle can sink to the bottom of the lake when turned one way, and turned the other way, it's a strong force, moving me and my board forward.

There's a metaphor in there somewhere, but for now I enjoy how silent my brain is. The worry is sleeping, so I can hear the soft slap of the paddle against the water, the rush of the eddies around its stem when it sinks below the surface. The activity on the shore is like a TV with the sound muted, and beyond our movements and the occasional bird, the lake swallows the noise of the town and of my worries.

We've passed the college now, and the lake meanders

into the Spokane River.

Win pulls his paddle out of the water and stands on his board, turned toward me.

"I'm coming!" I call.

He doesn't seem rushed. "You're fine."

I make three more slow, strong pulls and come alongside him, then promptly glide past him. "You didn't really tell me how to stop," I yell.

He laughs, waving his paddle. "Just turn the paddle wide and pull it back against the water. But brace yourself." He stands wide on the board and flexes his knees a little.

I do what he's shown me. I slow the board down, and Win comes even with me. I feel a little bashful all of a sudden, aware that I've been unguarded, unthinking, relaxed, and it feels almost as though I were younger, less tied up in all the stuff, all the baggage, all the fear, all the things that drag on me, like walking through mud with a pair of loose boots on my feet.

He notices. He notices most everything with me. "Nice job. Look, you're up on your feet. No big deal."

I speak for once without thinking. "I feel good. I can do this. I'm doing it."

He just smiles.

"Can we go down the river a little farther? Maybe past that building with the blue roof?" I'm brave. I'm tired of being meek. I wish I felt like this more often.

We move down the river side by side, and it gets quieter and quieter. The campus to our right is quiet, spring semester over and summer not in session yet.

His paddle up, Win calls to me, "Over there is Blackwell Island." He points out the wide pavement with white cubes—the tops of RV campers—rising from it to our left. "Sometime we can go down the slough, but it can be kind of gross, and that's not the place to fall in."

I look down and think about falling in. "What if I jumped in now, though?"

He's noncommittal. "This is a good spot. You're leashed to your board, so it won't go anywhere. Might be cold."

I think about it. It's not something to be afraid of if I've already done it by choice—if I've jumped in before I could fall.

"Kind of a metaphor," I say out loud, not thinking Win can hear me.

"Not sure where you're headed with the metaphor, but go for it." He pulls off his shirt and tucks it and his paddle under the strap at the nose of his board. He dives off in a gorgeous half-moon arc, the pale soles of his feet the last thing to slip under the surface.

And before I can decide to go in or not, he surfaces right by my board. "It's a little cold, but I'm sweaty from paddling, so it feels good. I'll hold the board. Make sure you hold on to your hat and your paddle."

I pull my hat off and jump in feet first before I can think of any reason not to. Cold and dark, the water holds me for a split second before I'm out in the bright air again. I whoop and yell, wet words out of my mouth without thinking.

"It's cold!"

And there he is, Win, next to me in the water. He smiles, water droplets catching the light in his hair, little mirrors and colors trapped in tiny globes. He shakes his head, whipping his hair out of his eyes. "Your smile gets crooked when you relax," he says.

Impulsively, I lean in and kiss him. His lips are cold and wet. I pull back, grinning.

He smiles. "And you get bold."

I panic. "Sorry." I pull the leash and drag my board closer to me, looking to escape.

"No, I liked it." He doesn't run away.

Of course, we're in the middle of the lake, so he'd have to swim away, but he doesn't do that, either.

I breathe in, and my lungs fill up with joy. "I want my life to be more like this, a lot more of this."

He dips his mouth to blow bubbles for a minute, treads water facing me. "That's my life in one sentence. In the moment, out under the sky, it's a lot easier to keep my head on straight." He pushes away from me with a few kicks and turns his attention to his board. He pulls himself up, and I can see his shoulders tighten and spread as he pulls clear of the water and retrieves his paddle.

"You make that look easy." I have one elbow on my board now, more to keep it from drifting away from me than anything else. I want to tell him he makes everything look easy, but I suspect that would be kind of hurtful.

He's struggling, and just because it looks easy for him, I don't know that it is. I saw him on the beach, that night at dusk, and I don't think things are as easy for him as everyone thinks they are.

I may not know much, but there was a girl in Issaquah who ran cross-country. She was wafer-thin, legs like willow reeds, and the girls in our English class, we always said things to her, envying her slim form. Girl things meant as compliments, like "you're lucky; you're so skinny" and "you don't have to worry about what you eat, as tiny as you are." We'd give her hugs and slip an arm around her waist and bemoan our big beefy thighs next to her tiny muscular legs.

And then she didn't come back from Christmas break. Her parents had checked her into an eating disorders clinic, and all the girls in our English class had the awful realization that everything we thought came easy was actually killing her. She was running and starving herself to death, and every day in English we'd stoked the fire of her disease with the comments we thought we were giving to someone who had it easy.

Win whistles to me. "Vivi, look at that. You're sitting up, out of the water, on the board, and this is your first try on a paddleboard. Well done."

Sure, I wasn't thinking much about getting from the water on to the board, but my legs tremble like Jell-O now. "I think I'm coming to the end of my beginner's luck, so I'm staying down." I position myself on my knees and put my paddle into the water.

"No need to show off. Quit while you're ahead," he says with an easy laugh.

I follow him back along the shore, tracing the borders of the NIC campus, then City Park, to the tiki shed and the sullen red-headed keeper of the shed.

We don't really talk. The water laps at our boards and talks around our paddles in eddies and swirls.

I don't want to come off the water, but we do.

I feel like the spell's been broken.

Win gets everything put away with Audrey and hands me my stuff from out of his backpack.

And the clutch of stress, the knot at the bottom of my stomach, comes back when I see my phone.

"God, my mom's probably having a coronary."

Win raises an eyebrow. "It's Saturday. You supposed to be somewhere?"

"Mom needs to know where I am. Kind of always."

He doesn't tease me. His eyes are serious, and I appreciate it. Being dismissive of my mom doesn't help me feel very great about the whole situation.

He looks to see the notifications her attempts to contact me have left on my phone. "She's a helicopter parent, then."

"She's a Blackhawk helicopter parent."

"Intense?"

"Yep."

I feel irritated. You know what? I'm pretty good. I'm not out smoking weed or having sex with a biker gang. I spend most of my time running around like a scared Chihuahua with my tail between my legs, cowering and waiting for the next swat with a rolled-up newspaper from fate or bad luck or the universe or whatever it is that makes things happen. Maybe Mom could just let me be for a couple hours.

And on cue, my phone rings.

Win puts a hand on my shoulder. "May the Force be with you."

"Hello?" I turn away from him, embarrassed that he

might hear this conversation.

"Where are you? Are you all right? Are you hurt?" She's frantic, and her voice is thick, like she's been crying.

"I'm fine, Mom. I ran into Win. We've been hanging out."

No way am I telling her about the lake, about paddle boarding. Instead of congratulating me on my adventure, she'd dissolve into the possibilities of disaster. She'd tell me I could've drowned, or been plowed over by a boat, or she'd tell me a story about a girl just my age that she read or saw on TV or on the internet who died somehow in some situation that was exactly like the one I placed myself in.

I don't want to hear it.

And I don't want to be mad at her. I'm happy right now.

I can tell she's trying, trying again to be different. She breathes into the phone, then I hear her speak. "You have fun?"

I try to have patience, or sound like I have patience. "Yeah. He showed me around. My phone must've gotten turned off on the hike. Sorry, Mom. But I'm fine. The weather's so nice, and we had fun."

Again I hear her breathe, very intentionally, and then she speaks. "Are you on your way home, then? I have a roast chicken in the crock pot."

"We're walking home now. See you soon."

"Love you."

"Love you." I hang up.

Win looks at me. "Was today worth it?"

"She's not going to beat me or anything. She just gets scared."

"Did something bad happen to you all when you were in Washington?"

Win hasn't really pried or pushed for more on my long story. It's fair that he's asking, I think.

I consider it, but I can feel the heat already spreading up my neck, just thinking about telling him more. "Code word palindrome, but I will say this: my mom's running from something."

Win looks out at the lake, and when he speaks his voice is low and resolute. "I wish you'd been safe from whatever it was."

I consider this. "But if we'd been safe there, I wouldn't be here. So…" I leave the sentence in the air.

He smiles and touches the inside of my palm. "And whose names would we be graffiti-ing all over the place? Our careers as defacers of property—"

"And persons," I remind him, since I've traced his name on the palm of my hand, after all.

"Yeah, our careers would be cut short, underdeveloped by serendipity or whatever." He stands there for a moment, then touches my hand again. "That kiss…"

I worry. It fit perfect out there in the water. Maybe talking about it here, maybe it doesn't fit. Is that what he's going to say? "Yeah?"

He looks down at the ground for a second and then up at me through a fringe of bangs. His face is tan, his mouth soft, his dark eyes wide and earnest. "I liked it. I don't want to rush you, but we fit. We know that, and I want more of that."

All the air goes out of my lungs. "We're going to have to get to know each other in condensed form. We don't have much time."

"We can spend every waking moment together as soon as school's out."

"Until you go away to college," I say, and I can hear a tiny tremble in the sentence.

He shakes a finger at me. "Don't get to the end before we even have our beginning." He comes closer and weaves his fingers in between mine. "You can't live life like that."

My phone vibrates again, and I remember my real life, which will be lying in wait when I make it back to my house. I start walking.

"Quicker to go on the streets or use the trails on Tubbs Hill?"

"What a buzzkill, this whole world of danger and threat and what have you," Win says, his expression revealing some connection that's reared its ugly head in his mind.

I know he's not ready to talk about that long story, so I don't even ask.

Mom's out in the front yard when I get home. I insisted that Win didn't need to walk me home, and we parted ways at 8th and Bancroft. He walked a block down and turned left on Young Street.

I don't know where he lives yet. I don't know why I haven't asked. I just keep thinking he's in my neighborhood, but why haven't I wanted to know where exactly?

I feel like he's this spirit, summoned to me when I emerge from my house, there for me when I escape into the air of the town, loosed from the walls that are closing in on me.

Most of the time, though, I'm happy to stay indoors, find excuses to stay in bed, read a book. This "go outside and do stuff in the world of nature" impulse is definitely the new Vivi, but it doesn't feel forced or put on, it feels inspired—by the town, the lake, and the clean, mountain pine-tinged air.

Who am I kidding? By Win.

His name in my train of thought puts a smile on my lips. I like it there.

"Hey, Viv, there's my girl. So glad you ran into Win today. Was he out hiking, too?" Mom asks.

The whole train of words is stitched together with such effort. It's fake as a three-dollar bill, but man, I can't fault her for trying. She's trying so hard I think sweat is beading on her brow as I watch her speak.

"He has a spot he likes to sit and write. I ran into him."

"A writer, eh? That's intriguing. Poetry?"

"I don't think so. Scientific observations, maybe? He's a watcher. Likes to keep notes on what he sees." I have this weird sense of pride, like I can take credit for what Win chooses to put in that thick spiral notebook he toted into the deep shade of the forest.

"He's a scientist. That's cool," she says. She takes a breath.

And I know it's coming, so I try to head it off at the pass. "Listen, Mom, I'm sorry about not answering your calls or texts."

"You know I think the worst."

I bite the inside of my lip. *Understatement of the*

millennium. I snap my inner voice off before it comes out of my mouth unbidden.

"I know," I say, trying to not sound like a robot. But I say that so often. I'm supposed to understand, you know, under the circumstances and all.

Mom gets a whole lot of latitude because of *circumstances,* our circumstances, those things notwithstanding, the backstory, the whole thing, most of which I know nothing about.

Sometimes, isn't it just time to not make excuses?

But I make plenty of excuses for myself, so I try to be forgiving.

Mom must read some of this irritation on my face. She's pretty astute, even when she's whipped into a frenzy.

"My first job is to be your mom," she says. "Moms are supposed to get you to adulthood in one piece."

"I know."

"Part of it is where we've come from. And you know that. I need to try to protect you from what we left behind. And I know I can't keep you safe from everything."

I feel my irritation easing. "Don't make me give you the *Finding Nemo* lecture again. Don't be Marlin, Mom; no one likes Marlin as their mom."

She smiles at our inside joke. It's been a good shortcut to try to get us back to reality and away from speculative panic.

"Fair enough."

I come to her and give her a big hug. "I love you for trying to keep me safe."

"If you were hurt…" She lets the sentence hang there, and I worry it's going to send her off into a train of worried thought about all the possibilities, possibilities we tried to leave back in Washington.

I see no reason to think any of that will follow us, find us here in Idaho.

And I'm not going to entertain any other possibility, not now.

Not when there's Win to think about. I'd like to entertain all kinds of life possibilities with him. Those are the right kind of possibilities.

Earthquake

Most of the planets in our solar system aren't rocks at all, but amalgams of gases, shrouded in clouds, caught in the blender of rotational pull and gravity.

Earth is different—it hosts a variety of life on its crust. The outer layer of the crust is about forty miles thick. It is made up of odd-shaped puzzle pieces, about a dozen large tectonic plates that slide over, under, and past each other, as they float on top of the partly molten inner layer.

When the seams between these plates bounce and collide and slide into one another, earthquakes are the result. Anthropologists believe early humans in oral histories passed down stories of gods and monsters to explain earthquakes. As late as the 1700s, people explained earthquakes as the emission of gases and air from huge underground caverns.

The first earthquake described or recorded in history was in China in 1177 B.C.

In the US, the worst recent earthquake was Northridge in 1994. Overpasses collapsed, buildings were destroyed, and the quake hit at 4:30 am, when many were asleep in their beds. Survivors describe waking up to shaking, pounding, and pitch-black darkness, as all the power was knocked out. One woman told of the noise filling her body as she tried to shout over the sound of the quake to her husband, but she could not.

The quake resulted in California making drastic updates to their building codes. Eighty-seven people were killed.

There are four earthquakes on the list of deadliest natural disasters in the world since 1900.

The greatest magnitude earthquake in the United States was the Alaska quake of 1964. Ground motion was so severe the tops of trees were snapped off.

Recent advances in earthquake detection include GeoCosmo, a system of forecasting earthquakes with semiconductor physics. Recent updates in safety and prevention include advances in building codes, though adoption of FEMA-recommended seismic codes has been uneven in the United States.

California's last big quake was the La Habra quake in 2014. USGS predicts an 85% chance of a magnitude 5 or greater quake in the LA area before April of 2018. California is a state that stands to be heavily impacted by earthquakes, as the population there is denser, and there are more multi-story buildings.

CHAPTER SIX
JACK BE NIMBLE

The next morning, I decide to run. I even almost *feel* like going on a run. I wake up and want to go out and be in the air.

Maybe this is what happy feels like. But I don't want to jinx it.

I have a predictable route now, and I cruise down the road toward the lake.

Jack McCann stands out on his corner in a banana yellow cycling outfit.

"Neighbor! Where've you been?" he shouts.

He could wait about twenty seconds and not have to yell, but I'm beginning to understand that waiting and speaking quietly are not attributes of Jack McCann. He says he's Steve Jobs without the turtlenecks and Bill Gates without the computer sense, but I think more along the lines of Richard Branson, who probably also lacks the ability to lower his voice.

"I hiked right over there yesterday." I point as I come closer to him. "I didn't see you out."

He sips his coffee. "The wife had me off buying supplies. These days I'm just a glorified errand boy."

"Supplies for what?"

"We're doing an open house tonight. You should come with your mom."

I shake my head. "Not likely."

Tilting his head, he looks confused. "What's that supposed to mean?"

I realize "not likely" might sound like it's likely my mom and I couldn't be bothered. *Making a good impression as always, that's me.*

"No, I mean, she doesn't like parties."

"Who doesn't like parties?" He honestly seems never to have heard of such a person before.

"Um, introverts? Shy people? People who'd rather go walk their dog? Lots of people."

He thinks for a minute and raises his coffee mug, making a point. "You're new in town. I know pretty much everyone. My wife expects people. This checks all sorts of boxes. Plus, Win will be here, probably."

"Win? Why's that?"

Jack gives me an exasperated look for the second time in less than five minutes. He seems to be humoring me, so he answers. "You know I know his folks. At what point are you gonna start listening? I know everyone in town. Everyone knows me. Ergo, I know Win because I know his parents. So Win'll probably come. C'mon, Vivi, I can't connect the dots for you all of the time." He hands me his cup of coffee as he leans over and swipes the newspaper off the curb.

"Fine. I might come, but I don't know about my mom. And I'm not sure you should use the word *ergo*." I hand him his mug back.

"My wife is good with women. They like to hang out with her. She's always off shopping or having lunch or doing charity or something with a gaggle of them."

I roll my eyes. "Gaggle? You could try to be a little less of a caveman. Honestly, Jack. And my mom isn't a lady who lunches. She works in the gift shop at the resort."

"That's fine," he says. "Plenty of women work."

"No, like, we don't have any money, Jack." I hear a little irritation in my voice. "My whole house would fit in the first bay of your garage."

"No, it wouldn't," he protests.

"Yeah, it would. It's 1200 square feet."

He thinks on that for a moment, strokes his chin. "It's bigger than the garage. The dock...it's about the same as that, actually. Fine, you're poor. So what? I was poor when I was a kid. Now I'm not. My wife would like people to come over. You and your mom are people. Come to the open house, and stop making it into a bigger deal than it is. Parties are just dinner with more people than usual and food on sticks. It's like the state fair with more complete sets of teeth."

I have to admire his cavalier attitude. "I'm not committing to anything, but I'll talk to my mom."

"This is why no one RSVPs anymore. Why does it have to be so complicated?" He turns his back to me and walks to his front door.

I call after him. "What time?"

"It's an open house; just show up. That's why they call it open." He waves a goodbye over his shoulder with the paper and shuts his front door behind him.

It's Sunday afternoon, school tomorrow, but I really want to go to this thing at Jack's. Win and I, we texted goodnight last night, but the kiss on the lake still feels like maybe I imagined it.

Maybe it was too perfect. I've had things like that before. I went ice skating with a neighbor girl and her mom and dad once at a little rink the local mall put up back in Issaquah, and it was so magical, all I could do was count down the days to the next Thanksgiving when we could go again. The next year, even though Mom and I had moved across town, I dragged her back to the rink. It was dinky, way smaller than I remembered, and it felt cheap and dirty. There wasn't anything different, not really, but I couldn't re-create everything about the first time.

This better not be an instance of that. Win's special. We've known each other two weeks now, but this connection, I think it's more than one impulsive kiss on the lake.

It has to be.

I take a shower, get all my homework done (there's not much—the teachers are coasting to the end of the year anyway), and put the dishes away in the kitchen. I try to do all of this as nonchalantly as possible, since I don't want to tip Mom off to the open house too early.

The gift shop's closed on Sundays, so I know that won't conflict. At about three o'clock, the opportunity to broach the subject appears.

Mom comes in from the backyard. "What do you want to do for dinner?" she asks.

Funny you should ask, Mom, I've got a dastardly plan to drag you to a social occasion you're sure to loathe. Instead I say, "There's an open house at Jack McCann's house. He invited both of us. He wants you to meet his wife."

Mom stops with the water pitcher still in her hand. "What?"

"The guy Win and I went golfing with last weekend. He's having an open house. He wants to meet you. He wants you to meet his wife."

"Where do they live?"

My heart sinks. She's never going to say yes now. "Lakeshore Drive, Mom."

Her eyes widen. "Down by the lake?"

"Well, it's Lakeshore, so that's a pretty good guess."

"It's a big place?"

I suppress the urge to roll my eyes. "I told you what Jack was like. Yes, it's big. It looks really cool from the outside, but I've never seen the inside. Jack's always outside when I'm over there." I regret the way I just said the last thing because it sounds as if I hang over at Jack's on a regular basis.

Mom licks her lips, thinking. "Fine. I'll go for half an hour."

I'm shocked. Seriously. I don't let her know that, though. "Cool. I'm thinking we go around seven."

She's walking to the bathroom. "That's fine. I'm going to take a shower."

"Okay." I can hear the shower start as I start plotting how to make sure I'm there when Win is.

Ten minutes later my phone buzzes, an incoming text from Win.

What are you doing?

I want to hear his voice. I might be a millennial (or Generation whatever they name those of us who come next), but his voice lights me up, and I want to hear it. I pick up my phone and dial his number.

"Hello?"

"Hey. I'm talking to you, that's what I'm doing." I can't keep the happy out of my voice. I make Minnie Mouse seem glum, I'm so upbeat.

"What're you doing tonight?"

"Going to Jack's house with my mom at seven for half an hour."

"So no specific plans, then," Win says.

"Nope. You?"

"My folks can't make Jack's party, but Toby might come with me. Or I'll come by myself. I want to see you." The last words thrill me. And maybe I'm imagining it, but I swear when he said the sentence it sounded lower, more intense.

I bite my lip at that thought. "I hope you're there. My mom's gonna hate it, so we won't last long, but maybe she'll be okay with me hanging out after she goes."

Mom walks into the room, hair wet from her shower. "I'll be okay with what?"

I suck in a breath. I put a hand up, stalling on

answering her. "Win? Mom needs to talk to me. I'll see you later."

"Okay," he says. The call goes dead.

I turn my attention to Mom. "Win's coming to the open house with his brother."

"Oh yeah?"

"Yeah, and I just said if you get bored and want to go, maybe I could hang out at Jack's with Win a little longer, and then Win and Toby could walk me home."

"Whatever makes you happy, lamb."

Mom comes to sit next to me on the couch, and her skin smells like oranges and vanilla. I have a pang of memory, a long-ago one, before I knew Mom wasn't perfect. When I was tiny, I remember watching Mom put on her perfume and comb her hair and line her eyes with dark kohl, and she was the most beautiful and perfect creature. Mom could do no wrong.

I wish it still felt more like that.

Mom and I walk down the street to Jack's house. I try not to fidget, but I've already chewed three fingernails down to the nub.

"What's Jack do?" Mom asks.

She's still working hard. I can't imagine what it's like in her head. In trying to reinvent herself and build a new, safer life for us, she's moved across a state, found a new job, and rented a new house, all the while helping her stress monkey of a daughter make the transition, too. That's a lot to juggle and also maintain an upbeat attitude. She's probably not very interested in Jack, and I can't imagine she's interested in having a new female friend who is all about shopping and lunching.

"It's okay if you don't like Jack, Mom. But I thought it might be good to get out and meet people in the neighborhood."

"I'm not sure this qualifies as our neighborhood," she says, gesturing to the well-kept houses on either side of us.

"I should've taken you down 10th instead. There are plenty of regular houses. We fit in here fine," I protest—maybe a little too strongly, but I want to give living here a fighting chance.

"You didn't say what Jack did for a living."

"He was a high school counselor. He's retired now," I say. That's partly true. I leave out the heir to the family lumber business part, but still.

"Huh. And his wife?"

"I don't know. I haven't met her yet."

We're in front of the house. Before Mom can even say a word, I see balloons tied to the gate to the backyard and drag her in that direction. If I trusted her not to turn around and head back to our house, I'd text Win so he knew we were here.

But I don't have to. He stands at the gate.

"Hi, everybody!" He waves, a little one, before pushing both hands back into the pockets of his khaki shorts.

He's wearing Tevas and a polo, and I'm glad I didn't give in to Mom's idea of wearing a dress.

"Win, good to see you," Mom says.

He kicks into gear. "Jack's down at the bar with Nomie. I'll take you down to meet him, Ms. Stone."

Mom relents. "Call me Samantha."

I'm glad she's backed off of that. Seriously, she's not Ms. Stone to anyone except maybe the nurse at school when the nurse hasn't ever met her and has to call home because I'm throwing up.

I consider this as we walk down the steps to Jack's outdoor bar. There are lots of mostly older people milling around, holding drinks and eating chips and burgers off of paper plates.

Despite the spectacular house, the barbecue looks pretty typical.

Jack stands behind the bar, and he's yelling. This isn't a surprise. And he's holding court—that definitely isn't a surprise to me at all. I *am* surprised that I couldn't hear him from the street, though, because he's so loud.

He spots Win and me. "The golfers! Come here, you two!"

Win must've done this before, because he holds out a hand and lets my mom and me go in front of him. Someone's taught him party manners. He seems at ease, too.

"Jack, this is my mom," I offer.

He's the happiest guy on the planet at this news and comes around the bar to meet her. "Hey there! I thought maybe Vivi would chicken out. So glad she didn't keep you at home all cooped up. Jack McCann. And where's Nomie?" he asks and wheels around, looking for his wife.

"Why are you yelling? I'm right here, Jack. Honestly, man." A tall woman with black hair pulled up into a ponytail and through a golf visor comes over. She has on a pink polo with white and black capris. I smile, remembering that Jack said he missed skirts.

"I turn around, and you disappear."

He slips an arm around her waist. She looks like she's about his age. I'm pleased that he's not a trophy wife kind of guy. Those guys aren't my kind of guys. And I've liked Jack a lot so far.

"I was going to show the Hernandezes the koi in the waterfall pool, but I will stay here and attend to my overly needy husband instead," she purrs.

Jack ignores her comment. "Meet Vivi and her mom— I'm sorry, what's your name?"

Mom steps up and shakes Nomie's hand. "Samantha. So nice to meet you. I appreciate the invitation."

Nomie smiles, wide and relaxed. "It's a gorgeous evening, and I wanted to have people over. We made a resolution that we were going to use the backyard more this season."

It looks like someone disputes this. "She's the social butterfly. When she says *we*, she's not talking about me," Jack says.

Nomie moves the conversation along. "And this must be Vivi." She reaches out and takes my hand in both of hers, which I usually would detest, but hers is the warmest handshake. Her smile and her eyes are warm and relaxed, too.

"Hi," I say and turn Jack for a minute. "Has Nomie met Win?"

Jack smiles. "Once or twice. I told you, we know Win's parents."

"Although we haven't seen much of them lately. What're they up to, Win?" Nomie asks.

Win looks queasy. "Mom's been traveling for work a little. Dad was up in Canada for a while."

Jack butts into the conversation. "Where's Toby tonight? Is he coming?"

"Just me, Jack. Sorry to disappoint." Win puts both hands deep into his pockets again. I'm starting to think that's his nervous tell.

Jack waves him off. "Let's get these ladies fed. Burgers for both of you?" He's off before either of us answers, headed to the grill at the bar.

"Okay?" I answer.

Nomie looks at Mom, and here's where I get nervous. The grown-up woman talk is about to begin, and I have no idea how Mom'll respond to whatever it is Nomie wants to talk about.

She'll be perfectly appropriate and polite, that's not the worry. But when Nomie walks away, Mom'll want to leave. She'll be anxious and want to go.

"So you feeling settled in? Jack said you've moved here recently." Nomie smiles again, and again my read on her face is that she really does want to know.

Mom smiles. "Vivi seems to be liking school, which was the biggest worry. I'm enjoying the sunshine."

"What brought you to town? Job transfer?" Nomie asks.

Uh-oh. Here we go. I look at my mom and bite the inside of my cheek.

Win jumps in. "Too much gray in Issaquah, that's what Vivi keeps telling me."

The women both chuckle, and I look to Mom's face for a reading. She smiles, but her jaw looks tight, tense.

I take Win's hand. "Do you mind if we show my mom the waterfall?" I'd take Mom's hand, too, and drag her off, but I know that'd look suspicious.

Nomie notices that I'm holding Win's hand, and her smile grows especially wide. "Please do! It's so nice to meet you, Samantha."

"You also," Mom replies, but she doesn't get a chance to say much more, as Win has taken my cue and drags me along the fringe of beach so we can go see the waterfall.

Jack yells after us, not surprisingly. "Burgers'll be done before long. Don't disappear!"

I can feel the expiration date of Mom's tenure at the party looming.

We admire the waterfall, then Win gets Mom to play a little croquet on the lawn with just the two of us. But after a few minutes, she begs out of the burger and kisses me on the cheek.

"I'm headed home, sweetie. Win'll walk you back later, yes?"

I nod. "What time you want me home?" And I grin a little, because I am 100% positive I've never had that problem before. When the highlight of your social life is Netflix, and you have no chill to go with it, a curfew is not a topic that comes up often.

Mom looks at her phone. "Just not terribly late. Maybe ten?"

I try not to spit. I was figuring by dark. This is huge. I feel like I've just been given wings. "I can do that."

"We'll start home around 9:45. See you then." Win gives her a wave as she leaves.

When she's really gone, I turn to Win. "That was

seismic."

"What?" he asks.

"My mom. Me able to stay out until ten. Either there's something in the water here, or she trusts you more than she trusts me."

Win looks at me and his eyes narrow slyly. His grin is conspiratorial. "Let's go be untrustworthy."

I panic for a second. *What can he mean?* I felt like we were on the same wavelength. "What do you want to do?"

"Let's go to Acapulco."

I laugh. "I'd like to not be put in a convent, but I appreciate the grand gesture."

"No, it's a swimming spot," Win says. "Over on Tubbs Hill. It's cool."

"I don't have a bathing suit." Now I start to sweat. I'm not even body-positive/free spirited enough to look at myself naked in a full-length mirror, much less strip to my underwear or—worse—skinny dip. Especially with someone like Win.

"You're wearing a shirt and shorts. You swam in T-shirt and shorts when we paddle boarded. No diff."

I consider this. "I don't know."

He touches my hand. "You need to see Acapulco. You'll love it, I promise."

Jack yells at us. Again. "Kids! Burgers are ready. Come eat."

Win waves him off. "We've gotta run. Thanks, Jack."

"I thought we were going to snoop around Jack's house?" I ask.

Win opens the gate for me, lets me go through first. "He says Nomie's the social butterfly, but we'll be able to swim and come back and he'll be the one giving lectures on the best way to make a s'more. We have time, trust me."

And I guess that's what it comes down to—I trust Win. Implicitly. Intuitively. He makes a lunch for me, for crying out loud. The guy's a saint.

Walking the trails of Tubbs Hill, everything glows. The trunks of the trees catch the slanted golden light of the evening, and the water throws sun and diamonds and little blue-and-rainbow prisms over the ground.

I follow close behind Win, my heart picking up its rhythm.

Swimming. Acapulco? When he suggested it, something felt a little more daring than just a swim. He's usually so mellow, but he seems revved up. I wonder if he feels the way I did when I kissed him. I wonder if he'll kiss me again.

I wonder how dead I'll be when I get home and I'm soaking wet. I'm definitely off script, and Mom doesn't do that well. About the worst boundary tests I've had in the past were staying a little later at school than I had planned, or getting stuck in traffic when a friend's parents were bringing me home.

Definitely not hanging out with a boy, alone, in the forest.

Mom's not a prude, that's not it. It's all the million things that could go wrong. We had the birds-and-the-bees talk when I still found boys repulsive. Mom was very thorough. No, she's less worried about my honor or virtue than she is about an axe murderer coming upon me and chopping me to bits.

Okay, probably not an axe murderer. There are other things she's more afraid of than that. All of them have a tiny grain of truth in them. Mom's fears are all the ones that are vaguely plausible.

For instance, when I was younger and went to a pool party at a classmate's house, Mom insisted she come along and be the water watcher.

I was a strong swimmer, and the parents already planned to have a lifeguard from the neighborhood pool come and help out during the party, but the tiny grain of truth that kids have drowned at neighborhood pool parties stuck in Mom's craw, and she couldn't trust anyone to watch me carefully enough.

And those aren't even the triggers that terrify her. That's just her being "vigilant."

I brush aside all of this heavy thinking. It makes my head hurt. We've come around a dusty corner of the trail.

The trees thin, and we're above the lake now. There are a good number of people sitting around on towels, chatting and sunning themselves.

And then there's a loud whoop and a splash.

"Welcome to Acapulco," Win says.

Cliff jumping. He said we were working our way up to it.

His idea of working his way up to something is way different than mine, clearly.

"Naw, this isn't…" I can't finish the sentence.

"Yes! Come sit here and watch a bit. It's fun. It's like a diving board, but with an enormous and much better swimming pool." Win sits on a rock and tilts his head to the sky, letting the sinking sun warm his face.

Two girls in soccer shorts take tiny steps to the edge of the cliff. It's probably about twenty-five or thirty feet to the water, but I'm too chicken to get close enough to look.

"What if you hit the rocks?" I ask. My brain is already running through nine hundred different ways this can end in calamity. Bashed-in heads, bodies sinking to the bottom—you name it, my gruesome, sick brain has already considered it.

"You don't. You just take a good run off the edge, and the water's deep. Probably a hundred kids jump off every day in summer. Maybe more." Win lounges, the model of relaxation and chill. The opposite of me.

"Really?" I hear it come out of my mouth, and it almost, almost sounds like I'm entertaining the idea of jumping off of a cliff.

"Yeah, really." He points to the two girls in front of us. "See, there they go."

The girls both take a running leap, plug their noses, and drop from sight. They squeal, then a splash and laughing floats up from the water below us.

Win slowly, so slowly, turns his head to look at me. He pulls down his sunglasses and looks at me over the top of them. "What do you think?"

"Gah, Win, I think I'm gonna throw up." I can't feel my legs. My stomach is upended.

"It'll be cold, but I'll be right next to you. If you hate it, we can be done." He stands up and strips off his T-shirt, hat, sunglasses. I look at him, standing silhouette against the blue summer sky.

"I can't think about it." I stand up and pull off my

shoes. I put my hand out. "If I die, you are in so much trouble."

"You'll kill me?" He leads me closer to the edge, dust under our feet.

"Something like that." I look down, and I can see the blue water, greener below me, and the beige of the sandy slope of the rock disappearing under the water. I back up a few steps, plug my nose, and take a running jump.

And I'm free, limbs weightless. My stomach floats up in my throat, and I plunge into cold, wet darkness. Then I'm up out of the water, shivering and laughing.

There's a splash next to me. Win bobs up. "Hey! You didn't even tell me you were going!" He yells.

I laugh loud. "If I'd said it, I would've chickened out." I kick and wiggle in the water. Adrenaline rushes through my blood, pushed to my extremities by my thudding heart.

"You did it!"

"I did it!" I look around for the path I saw out of the water, start to kick toward it.

Win follows right behind me. He comes up next to me as I breaststroke toward a rounded rock where the girls who went before us are sitting, drying off.

"Well?"

I can't help it, I'm grinning. "That was great. I'm proud of myself."

"And you're never doing it again?" he asks as I find a grip on the rock and pull myself out of the water.

I feel the rock scrape my knees, then a bit of a sting. I'm going to be all bumped up, but I remember my toes bleeding from scraping on the bottom of the swimming pool when I was in second grade. The war wounds of summer are worth it.

"I might do it again, but I'll have to sneak up on myself. If I think about it too much, it'll never happen."

Win's out of the water, and we both stand up on the rock. I'm shoulder to shoulder with him, and I put my arms up high over my head in victory. "I did it!"

Win puts his arms around my waist. "Watch the enthusiasm. This'll be when you pitch over and crack your head open."

I turn toward him and hug him, hard.

He threads his fingers through mine and leads me back to our clothes and shoes.

I pull my shoes back on. "You understand, of course, that you'll now need to take a blood oath of secrecy."

"About what?" He smiles.

"My mom finds out we just did that, she will kill you, then kill me, then ground my cold dead corpse until it graduates from college." I shiver. How am I going to keep this a secret seeing as I am currently dripping wet?

Win knows. "We're heading back to Jack's. He's got towels and a big bonfire going. Stop worrying. Your internal anxiety is so loud you have a thought bubble over your head."

We walk back along the trail.

"Tell me what I looked like," I say.

He laughs. "You just gritted your teeth like you were eating broccoli or something, which was reinforced by you holding your nose, and then *boom*! You took off and jumped."

I smile. "I like that you were my witness."

"Sorry for no pictures."

"Good that there aren't. Mom would use them in court for defense in her double murder trial."

When we walk back up to the gate to Jack's backyard, he's standing there with two towels.

"Your burgers are stone cold," he says.

"We had to take a little detour," Win says. He tilts his head at me. "Vivi wanted to jump off a cliff."

"As one does," Jack says. He hands me a towel. "Your mom know about this?" he asks me.

"Lord, no." I feel like I can trust him. I don't know why, I just do.

"Don't get uppity about that. Parents aren't dumb. And they can get pretty retaliatory when you sneak around and they find out."

I frown. "I've been a complete angel. Just because I went swimming doesn't mean I'm gonna steal a car next."

Win laughs. "Cliff jumping is a total gateway drug. You'll be a member of Brother Speed within the week."

Jack shakes his head. "It's called Brother Speed for a reason. No girls allowed."

We walk back to the grill, which is crammed full with a fresh, sizzling spread of hamburgers and hot dogs.

"I'm just saying, relationships are built on trust, and your mom needs to trust you," Jack adds. "Don't push it."

I kind of want to smack him, or at least pelt him with hot dogs. He's right, but really, I've been so dang well-behaved.

Win looks at me as Jack moves behind the bar to man the grill. "Are we okay? I didn't peer pressure you into that, did I?"

"No. I mean, Jack's right—I definitely don't want to be that guy. But no, I did it on my own."

"What do you mean, 'that guy'?"

"You know, the cliché teenager rebelling against the overprotective mom. I don't want to be the cliché."

Win fakes a yawn. "How predictable. Really."

"Exactly. Just like I hope you won't turn forty and buy a sports car."

"What if I'm losing my hair and really, really need to prove my virility in the face of imminent death?"

"Geez, imminent at forty? How about just eventually inescapable mortality instead?"

He sits on a barstool and picks up a plate. "Right now I'm gonna eat one of Jack's hot dogs and bring myself one step closer to my demise. Maybe consume a s'more. Then I think you and I should dry off and go walk down the beach."

I try my best to dry out. I watch Win eat a hot dog, and another one. I don't eat—my stomach's still upside down from the adrenaline rush. I hear Jack telling some guy sitting next to him in the Adirondack chairs that a golden retriever is superior to a Labrador.

We sit, content, listening to Jack spin stories and watching two little kids make s'mores over the fire pit on the beach. I really could just sit here, and that would be enough. One of the young boys keeps bringing Win s'mores he's made for him, each of them more charred than the last. I laugh as each time, Win thanks him and takes a bite, smiling through the charcoal. Finally, the little one gets scooped up by his mom, as she declares that he's hit his marshmallow limit for the night.

Win dumps his plate in the trash and motions for me to follow. "Come, let's go walk on the tiny strip of public sand below the high water line," he says, obviously trying to get a rise out of Jack.

Jack waves a hand in dismissal. "I hold property. It's what we capitalists do."

The air cools, and the lake shimmers in the night air. I check my phone nervously. It's almost time for me to get back, and I've done so much envelope-pushing tonight, I think making it home on time is the least I can do.

Win walks next to me. "What's up?" We walk close to one another.

I wish he'd hold my hand, but I don't want to push it. "I wish my clothes would dry out a little more."

"You could've waded in at Jack's, you know. You can admit to swimming without admitting to hurling yourself off precipices." He smiles at me.

We make it down the sand, to the spot where I saw him sitting not long ago, in apparent despair.

"You know my mom's a worrier," I say.

"Yeah. We all have moms, what're you gonna do? Mine calls me Winnie." He sits and puts his hands deep in his pockets. Nervous again, I guess.

"I have more to tell, but what about you? Any hints to your palindromes for me?" I try to sound light, casual. "Nothing to do with your mom's nickname for you, is it?"

"I don't think the night's long enough tonight. You'll probably have to break curfew for us to get to the bottom of our issues."

I don't push. I sit next to him. He looks up in the sky.

He points to the moon. "Look at that. Twenty-two degree halo. Nice."

"And that is what?" I ask.

He leans into me, and I can feel the warmth of his torso through the fabric of my T-shirt. Pointing, he traces the hazy ring that forms a perfect circle around the almost-full moon. "Can you see it? Almost a rainbow around the moon."

"Where are you pointing?" Under the guise of getting a better bead on the rainbow, I rest my cheek against his strong arm. His skin is soft, and I can feel the taut sinew underneath. "I see it. What's the twenty-two part?"

He puts his arm around my shoulder. I turn my face up to his, and he leans in and kisses me. I close my eyes for a moment, feel his lips on mine, and wonder if I am imagining the stillness of the shore, imagining the water and the wind holding their breath, waiting for us. He breaks the kiss and the silence.

"Do you really want to know or are you humoring me?"

I nod and resolve to continue to listen to him, but my attention wanders, even as he speaks. "It's moonlight refracted through ice crystals. The angle is always twenty-two degrees."

I lean out and look at his face. "You sound positively meteorological right now. A news team's going to spring up and hire you on the spot."

"Naw, not a weatherman," he says. "That's too tame. Fire or hurricane forecaster. Or if I can manage the math, volcanologist. Something more daring."

This is the second or third time he's mentioned

wanting more danger, not less. This will not wash with Mom's vision of my first boyfriend. Pretty sure her idea is an Amish wheelwright. Maybe an actuary. Someone who upholsters chairs. Not, *definitely* not, a storm chaser.

"So putting on one of those big silver suits and falling into a volcano is your preferred vocation?"

He crinkles his nose in thought. "I've devoted a lot of headspace to the amazing planet that lives and breathes underneath us and around us."

"You're geeky like that."

"What're you passionate about?"

"Nothing. I told you, I'm aimless. Lost."

He stands up. "I don't accept that. You've got something inside of you. Maybe it's just hidden."

Piled under baggage and fear. Too bad I don't know what I'd be looking for if I started digging.

He pulls his phone out. "We better go. I promised your mom."

"Yeah, you did," I say, but I wonder if he realizes the level of commitment to safety my mom really expects. I doubt he does.

The next morning, I go on a walk. I miss Tacocat and Racecar. I need a puppers fix. But it's early; the streets are empty.

Until I get to Jack's house. He's taking out the trash.

"Good morning," I say to him.

"You're not running," Jack notices. "You hurt something being adolescent yesterday?"

"No." I bend down and grab his paper, walk with him

as he walks back toward his front door.

"So just lazy then. That's fine." He points at the open door. "You want a cup of coffee? Nomie made tea. You can have tea if you want."

I check my phone. "Sure. It kind of has to be quick. My mom doesn't like me out longer than normal. And I have to get back to shower for school."

We walk inside Jack's house. In front of us are two armchairs, and then we walk down a wide hall with recessed cubbies that display stuffed antelope heads, fly-fishing gear, sleek antique rifles, ducks, and a mounted buck whose rack threatens to snag my T-shirt when we walk by. The floor is covered with bright, thick-pile Oriental rugs. I take a step to the right.

"You're not going to give me a PETA animal-hugger lecture, are you?" he asks.

"Jack, when has a lecture about anything changed your mind?" Nomie asks from the kitchen table.

We walk into the kitchen. It has a wide island and state-of-the-art shiny appliances. Jack bypasses all of the chrome gadgets and pours two cups of coffee from a battered old coffee carafe. He uses one of the mugs to point at me. "I just don't want to hear it from the whippersnapper."

Nomie gets up and gives him a kiss on the cheek. "Don't forget to see if Vivi here can housesit. I'm going to get ready. I've got Ladies Auxiliary at the hospital this morning."

She glides across the kitchen, and I'm amazed that my presence is such a non-event. I suspect I'm not the first stray kid Jack's roped into his schemes and plots.

"I can housesit," I offer.

"We're going to be in Michigan for a couple days at the end of the month."

"What do I have to do?"

"Water the plants and pick up my newspaper. Think you can manage it?"

I nod. "I can do that."

"Good. Nomie can give you a key later."

Nomie looks at Jack. "And let Vivi know you're paying her, of course."

"Of course. Some of us know what it's like to not have a lot."

Nomie shakes her head. "Jack's dad hit it big in the lumber business when Jack was fourteen. Don't let him tell you a sad Oliver Twist story." She picks up her tea and starts to leave. "Be sure to give her the housesitting dates." She disappears down the other hall.

But Jack's not super interested in the housesitting. "Tell me more about your mom."

"You want the pleasantries or the truth?" I think my heart might be beating a little harder.

"Try a tidbit of the ugly unpleasantries. Try it out on me before you get real with the boyfriend."

"Win's not my boyfriend."

"Okay, whatever. Try the truth with me."

"My mom's got anxiety."

"Who doesn't?"

"Who's been in the hospital because of it?"

"Okay, keep going."

"I think the biggest part of it is—" I stop. The words freeze, caught like icicles in my teeth on the way out of my mouth. "I can't do this."

"What?"

"I can't. It's not me, it's my mom. I can't say anything." I hate, hate this. I wonder how it feels to just be normal.

"Fine, but I'm here if you want to disclose. You might consider how far you want to involve yourself with Win if you're not willing to share the big elephant that you and your mom are running from."

"Win and I can't get 'involved'. He's off to UNR in the fall, and I don't even know my way reliably from one class to the next at CDA High yet. We're basically ships passing in the night—we've had a nice conversation from one deck railing to the other."

"You jumped off a cliff for him."

"Lots of people are thrill seekers."

"You're not one of them." He takes a sip of coffee. "Listen, Viv, I drink out of the Wal-Mart water fountain once a week."

"For the love of all that is holy, why?"

"Best immune system booster—it's like a vaccination but without the sore arm. Would you do that?"

"I'm not trying to die. No way."

"You who will not even take that chance is jumping off a cliff. Think on that, and then decide what you need to be honest about with Winnie."

"You just called him Winnie. I thought only his mom did that."

"I think I've earned the right to do it, too."

"Why?"

His phone rings, and he looks at the clock on the oven.

"A story for another time. You best be running back unless you're rounding out the year with a nice Saturday school session for tardies."

"Fine. I'll be by later to get the key to housesit."

"Make it a great day or not, Vivi—"

"I know. The choice is mine." I pour the rest of my coffee down the sink and dodge the antlers of assorted taxidermied animals on my way out.

CHAPTER SEVEN
MAY DAY

School has always been underwhelming for me. I can put all kinds of spin on it, post all the inspirational Instagram pics I want (tabby cats with lion shadows, quotes about fountains vs. drains). But it just kind of sucks. Before I moved to Coeur d'Alene, the only class I ever found even slightly bearable was art. English? The reading was fine, the Socratic seminars, not so much. Class participation and I, we've never seen eye to eye. Art has never been boring here, thanks to the company, and I do still love to draw, though I wish I hadn't missed the ceramics unit, my real favorite. My other classes mostly involve me trying to find a way to participate in lessons and units that began four to five weeks ago, prove that I'm competent enough to graduate, and remind my classmates and teachers who the heck I am and why in the world anyone would appear in a new school mid-April of senior year.

But there's something about school now that helps it suck less. Today, for instance, on the first day of May, my outlook on school is pretty great.

I swear I practically skip down the street to the city bus stop. Because the bus ride means sitting next to Win, the bus ride is awesome.

My first four classes are painful ordeals, but then art and lunch bring me all the endorphins I need. I just sit and draw or listen to Fiona and Phoebe, knowing that Win is coming to see me, to bring me a sandwich, to eat lunch in the art room, with me, of all people.

It's kind of pathetic, it's so sappy.

In art, I sit at my regular table with the Fi twins (as Win and I have started calling them). Phoebe has been drawing prom dresses for the last two weeks, and now she's coloring pictures of basically Barbie heads with her prom makeup demos on them. I'm waiting to have nightmares about them.

Today Fiona and Phoebe are close to fisticuffs.

It's serious business: to spray tan or not to spray tan.

"It's terrible. You'll be orange. No one wants that. Plus, it's probably toxic," Fiona says.

Phoebe isn't convinced. She sits beside me and won't make eye contact with Fiona. She draws eyebrows on the latest Barbie head. Once in a while she casts a look up at me, and at first I think she's trying to get me to agree with her and join the tan debate. But then it seems she's just trying to get a good look at my eyebrows so she can copy them for the latest makeup example for her prom "look book."

"Phoebe. Seriously." Fiona calls her out.

Phoebe looks up, and her lips are pursed tightly. "What."

It's not a question.

"Don't do it." Fiona looks at me. "Right, Bébé?"

"Yeah, on this one, I think Fiona's right. You've got gorgeous skin, and the spray tan will just cover it up."

Phoebe holds up the picture. "Will these colors look good if I look like I died two years ago? I think not."

I point at her drawing. "Save the money. You'll be gorgeous, and those colors match your skin right now."

Phoebe shakes her head, disagreeing. "You shouldn't even talk. You're the color of mocha or something else amazing and light brown. You're disqualified from this talk."

"You could spend the money you save on a Brazilian?" Fiona offers.

I agree, nodding.

Phoebe rolls her eyes. "Fine, you guys win. Let's talk about something else. I need to stay calm. If I stress I get zits in the crease of my chin."

I begin the daily ritual of praying for the bell to ring.

Fiona points her phone in my direction. "Are you going?"

"To prom? Of course she isn't." Phoebe answers for me.

I appreciate it, really. I can participate and not even be present. I could be out getting my lunch, and the Fi twins would hold up my end of the conversation. But now I'm curious.

"Why not?" I interject.

"We told you already, Win doesn't do prom."

"Who says I was going with Win?"

The girls' eyes widen. "What's wrong? Are you fighting?"

"No. We're not boyfriend and girlfriend, you know."

"We do not know this. We dispute this. You two are OTP." Phoebe's not having any of it.

Fiona goes in for the kill. "You like him, Bébé."

I blush. I can feel the heat off my cheeks. "Yeah."

"He likes you. You do a ton of stuff together."

"Have you kissed him?"

"She has—look at her. She's a red lobster."

"Oh, that's a place we could go."

"What?"

"For dinner before prom. We could go to Red Lobster."

Fiona pauses, considers this. I silently thank red crustaceans everywhere for getting the girls off on another conversational topic that is not me and my love life.

The bell rings.

"Later, Bébé. Give Win a kiss for us," Fiona calls as she gets up to leave.

"Not eating with us today?"

"I'm going to go outside and make a couple calls for limousines and check prices."

Phoebe follows Fiona out.

A second later, Lulu pokes her head around the door. "Are they gone?"

"For now," I caution. "They'll be back after they book the limo."

Lulu glides through the door. Orion follows, carrying

his lunch and a black and pink Hello Kitty lunchbox. He sets both of them on the table next to me.

"Am I supposed to get a limo?" He looks sweaty just saying the word.

"No, that's totally over the top. Ask Lulu, she'll tell you." I try to give him a little hope.

Lulu puts a hand up. "It's not over the top, but it's expensive, and we're not buying into monetizing prom."

Orion points at her. "Nice pun."

Lulu just looks at him, raises an eyebrow, and shakes her head no. It's not easy being her significant other, obviously.

"I thought prom was all about spending money," I say.

"Fine, about monetizing it more than it already is." Lulu pushes back on anything that might be traced to "The Man." Money tends to have a direct link to said Man.

I really don't mind all this prom talk. What I do mind is that I don't know where Win is. I don't expect him to take me to prom—the Fi twins are relentless in reminding me that they know something I don't, and that it's a big deal, possibly traumatic. I don't need prom. I need to see Win. Preferably lay hands on him. Or a hand. Or a finger, but in a nice way, maybe as a greeting.

"He'll be here. He had to check in with the counselor." Lulu knows. It's that obvious, I'm sure.

Orion coughs. "Oh man, which one?"

"Haggerty," Lulu answers.

Taking a big swig of buttermilk straight from a quart carton, he explains to me. "He hates her. She uses the phrase 'lean in' way too much."

Lulu rolls her eyes. "And she's got a heavy hand on

the injections."

"What do you mean?" I start to imagine terrible prescriptions and wonder how a counselor could possibly get away with that.

Orion clarifies. "No, she means Botox, collagen in her lips, stuff like that. She isn't doing anything to Win except asking him to 'lean in' on tough issues." He chews his bologna sandwich thoughtfully. "What if I wanted to lean out? Would that mean I'd fall off the ledge of the problem or what? I don't get it."

Lulu waves a chopstick at him. "Read more intersectional activism stuff or watch some TED Talks. I swear, it's like you don't even know me."

Orion sighs and goes back to chewing without answering Lulu. I'm not sure how the two of them ever came to be a couple. Oil and water maybe, or yin and yang, or something.

"You two aren't fighting, are you?" Win walks in. He smiles at me, and I get up and walk to him without thinking, kiss him on the cheek.

Lulu yells. "What was that! Did you just kiss my friend?"

I cower. If I could hide behind Win, I would. "It was just a smooch. No big deal," I say.

I think it's no big deal. I've never liked a person before who liked me back. I wanted to kiss him on the cheek. So I did.

Win puts an arm around my shoulder. He comes to my defense. "We don't get to spend hours together like you two. She's allowed to greet me with a—what'd you call it?" He looks at me for the word.

"A smooch." I'm embarrassed. Maybe that's not what people call it.

Win grins at me, and I'm so grateful, so relieved. I thought my instincts were okay, and apparently they were.

"Oh, that feels like a nickname. Smooch." He leans over and kisses *me* on the cheek this time.

Lulu stands up from the table. "This is ridiculous. My friend, Win Kemper, participating in adolescent school PDA. I never thought I'd see this day." She gathers up her things and gives Orion a nod.

Orion sighs again. "I just sat down not ten minutes ago," he says. "Can I at least finish eating?"

Lulu looks like she'll relent. "You can. Or you can participate in a *non-public* display of affection if you come with me."

Orion listens, thinks, and then his eyes go wide when Lulu's words register meaning. He looks at Win. "Hope Haggerty wasn't too irritating. Must go." He scoops up all of his food and books and follows close on Lulu's heels.

Win and I are alone in the art room.

"I hope it was okay." My voice is really small.

"What? A kiss on the cheek?" he asks. "I liked it."

We haven't been alone with each other all day. I get a bit brave. "I'm just not sure where we are on the dating spectrum. Are we friends who hang out and like each other a lot so once in a while there's a spontaneous effusion of kissing?"

Win laughs. "I think we're dating. But we're also careful because we have to pack in a lot of getting to know each other while also realizing we might be a really good fit. So the balance between chill and 'you are my destiny' is tricky, but, you know." He says this in a light, casual tone, but then he looks straight into my eyes, and I can't help it, I swallow hard.

He does, too. And then we're really quiet for a second. He leans in close, just as the art teacher walks in with her boxed salad from the cafeteria.

"So close," he says, still near enough that I can feel the breath of his words on my collarbone.

"And yet so far," I whisper and then lean back. I laugh. He's curious. "What's funny?"

I wave a hand. "Orion was talking about the counselor, and how you hate her saying 'lean in', and then he was wondering about leaning out. I think I just did that."

He smiles. "You'll have to tell him when he's done macking on Lulu."

"If she doesn't eat him alive," I worry.

Patting me on the back with one hand, Win pulls my sandwich from his lunch bag with the other. "She's all bark and no bite. She moved here in sixth grade and had long black hair and wore polos buttoned all the way up. Her parents are both from Japan. They're engineers for GE. She's just in her 'be the opposite of my parents' phase."

"I guess that makes me feel better. I know that phase."

Win pulls open his math book. "You don't have to worry. You're not much like your mom. I can tell that, and I've only met her twice."

I don't really want to talk about me and my mom. "Tell me more about the leaning counselor of Pisa."

He looks up from his math. "She checks in on me."

I broach the subject, just a teeny, tiny bit. "Fiona and Phoebe seem to know that this is a bad time of year for you, but they won't tell me why."

"I appreciate and am amazed that they don't blabber on about that. It is a tough time of year. I guess that's why Haggerty checks in."

"How long has it been bad?"

"Two years." He crosses his arms over his math book and sinks down to rest his head on his arms. He looks up at me. "I do want to tell you about it. What if we do something fun on prom night?"

"Something non-prommy?" I ask.

He nods.

"I'm definitely in, but I think we shouldn't call it a date."

"Why not?" he asks.

"I'm comfortable with where we are in our 'really intense but also balanced and chill' situation, but the more casual we can make it appear to my mom, the better." I look at him to read his face, hoping I'm not ruining everything with this request. "If we're mostly friends in my mom's eyes, I'm pretty sure we'll have a whole lot less trouble from her too."

"I get it. We can call our situation whatever we want to, and we can also concoct another code word if needed. We're cool like that."

"What do you want to do?" I ask. I just want to be with him. I don't care.

His eyes light up, an idea clearly coming to mind. "I have a plan. It's a good one, too. I'll just pick you up at your house next Friday after school."

"Where are we going?" I ask.

"Wear sneakers," he says. "That's all I'm giving you."

The next eleven days crawl by. I spend each day in art class listening to Phoebe and Fiona obsess over the minutiae of prom: which eyeliner Phoebe should wear, how should they stick Fiona's dress to her bra so her boobs don't fall out, when does it make sense to go get pictures at the park to miss the crowds, and on and on. I survive with my wits, but just barely, and if I ever have to save my own life by commenting on the intricacies of Kylie Jenner's lip kits, I have all the details I need.

Finally, I sit on the front porch of my house on a lovely Friday afternoon, waiting for Win.

Mom comes to the door with a kitchen towel in her hand. "So you're not going to prom, but you are going out?"

"I don't know if I'd call it 'going out'," I say. "We're hanging out." I smile, proud of myself for how calm and collected I sound.

I'm not, really.

"Whatever. And you really don't know what you're doing?" Mom sounds dubious.

"No, I was told to wear sneakers. That's all I know." I worry for a second that I should know what it is, that Mom will overreact to the surprise of it and not let me go.

"Well, holler at me when you leave. I'm going to finish the dishes." She drifts back into the house.

Maybe I'm not giving her enough credit. She doesn't seem worried at all right now.

I see Win come down the sidewalk, and Tacocat and Racecar are with him.

145

Tonight's going to be a good night.

"Hey," he greets me, and Tacocat tries to climb up into my lap.

"The dogs get to come tonight?"

"They insisted on it," he says. "Remember, they're vicious. There's no saying no to these killers."

Racecar rolls in the dandelions on the front lawn.

"I can see what you mean." I put Tacocat on the ground and take his leash from Win. "Where to?"

Mom pops out the door. Her timing is impeccable, or her sixth sense of worrying has alerted her to my departure. "You two headed out?"

"Off for a walk with the dogs," I say.

She smiles, and I can't tell for sure, but it looks as though she's biting her lip—actually biting her lip to avoid prying, lecturing, or otherwise overprotecting. I knew the nonchalant attitude earlier was for show.

"You two be safe. Have fun."

I hold up the leash. "We've got the guard dogs. We're in good hands."

"Paws," Win adds. "We're in good paws."

Mom's façade probably has two minutes and counting before it completely falls apart. I feel the urge to flee.

She waves at us with the dish towel. "Love you, Viv."

"Forward and backward, up and down and always, Mom." I go to her and give her a quick peck on the cheek.

Win turns toward the end of the block and the library. The dogs and I follow his lead.

"Give me your phone?" he asks.

I unlock it and hand it to him. "What are you up to?"

"We are up to geocaching. Ever done it?" He's done

with my phone and hands it back.

"Nope." I wave goodbye to Mom, still standing on our front stoop, and follow him as we turn the corner.

He explains as we walk. "People stash various treasures and leave coordinates on where to find them. A lot of times the cache is a little box. It's treasure hunting, basically."

"What kind of stuff is in the caches?" I have to skip a little to keep up. Win's excited, the dogs are excited. Everybody's basically running, at least those of us whose legs are shorter than Win's.

"Little stuff. You sign a log, and you can leave trinkets, too. When Toby and I were younger, he loved to take stuff, so I was the one who made sure we had good stuff to swap out. That's how it's done."

I look at the app. The map has little green treasure boxes in the area around us. "There's one at the base of Tubbs Hill."

"Yep. We're headed there first." Win puts on an accent. "Treasure awaits!"

I catch him by the arm. "You have to slow down a tiny bit unless we're jogging all night. You said sneakers, but I can't keep up with this pace."

I smile, and he leans forward and kisses me.

"Enthusiasm," he says. "This is why I'll never be cool."

I take his hand, and the dogs slow a bit, too, walking side by side in front of us. "You're cooler than anyone else I've ever met, Win Kemper. Keep doing you. It's lovely."

We've walked a little farther when we hear a voice. "Hey! Win!"

I turn as Win does. He laughs.

"Oh boy, there's Orion."

Orion drives up in an old Chevy Impala, metallic green and straight out of the sixties. The windows are down. Lulu sits shotgun, a pale blue confection of a prom dress rising up on all sides of her like bubbles in an overfilled bathtub.

"Hey, it's the happy couple!" Win laughs. "Where are you off to?"

Lulu leans over to the driver's side. "Pictures at the park before it gets crowded. Then dinner downtown, then an appearance at the dance, then dessert at Beverly's."

Orion's just riding the Lulu wave at this point. He simply nods.

Win looks at him. "Top of the resort to finish the night off. Romantic."

Orion shoots him a look. "Just a great night between friends."

I can't resist. "Who participate in non-public displays of affection."

Lulu points at the both of us. "You both shut it. It's going to be a great night, and we're on a timetable." She thwacks Orion on the side of the arm. "Let's roll!"

Orion shrugs. "Grandma wants the car back by midnight. You know."

Win smiles. "Grandmas. What're you gonna do." He waves them off as Orion floors it and peels out. The dogs bark at their noisy retreat.

"That is going to be a date for the ages." I laugh.

Win looks at me. "They are way cooler than both of us, and they don't even mean to be."

"Definitively." I take his hand, and we continue on our

quest.

The cache is near the statue of Mudgy and Millie on the other side of Tubbs Hill. We both have our phones out, and the dogs sniff around, giving the appearance that they're helping in the search, too.

"It says to keep an eye out for Muggles," I read.

"Yeah, geocachers don't want regular people to see you get a cache and then come and steal it. You're supposed to be subtle about it."

"Interesting." I look back at my phone. "It's really, really close."

"Check the hint." Win's crouching on the trail, his eyes sweeping the brush next to us. Tacocat comes up to him and tries to lick the inside of his right ear.

"Your dogs don't seem to get the point of geocaching."

"They're just happy to be along for the ride, I think."

I check the hint on my phone. "It says it's in a natural cubby against the rock face. So basically a snake hole. Or a badger hole—badgers have holes, don't they?"

"It could be a little grotto. Doesn't have to be the lair of an animal destined to maul me."

"What can I say, I'm my mother's daughter. Always waiting for the danger to catch up with us." It's an unguarded moment, and it slips out before I realize I've said it.

Win stands up with a small, green, metal container in his hand. "Tell me which danger is going to catch up to you, specifically."

"You found the thing! Let's look inside."

I'm not completely trying to change the subject. I'm actually really intrigued to peek inside the little container in his hands. But I'm also trying to change the subject.

He holds it up above his head. "Be real, Smooch. What's your mom so afraid of?"

Although I'm thrilled to hear him use my new nickname, I'm not about to edge closer to this discussion of my mom's failings.

"Stuff back in Washington. I thought we weren't ready to get into all of that."

"Maybe tonight's the time to do it. We've got all night." He looks at me as he turns the little container over in his hands.

"Okay. We moved here because Mom didn't feel like it was safe in Washington for us anymore. My mom's always prepared for the worst-case scenario. She had escape routes planned out of our apartment, always carried cash and a bug-out bag in the car in case it wasn't safe to go back to our house."

"But now nobody knows you're here?"

"There's no one who loves us besides us, to be honest. Mom's parents died a long time ago. Nobody else. Just me and my mom." I don't think I've ever said it that way before, and it sounds really dang sad. "Huh. Sorry. We're supposed to be having fun."

He comes close to me. "It's okay. We've got all night; we can take a breather from the heavy stuff. But I'm not kidding when I say this: I can help keep you safe, make you feel safe and sound. We wear the same 'like me' label, remember? If we're a match, we take on each other's issues. We do that for each other."

Shame bites at me, and I try to dismiss it. As much as I love that he says that to me, I can't help but doubt it. If he really knew what my issues were, what Mom's were, I don't know if he'd be so certain about hanging out to help.

I've been trying to fix things for most of my seventeen years, and it just makes me tired. Nothing's fixed, and Mom's not fixing it either.

"Okay. Show me what's in the cache." I take the item out of his hands.

Both the dogs sit in anticipation. They think it's got treats in it.

The top of the little container screws off, and rolled up inside is a bunch of little notebook pages stapled together. There's a golf pencil, presumably to write on the paper, two Canadian coins, a frog eraser, and six tiny onyx buttons.

Win plucks the notebook paper and the pencil out of my palm. "I'll sign it for us. Then we mark it as found on the app."

I look over his shoulder. There are at least a dozen names from all over on the log sheet. One of the last is from Germany. "This is cool. I want to leave something."

I wish I'd gone through my backpack before we left. Surely there'd be something fun and colorful to leave in the cache for the next person.

"I've got a couple things." Win digs into his pocket and then opens his hand for me to see.

In it are three jacks and an orange and green bouncy ball, two purple zigzag paperclips, and a tiny, tiny white shell.

"Perfect."

We finish and put a few of the new little treasures into

the container, stash it back where Win found it.

"Can we do another one?" I ask.

"You bet. The dogs will need a water break and a snack at some point, but by then we will probably, too." He leans over my shoulder and looks at the map on my phone. "We could do that one. It's not far from here."

"Let's."

We find the next cache hidden by the "Welcome to Coeur d'Alene" sign near the community college campus. Someone's signed the log from New Zealand.

Then we look at the map on my phone. "The next one's down the road here on Government Way," I say before I realize that this is a place I've been before.

It's the cemetery. I look at Win's face. Nothing.

Maybe he doesn't know Toby took roses there. Maybe it's not part of what makes prom bad for him.

"Sure, we can do that." He says it casually, but then he turns his face the other direction, and for a split second, I see him press his lips together, like he's holding something in.

I wonder if I should say something. How do I mention that I tailed his brother all over town and he ended up at the cemetery?

We walk the dogs down Government Way, and we follow the coordinates into the cemetery. The sun filters through the trees as it begins to sink lower in the sky. I wonder immediately if the cache will be by the statue of the angel, but we end up close to a park bench and a trash can.

"I'm not looking in the trash can, just sayin'." Win sits

on the park bench and pats Racecar on the head.

"I've got a hunch." I kneel down between the dogs, and sure enough, there's a shiny silver tube under the bench. "I'm reaching under here, but if a black widow bites me, I expect Racecar to kill it dead." I pull the tube, which is stuck to the metal underside of the bench.

It's got a big magnet on its side. The end of the tube swivels, and I look in to find the log is there, along with a little keychain with a red heart on it. I pull it all out, and a beaded bracelet drops on the ground. The bracelet has a tag on it: *In Memory of Ayla, beloved sister.*

"That's nice. I think the people who made this cache might have done it to remember their sister." I tuck the little bracelet back into the cache.

On the back of the log is a photocopy of the grave markers in the cemetery with one starred. It has the word Ayla marked on it, too.

"I like that," I say. "People will know a little about her."

Win only nods.

I take his hand. "I guess we should go."

"Yeah. The dogs are ready." He leads me out of the cemetery.

He's quiet for a long time as we weave our way back through the neighborhood to the lake. The dogs trot along, happy and blissfully unaware.

I follow him, not sure what's coming next, and we close in on Lakeshore Drive.

"Are you okay?"

"I will be," he says.

We've come to the end of the road.

"You want to take the dogs out on the beach?" I ask, ready to let them off their leashes.

"Actually, I planned a little something to finish off our adventure." He takes me through the gate in front of us. There's a sign to the right of it, one I've not read before: *The Jewett House*.

"Are we supposed to be here?"

He laughs. "You are the most law-abiding creature I know. But you're in luck. I know the manager. She knows we're coming here tonight."

We clear two large Douglas firs and come face to face with an old, white house, its wide front porch decorated with twinkle lights.

"What's the Jewett House?"

"Old lumber company exec's house, but now it's the senior center. They sometimes have weddings. Often have bingo."

"You seem like you know about the bingo."

He smiles, just a tiny pull of one corner of his mouth. "I won't comment on that."

He takes my hand, and the dogs trot along with us, Tacocat stopping from time to time to snuffle a particularly intriguing tuft of lawn.

The shade deepens as we come along the back of the house.

There's a lawn surrounded by old, tall evergreens, and a little gazebo.

And a big white inflatable pool. It's knee high and kidney-shaped, probably fits five or six overactive toddler swimmers, or three or four bigger kids.

"What's that?"

"That's our surprise. You'll laugh."

"Why?"

We come closer, and I see that the pool is filled with pillows and blankets. There's bug spray, little flashlights, a big bag of popcorn, one of those tubs of licorice from Costco.

"Did you do this? This is amazing."

"I would love to take credit, but your art buddies were all over this."

"The Fi twins?"

"They love their Bébé."

"Man, that's really nice of them. They were so wrapped up in prom; I'm amazed they could pull this off, too."

Win laughs. "They're coming in a while, I think. One of their dates has a really big truck, and the girls filled the back with pillows."

"You know, that's crazy."

"What?"

"After all the play-by-play about prom, I don't even know who they're taking."

"I just assumed they were going together. Guess not. Some brave guys must have stepped up to the challenge."

"I hope whoever it is has fantastic eyebrows. Phoebe has high standards."

I walk over to the inflatable and turn around, falling back into the pillows and blankets. "It's kind of awesome. Don't tell them that."

Racecar and Tacocat immediately try to climb in, too.

Win gives the fat little Corgi a boost, and he flails in the deep pillows. We spend a few minutes trying to get the dogs to settle before they pop the pool with their toenails, but the popcorn finally distracts them, and they sit for Win's commands.

Win steps into the pool and wades through pillows and blankets as though it's filled with water.

"This is fun." He wades over to me and flops down. The dogs try to leap up, and he has to calm them down again.

"We have movie snacks. Are the girls bringing a movie theater with them, too?"

"Fiona's got a portable projector. She was going to pop it up on the broadside of the house."

"Clever. When are they getting here?"

Win smiles. Maybe he doesn't want the company, either. "In about an hour. Is that okay?"

"Sure. I'm glad we get a chance to be alone, though."

"The dogs are glad, too." Win laughs.

"Can I ask you about the bad thing?"

"Yeah, you can."

"What is it?"

"You just cut straight to the chase, huh?"

"If I guess something wildly off, it'll be in poor taste. I don't want to hurt your feelings."

"So I have a sister, Franny."

"Yeah?"

"She ran away two years ago."

"Oh, no. I'm sorry, Win. Did they find her?"

"Mom and Dad were wrecks. We looked for almost four weeks. Everyone was thinking the worst. They had divers in the lake. There was even an Amber alert."

"What happened?"

"Sheriffs found her in Spokane on prom night. She was a senior. She was supposed to be at prom, having fun. They found her using, at some crackhouse. She's an addict. I guess she'd been using with a boyfriend, but the last weeks of senior year kind of sent her over the edge, and she ran away with him."

"Where is she?"

"I only kind of know now. Mom and Dad brought her back; she did a stint in rehab, but when she turned eighteen, she ran away again. Last time I saw her she was in really bad shape."

"I'm so sorry. That sucks."

"Here's the worst part. When they found her, I was ashamed."

"What do you mean?"

He looks down, pats Racecar on the head, avoids looking me in the eye. "Of course when they found her I was so glad she was safe. Alive. But we'd looked in the lake. We all thought someone had kidnapped her. And it turned out she was just a mess, a user."

"But she wasn't dead." I say it and worry I've been too blunt.

He laughs, a dark, bitter scoff. "I swear, and I wouldn't tell anyone but you, Vivi, but I swear it felt like the town wished she were still the clean-cut kid and at the bottom of the lake, like that was more acceptable to them." He shakes his head, saying a silent no to that screwy logic.

"I'm sure they didn't feel that way, Win. And which 'they' are we talking about, anyway? The people who love you and love her were all glad. I know they were. Anyone thinking any different doesn't matter."

He leans all the way back in the pillows, stares up at the darkening sky. "I felt ashamed. That's screwed up. I was embarrassed that Franny had all these people looking for her, made us look bad. How wrong is that?"

His eyes close for a moment, and I look at his lashes, a thick dark fringe. They're tangled with teardrops.

I take his hand. "I'm sorry. But what you thought, it was normal. Understandable." I want to say more, but it feels like a time to be quiet.

"I miss her. We used to paddleboard all the time together. Dad used to call us Frick and Frack. I don't even know if I'd recognize her now. Now I just cross my fingers that an officer doesn't knock on our door." There's a pause before he speaks again. "That's my longest long story." He opens his eyes and looks at me.

I hold his gaze. "I'm honored that you would share it with me. Thank you."

"We should share things. We're good together, Smooch. We are."

"I know." I lean to him, forehead to forehead. The dogs wiggle in, wanting to be in the middle of the two of us. Win kisses me, but Tacocat starts to wedge himself in between us, tapping Win with his paw for attention.

"Who thought bringing the dogs was a good idea?" he asks.

I look at my phone. "It's getting late, anyway."

"It's prom night. That's usually an all-nighter."

"In my mom context, we are on the outer edge of the envelope." I lie back and look at the stars.

Win lies back, too, and the two dogs flop happily between us. Between thwacks with Racecar's tail, I feel Win take my hand. He gives it a squeeze.

"Here we are. Safe and sound."

I close my eyes and concentrate on the warmth of his hand, the waggly tail of the dog next to me, the smell of pine trees. I let my mind clear, and I feel sleepy, warm, content.

Safe. I feel safe. I can't say I've felt completely safe in any recent memory. I can't remember when.

"If I fall asleep, you have to stay awake to wake me up and take me home before it's too late," I murmur.

"Fair enough." Win strokes my hair, pulls me into the crook of his arm. "I won't let anyone hurt you," he whispers.

I'm dozing off, but my brain registers his words as I fall asleep.

I've lied to Win. Even if I didn't mean to, I've lied.

CHAPTER EIGHT
SHAME ON ME

I think the worst thing about shame might be that when I am in the throes of it, I am utterly alone. I feel as though I am the only one who screws up, who is left out, who doesn't do things the right way. Shame feels like self-inflicted loneliness, self-imposed solitary confinement, my own fault for not being good, or not following directions, or not fitting. For not being like them.

It might not be a logical thing, what I blame myself for. It might not be something anyone who is healthy should ever take the blame for. But I take it and carry it like a boulder, its weight crushing me and pulverizing my sense of self-worth.

Shame's the most ugly and powerful emotion. I am hunched over, tiny, curled into a ball by it. If I had a tail to tuck, I would. Disappearing makes more sense than anything, and I'm not going to lie—there are certain kinds of disappearing that are really, really appealing when I'm ashamed.

I will do almost anything to avoid feeling that way.

I can point out how I played fortune's fool all over my mess of a past. First time I can remember, I was probably five. I walked home from half-day kindergarten one day without my mom. Little did I know, she was stuck in a meeting and losing her mind with worry. I don't really remember deciding to go it alone; I just remember standing on a street corner with the crossing guard.

My memories of this are remarkably tunnel-like. I can't see anything else; I can only see me and the taller kid and the curb. No idea where we were, how close or how far away from the school. I don't remember the route home, or what it looked like, even though my mom walked it with me every day that year.

But what I do remember is stepping off the curb. I don't remember cars. I don't remember noises, either, except for the crossing guard yelling at me. A voice, a bark, the guard yelling and yelling because I'd done something wrong. I was in trouble.

And then the feeling that came immediately afterward. It was hot, it was tears, it was staring down at the ground, it was feeling every other pair of eyes on that street corner judging me and yelling at me too, except I don't remember another word being spoken.

Other memories of shame are lot more detailed.

Standing at the self-checkout in Safeway, with a basket full of a week's groceries, while the checker told me the card's been declined. The checker wondering in a loud voice where my mom was since it was her credit card. Lying, telling her she was in the car, when Mom was really in bed, and had been for a week.

Getting fed the "special lunch" at school because Mom wasn't functional enough to reload my lunch account.

Sitting in front of a counselor, being told I should have known we couldn't enroll in a school without a utility bill to prove we lived within the boundaries of the school, when I knew we didn't have a utility bill because we didn't have a signed lease yet.

The school secretary looking at my enrollment history and rolling her eyes, then pretending to be nice to my mom and me.

Knowing in second grade that when someone asked to have a playdate with me, it would never be at my house. Going on a walk in the neighborhood and seeing the rest of my fourth-grade class at one of my classmate's houses for a birthday party.

Lying about why I couldn't sleep over.

Lying about why I couldn't go on the class field trip.

Honesty is a luxury. Lying is survival. Lying keeps the shame away, at arms' length. Little lies about having plans (when I don't have money to buy the movie ticket) or bigger lies about "businesses" transferring my mom, or why my dad doesn't live with us.

It's exhausting. I suppose that's why I've been awake all night, staring at the ceiling since Win dropped me off.

I decide someone has to know something fundamentally truthful about me.

And it's going to be Jack McCann.

He's a counselor. He can be my test confession, just

like he said.

And he's right. If I'm willing to jump off a cliff for Win, I should be willing to take a risk and tell him the whole truth about me.

Most of the truth, at least. I reserve the right to keep the time I wet my pants in kindergarten to myself. (The teacher wouldn't make eye contact with me, and she only allowed us to use the restroom if we made the sign language sign for toilet. I was afraid to say anything—she'd told us not to.)

When morning finally arrives, I get up and get dressed in my running clothes and sprint to Lakeshore Drive. The beauty of this ridiculous plan is that Jack McCann is nothing if not predictable, and there is he, God bless him, standing in his bathrobe, at the corner, getting his newspaper.

I could kiss him.

"Morning, Vivi." He looks at me, and I swear he knows already. I have no poker face.

"Can I talk to you?" I ask. "I promise it's not for long. I only have a little time—got to get back before Mom worries."

He waves an arm to the house. "Sure. Nomie's doing yoga, but we can sit on the back porch."

He guides me in, pours me a cup of coffee, loads it up with vanilla creamer, and takes me out on the back porch.

It's hard to stay on track with my pathetic story and confession when Lake Coeur d'Alene wants to say good morning. There's a float plane taxiing over by the resort, getting ready to take off from the water. The morning is fresh, and the breeze brings the calls of birds in the trees, sweet melodies on pine-scented air.

"Okay. Hit me with it. I can tell you're all chewed up about something. So just do it. Spill."

I look at him. He's not teasing me; he's all business.

"Fine. Remember when I tried to tell you what the story was with my mom?"

"Vaguely. What's the story with your mom?"

"She's terrified of natural disasters. She has anxiety about keeping me safe from all sorts of stuff, but natural disasters, that's her Achilles heel."

He slaps the paper on the railing of the deck. "Really?"

"Yes."

"I thought your dad beat her. Or beat you."

I collapse into a chair. "That's what Win thinks, too. But I swear to you I didn't ever say anything to give him that impression."

"You say 'My mom's just trying to keep me safe' constantly. I've even heard you say it."

"Wait, has Win been talking to you?"

Jack looks at me, another one of those "inspecting me for defects" looks. "Of course he has. People talk to me, Vivi. You don't pay attention to anything I tell you, do you?"

I roll my eyes. "You're making this really, really hard. Win thinks my dad is the threat."

He sits down, puts his feet up on the ottoman, stretches his arms out, and clasps them behind his head. "Explain this to me."

"What?"

"Her big thing. Explain it."

"I don't know where it comes from, but ever since I

can remember, Mom worries about things she can't control. Some of it makes sense. She was always afraid that I'd fall down the stairs, or choke to death on food when I was really little—stuff that can happen to little kids. Leaving me with a babysitter terrified her."

"Why? What happened when she left you with a babysitter?"

"She never did. She was afraid to leave me with someone."

His face falls. "Oh."

"But more than that, she was afraid of things like earthquakes and tsunamis and hurricanes."

"In Issaquah?"

"At first, when it was me and my dad and my mom, we all lived in California. I was too little to remember that."

"Well, California is going to fall off the continent, so she's got something there."

"She really is afraid of that. In her mind, that's going to happen at any moment."

"I guess it might," he says.

"But do you sit around waiting for it to happen? I mean, is your first thought when you drive to the grocery store to park the car facing out so you can hit the evacuation route faster? Because my mom's is."

Jack processes this. "Huh."

"Yeah." I take a deep breath, and the tears come.

"Hey, you can tell me all this. It's not the worst thing anyone's ever told me. Nothing to be ashamed of."

"Really? All I feel is shame. I want to shrivel up and blow away, be invisible."

He picks up his coffee. "You know what the dictionary

says about shame?"

"Tell me."

"That it's a mix of regret, self-hate, and dishonor. You have any reasons to be ashamed of your mom's fears? They don't dishonor you. You can't regret them—they're not your burden to carry."

"Self-hate." I whisper.

"For why? For having a mom with a problem? Every mom in this world has something she isn't proud of. I can personally guarantee you that every dad does, too. There's not a person in the world who is perfect."

I look at him. "'All happy families are alike, but each unhappy family is unhappy in its own way'."

"Where'd you get that?"

"*Anna Karenina*," I say.

He spits coffee out. "You cannot use Tolstoy to prove anything. Lord, *no* family in Russia was happy. And he published that in installments, so it's basically a soap opera. A *telenovela*. Don't believe him about happy families. Families have ups and downs, and almost every one of them has a big, ugly, messy, tragic event hiding under the glossy surface."

I look at him. "Win told me about Franny."

He sighs. "I figured he would. So see? You should feel completely at ease."

"But that's something real. My mom's tilting at windmills."

He presses the bridge of his nose between his thumb and forefinger. "If you reference one more work of literature, I'm going to have a massive migraine. Her fears, they aren't imaginary."

"Yeah, but—"

He interrupts me. "I bet she was in an earthquake if she lived in California."

"She was there for the Northridge quake."

"Then she has PTSD, not anxiety. For crying out loud, Vivi. Has anyone gotten her help?" He seems like it's urgent.

"She's seen people before." I don't know the details. I've never really asked.

He stands up and strides to the railing, takes a big swig of coffee, and points his newspaper at me. By now I'm 100% sure he never reads the thing—it's just his prop for occasions like this.

"Dig in with your mom. Have a conversation. She's probably not had anyone to talk about this with in, what, sixteen years?"

I nod, tears all over my face. "She tried. After Northridge, she tried. She stayed with Dad in California until she got pregnant with me. She lined up a job in Washington, where she thought we'd be safer. But Dad wouldn't move with her." I let out a big breath and feel little shudders of sobs fight their way out of me.

He comes over and pats me on the back. "You've been to a counselor before, right?"

"Not one that knew me. Or believed in me. Or cared about me." I smile at him hopefully.

"Well, you're very kind, but let's get you and your mom hooked up with someone you can talk to who isn't usually wearing his bathrobe."

I laugh. It is ridiculous. "Good point."

He starts to connect the dots. "So something made her

move here, then."

I think back to all the moves. "We've moved a lot, but the Japanese tsunami took us from Tacoma to Issaquah. More inland."

"What about to Coeur d'Alene?"

"The Oso mudslide didn't help, but she stayed strong for as long as she could. There was an article, and then a FEMA exercise."

He snaps his fingers as it occurs to him. "Cascadia. The article about the subduction zone."

"If I ever get a chance to meet the lady who won the Pulitzer for that article, the one that set Mom off, I'll smack her across the face."

"That's a little much."

"Then Cascadia Rising was the nail in the coffin."

"Cascadia Rising?"

"A bunch of government agencies did a big exercise to prepare for the huge, cataclysmic seismic event that will swamp everything west of I-5. When Mom saw the news about that, it was over. People practicing a disaster, with pretend casualties, and police and National Guard troops? She couldn't take it anymore."

"And now?"

"She seems better. Not much in Idaho to be afraid of," I say, holding up my fist. "No hurricanes. No tsunamis. No tornadoes. No big earthquakes." I put up a satisfying finger at each non-existent hazard here.

"Don't let her know about the Big Burn of 1910."

"What?"

"We have some doozies when it comes to forest fires. And there's always the Yellowstone caldera."

"If you mention either of those to her I will gut-punch you. I'm not kidding."

"How can you keep her away from things like that?"

"We can't afford internet at home; she works retail. Staying away from computers and doomsday cable TV shows really helps."

Jack shakes his head. "It's more about keeping her healthy. I'm not kidding about a good counselor and the PTSD. Here's another thing, kiddo."

"Because I need another thing?" I wince.

"Change. Any change. I'm not Sigmund Freud or Jung, but I will tell you one thing I know from my years in counseling. These fears hide other fears. Fears about things that are inevitable. Like your own mortality. And your little girl graduating."

"Graduation. Really."

"And your little girl falling for her first real love. It's about losing things, about things we mere mortals can't control.

"Ever since we've been aware, since we got wise and moved into caves, maybe, we keep trying to put a lid on the chaos around us. Sometimes we manage it pretty well, but let's face it. What's scariest about a tornado?"

I shrug. "Getting impaled by a 2x4?"

"The fear of the unknown. What *might* happen. Not being in control."

I turn this over in my brain. I get it. I do. I just wish my mom wasn't at ground zero of trying to control everything for the two of us.

Something occurs to Jack. "Oh. Oh, that's not good."

"What?"

"Your mom doesn't know about Win's chosen profession, does she?"

I can't keep the sarcasm out of my voice. "You mean as a storm chaser? Yes, she's thrilled. Encouraged me to get on out there with him."

Unamused, Jack waggles his finger at me. "Sarcasm doesn't suit you."

"Maybe I could just tell her he wants to be a meteorologist. But it doesn't matter anyway."

"Why?"

"He's going off to school, and we've known each other less than a month."

Jack stands up and swats at a fly with the paper. "So what?"

"So it doesn't matter, that's what," I say, and it comes out almost like crying. "He'll be gone, and it won't matter what Mom thinks of him."

"Where will you be?"

"What do you mean?"

"If you wanted to be with him, why not? Why couldn't you?"

"That's not what you do. I'm seventeen."

"Fine. I think you can pick a school where a friend of yours is happening to attend. People do it all the time. You'll get an aid package if you want it."

"I don't know."

"What was your plan?"

"I hadn't thought about leaving Mom."

"Because?"

Now I realize what he's doing. "That's dirty pool."

"Standard counselor trick. You've been to more than a

few—I'm surprised I caught you on that one."

"I hadn't thought about leaving Mom because it would totally freak her out, and I don't like to think about that. Well played."

He stretches and finishes the last of his coffee. "My work here is done. Let's recap: get you and your mom in to a counselor, and be sure to specify PTSD. Talk to Win and be honest. Everybody's family is jacked up. And apply to whatever school you feel like—you'll need to cut the apron strings at some point."

"Okay, I see why you had to go into lumber. Pretty brutal on the recap, Mr. McCann."

"Tough love, Vivi. But you're a strong girl. Time to cut yourself some slack and start living."

In art on Monday, things are pretty chilly with Phoebe and Fiona.

"I'm sorry, really, you guys." I try to sound really sorry. I'm kind of a lousy actor.

"You went home," Fiona says.

Phoebe tosses her hair in my general direction. Pretty sure that's a cold shoulder in Phoebeland. "Yeah. Before the movie was over. And you weren't even doing anything with Win."

I try to plead my case. "It was midnight. I was asleep, anyway. Win just took me home."

Fiona points her phone at me. "See, that's the biggest problem. You, in Win Kemper's arms, and you fell asleep. Who does that?"

Phoebe nods in agreement, crosses her arms over her

chest. "Yeah, who does that?"

I give up. "Me?" I come over and put an arm around each of them. "You all did such an amazing job with the pool full of pillows and the movie snacks."

"Yeah, we did."

"I'm sorry I was so lame that I couldn't stay awake." I give them a little squeeze.

The hugs seem to placate them.

I sit back down across the table, and a girl in a wheelchair glides in with a call slip. She hands it to the teacher, but I'm already out of my seat.

"Bébé, you okay?" Phoebe asks. She's over my infraction now, her voice full of concern.

"Don't worry," I say, giving the Fi girls a wave.

What's crazy? They're growing on me. They might really be my best friends in Coeur d'Alene, not counting Win.

And not counting Jack McCann.

Jack can be a pretty persuasive guy, and today I'm taking some of his advice. I take my call slip to the counseling suite. After his tough love talk, I'm talking to the school counselor.

"Come on in, honey." A lady with impossibly curly hair calls me in to her office.

"Mrs. Haggerty?"

"One and the same. You're Vivi?"

"Yes."

"What can I do for you today?"

I try to get to business, try to channel my inner Jack McCann. Never in my wildest imaginings would I have thought I'd use an old guy in a bathrobe as my role model, but "What Would Jack McCann Do?" might as well be on an obnoxious pink plastic band around my wrist, because coming to the counselor's office is not a Vivi Lewis instinct at all.

"I want to apply to UNR."

"Nevada Reno?"

"Uh-huh, and I need the full rundown on financial aid, and probably the Western Undergraduate Exchange thing. My mom and I are pretty much broke, so any help past the FAFSA would be great, too."

She grabs a green Post-it note and scribbles these things down. "Give me a couple days to check your transcripts, since you're new, and I'll call you down again to get the forms filled out."

"Okay." I stand up, my business here done.

"You settling in all right? Meet anyone you click with?" She looks up at me.

"Yeah." I consider who I click with, and I decide to make a move to fix more of the list Jack gave me. "And if you have the name of a counselor who's good with PTSD, I'll take that, too."

Her eyes widen. "For you?"

"Little bit me, mostly my mom. Long story, but I think it's mostly handled." I feel almost giddy, taking care of business like I am.

She writes a private counselor's name and phone number on another Post-it. "I'm following up with you about both of these things end of the week. If you're not ready to lean in on the PTSD thing with me, that's fine, but I do want to circle back and check on you."

I suppress a giggle and the urge to lean really, really

far out, just for Orion.

CHAPTER NINE
HOPE IS THE THING WITH FEATHERS

When I became a senior, it didn't really strike me as a milestone. It was another year of school. School drags on, one year into the next. But at the same time, I remember first grade like it was yesterday, and here I am, a senior.

Grown-ups, on the other hand, boy, they like to behave as though senior year is the second coming.

Okay, some grown-ups. Seems to me it's the ones for whom high school was awesome—maybe so awesome that nothing's topped it since. You know, they were cheerleaders and homecoming king and featured on twenty pages of the yearbook, and since then it's been all downhill.

Sometimes I think these adults show back up as super overzealous moms of high schoolers—the moms and dads who plan the senior lock-in on graduation night, or, say, the Senior Day at Coeur d'Alene High School.

Today, because of some booster parents and a guy at the local Coca-Cola Bottling Company who took pity on us poor public high school kids, the seniors are all going to Silverwood, the amusement park north of town.

"It's not dinky. Really, my grandma and I go every summer. The rides are pretty good." Orion explains to me what to expect. He sits across the aisle on the school bus from me and Win.

Lulu wasn't going to come, as she was thinking about making a stand against the capitalism of it all, but Orion asked her to come, so she sits behind him in her own seat.

I think that means there must be something there with them. It's something that she would come with us, just because Orion wanted her to.

"I'm glad to hear it's not dinky," I say. "I like rides that are bolted into the ground. Never felt super on-board with the state fair rides."

Win nods. "Portable roller coasters. When you say it that way, it doesn't sound great, does it?"

He takes my hand and sits back, looking out the bus window.

His dark eyes and dark hair are reflected in the glass, and I see him close his eyes for a moment.

I wish I could have known him before Franny left. I wonder if he carried himself just a little taller, a little lighter.

But we all are made of our history. Like sand deposited on a faraway beach, our lives add little grains to who we are every day.

Of course, I feel like my beach is Jersey Shore and Win's is Bora Bora, but what can I do.

Lulu speaks up from the seat behind. "I'm telling both of you boys right now not to fall victim to the carnies who want you to win big dumb stuffed animals in the name of your girl."

Orion turns around and lifts himself up on a knee to see her over the back of the seat. "Did you just say you're my girl?"

Lulu blanches. "I'm just saying, don't fall for the gendered stereotypes. Men have been suckers for that since they were jousting in the 1400s."

Orion sits back down and points at her while getting my and Win's attention. "You heard that, right?"

I smile. "I will stand witness to the 'girl-ing' of Lulu to you."

Lulu glares at me. "I'll cut you."

Win puts an arm around me. "Don't make me defend my girl."

Loving this exchange, Orion eggs Win on. "We'd have to fight each other for our girls' honor."

Lulu puts her headphones on, practically growling. "I'm going to retch. Knock it off."

The bus pauses at a stoplight, and Fiona and Phoebe rush up the aisle from the back of the bus to sit behind me and Win.

Fiona takes a picture of Win and me with her phone. "Here's the plan: we ride everything on the south side of the park first, so we'll have to get off the bus and run over there to beat everyone else."

Phoebe taps Orion on the leg. "Can you pretend to tie your shoe and keep everyone on the bus for an extra forty-five seconds or so? It'll give us a head start."

He's not buying it. "What if I want to get across to the rides ahead of everyone else too? Why do I have to take one for the team?"

"Because you're bigger than us. They'd mow Bébé over." Fiona and Phoebe both plead with Orion.

I speak up. "How about Win and I distract them for a bit? Then you two and Orion can get over there and get going."

"What're you going to do?"

"I don't know, but I can figure something out," I promise.

Win agrees.

When the bus rolls in, all the seniors start to rustle with anticipation. It's not every day a whole theme park is at your fingertips.

Of course, no regular person worth her salt probably wants to be in an amusement park with an entire senior high school class, but still, the idea that it's all ours is fun.

My phone vibrates.

Have fun. Be safe. Love you up and down.

I text Mom back.

And backward and forward. And always.

She's back at me immediately.

Text me when you're on the way home.

Win leans against my shoulder, looks at my screen. "Your mom?"

Another opportunity to be honest. "Yep." I take a breath. "You know, Win—"

Fiona and Phoebe stand up as the bus comes to a halt in front of the park entrance. "Do your magic, Bébé."

Win pats me on the back. "Godspeed, girls and Orion.

Don't trample little old ladies."

Lulu sighs. "Fine, I'll come, too. At least I can get away from some of these people." She waves in the general direction of the rest of the bus.

The truth opportunity is gone. I place my phone on the floor and stand up, then give it a good boot toward the back of the bus. Standing tall, I call out to the back of the bus as Fiona and Phoebe and Orion slip down the bus steps. "Who knows where my phone is? Is it back there? Can anyone see it?"

Win smiles wide and joins in, yelling loudly, "No one took it, did they?"

The whole rest of the bus yells at one another now, some kids getting down low to find my phone, one kid laying blame on another for stealing my phone.

Mrs. Haggerty whistles with her fingers. The bus stills.

"Everybody stand still and look at your feet," she says. "We find Vivi's phone, then we can go."

I cast a glance over my shoulder. Orion and the girls really are sprinting, and I see them run out of view under the trees of the main street of the park.

Win whispers, "Mission accomplished."

"Here it is!" Mrs. Haggerty holds my phone high, wades through the impatient students, and hands it to me. "How it got all the way back there, who knows."

Win and I let all the other kids filter off the bus, then we get into the park. I buy him cotton candy, and we ride the little train around the outside of the grounds. We ride the log flume and shoot water cannons at the bumper boat riders; I decline to ride the Panic Plunge ride that drops its passengers seven stories straight down, and we eat lunch with Orion and Lulu.

And the whole time I don't take a minute, thirty seconds, to correct the record about the imaginary villain Win thinks wants to hurt my mom and me.

The afternoon gets late.

"We've got time for one more ride," Win announces.

I'm hot, and my feet hurt. Shockingly, my mom and I didn't really do theme parks when I was younger, so the day has been long and fun, but mostly kind of long.

"What about the Ferris wheel?" It's right in front of us.

He takes my hand and leads me toward the back of the line. "Low adrenaline and short line. Brilliant."

We stand behind three guys from the yearbook staff who are looking over pictures they've taken on their phones, ready to load them up on the senior slideshow for graduation night.

"Graduation." Win just says the word and lets it sit there.

"Yep." I don't know what else to say.

"We've got summer, though," he replies.

"I might do something," I volunteer.

"Do what?"

"I might apply to UNR."

He smiles. "Really?"

"I might have already started the app last night. Haggerty helped me do the FAFSA on Wednesday."

"You really hadn't done anything about college apps before that?"

"Nope."

"Why not?" We edge forward in the line, and the breeze picks up, clouds starting to fluff up in the sky above us. It feels good, a welcome relief to the unblinking sun we've been under all day. (I put on sunscreen, of course. Mom wouldn't have let me out of the house without it. And without her list of approved rides. And without a lecture on staying with the group. Really, it's a miracle I got out the door at all.)

Trying to think of a short answer, I tilt my head. "Jack McCann boiled it down in his last lecture to me."

"Oh, he did now, did he? Please, impart his wisdom to me." Win's not often sarcastic, but he sure is right now.

"No, he's been a help to me. Really." And here I am at the same old topic of needing to tell Win the truth. I edge toward it. "I'm afraid to leave my mom."

"I can imagine." He takes my hand and gives it a squeeze.

"No, it's not really why you think, though." I say.

"What?" Win asks.

"Let's go." The ride attendant, a slim man with a very fierce-looking tattoo of either Jennifer Lopez or Javier Bardem in *No Country for Old Men*, I can't tell which, waits to close the ride gate behind us.

"Last on, top of the wheel," Win says.

"What do you mean?" I ask.

"He puts us on, then rotates the wheel to check everyone's seatbelts. We end up at the top before he starts the ride. Bonus."

"Cool," I say. I wonder if my mom has a story of someone falling from the top of a Ferris wheel.

I wonder why I even wonder. I'm sure she does.

Win pulls out his phone. "I want a picture with you." He puts an arm around me and pulls me close, as the wheel slowly begins to turn, our seat rising little by little.

And he leans in and kisses me on the cheek. I turn, surprised, and he kisses me again. It's the first time today that we have a moment to ourselves to focus on just us.

I kiss him back, and he puts the phone down, slips his other arm around me, and really kisses me deeply. The sensation of it flashes through my body, my heart revving up and my skin prickling.

It's amazing.

Then there's a crack of thunder.

I jump, and Win pulls away from me. "Wow. That's crazy."

I turn around, and coming up from the south is a dark, angry cloud. "Oh, crap."

"We're fine. They'll unload the ride right now, not a huge deal," Win says.

I look down at the attendant. It looks like Win's right, the guy is on the ride's phone, and he looks in the direction of the big cloud as well.

"That storm really came out of nowhere." Win sounds a lot like he's trying to reassure me.

I don't want him to worry. This is not anxiety-attack-making for me. At least I don't think so.

"I'm fine."

Then my phone buzzes.

Where are you? There's a severe thunderstorm warning.

"Oh boy." I look at my phone and immediately go into crisis-management mode.

I text Mom back.

We're in the restaurant by the entrance of the park. No worries. I think we're staying put until the storm clears.

I hate lying to her, but she'll drive up here. She really will. I feel my stomach start to churn.

"Gah."

Win looks at me. "What?"

"My mom. My mom is worried."

"About us being on the Ferris wheel?"

"Yeah," I say. "Well, no, because I wasn't that specific. I guess there's a severe thunderstorm warning."

"Oh, my mom would be freaked about that if she were in town."

"Yeah?" I ask. But I wonder in my head if she would ponder moving to a different region of the country if she felt it were a profound enough threat.

Because my mom would. And Win doesn't know that.

We have to go up and over the top before we get our chance to unload. It starts raining. The view is pretty amazing, but now I actually am a little worried. The J-Lo-loving ride operator looks as bored as he did when he loaded us on the ride, and he keeps checking his cell phone as he moves each carriage to the platform and lets its riders off.

"This isn't a rush job, I guess," Win observes.

"I guess not."

The wind blows in, and the air temperature drops about five degrees, dust blowing up out of the parking lot. The rain opens up, and there's a flash, followed before long by another big boom of thunder.

"Now I'm a little nervous." I shiver.

Win pulls me closer, and the rain soaks through our shirts and trickles down our foreheads. The little carriage begins to sway, ever so slightly, as the wind buffets the Ferris wheel.

Win smiles broad and puts his face up into the rain. "I counted between the flash and the thunder. We're still like five or ten miles away from the center of the storm. No worries."

"Is that your inner storm chaser talking? You're trying to stall so you can ride it out on the Ferris wheel, aren't you?"

"I'm not a thrill-seeker; I'm a scientist."

"You're an aspiring scientist who won't be much of one if we get electrocuted."

He holds me close, and with one hand points to the center of the ride. "Sorry to be a buzzkill, but there's a huge grounding cable right there. The lightning would travel right down that and into the earth. Dunzo. No dramatic cooking of the riders, unfortunately."

The wheel continues to glide around, little by little, each carriage unloaded.

If we don't get off soon, Mom will show up and freak out and I'll be done. No more Win and Vivi, no more school in Coeur d'Alene.

Win nudges me. "Hey, it's going to be okay."

I lean forward and kiss him again, close my eyes tight, wish the world away.

It occurs to me that she can't make me move anymore. I can stay or I can move, and I can even choose to move to be with Win. I'm in charge, really. I turn eighteen in July, and I can be my own person.

"I love you." I hear it out of my mouth, and it surprises even me, but I'm in love with this person. I want to be with him, and I want him. I love him.

He wipes my soaked hair out of my eyes, takes my face in his hands, and kisses me. "I love you, too, Smooch."

"Get off."

We've made it to the bottom of the wheel. Clearly our carnival host is over our profession of love.

"Okay. Moment over." Win laughs and takes my hand. We race to the entrance gate of the park. The buses are loaded, and Mrs. Haggerty waits for us at the bottom step of our bus.

"You two get lost?" she asks.

"Something like that," I say with an unnatural amount of cheer.

Win gets on the bus with me, and he breaks into laughter.

Orion sits next to Lulu. In her seat behind him is a gigantic stuffed panda bear, hogging the whole seat.

Win looks at Lulu. "You change your position on the whole 'win something for me' argument?"

Lulu folds her arms over her chest. "I'm aware of the construct of gender, and Orion let me know that he was really good at the softball toss. I think in the whole scheme of things, him winning the panda bear for me was an act of rebellion."

Phoebe cuts into the conversation from her seat with Fiona across the aisle from the panda. "And it's sooo cute!"

Fiona and Phoebe give me and Win a ride to my house. The

rain's gone now, but the air is cool, and the sky is gray and pink in the waning light.

"That sure beat any regular day of school," Phoebe says as she pulls her little car to the side of the road.

I nervously look for my mom. She's not out on the lawn waiting for me, so I guess that's good.

Fiona texts someone with furious speed.

"What's on for tomorrow for you two?" Win asks Fiona.

She looks up for one second. "I have not a clue. If you two want to do something tomorrow, text us. Sunday's out."

"Why?" I ask.

"We run the day care at our church," Phoebe answers.

"Interesting." Win says.

"We like the little babies." Fiona says, but she doesn't look up from her phone.

"Good night," I say, and Win and I get out.

My mom still hasn't come out of the house. Something is up. It has to be.

Win pulls me close, hugs me tight. "You're still a little rain-soaked."

He smiles, and I think he's about to kiss me, but I point at the front door of my house.

"I better go in," I tell him.

He nods. "That's right, we're chill, casual, no big deal." His grin gets really, really wide. He pulls out his phone and types something.

My phone buzzes. He's sent a text.

I liked saying I love you. Chill or no.

I look at him, look around. The front door is still

closed.

Me, too. I type back.

The door opens. I hear it.

Win gives me a little wave, then a wave to my mom. "Ms. Stone, you missed a fun time at Silverwood today. Have a good night."

Mom comes out on the front porch, gives him a wave back. "Goodnight."

I watch him walk down the street and turn left. I turn around and look into Mom's eyes.

"You okay?" she asks. She pulls me close into a hug, and I can hear her pounding heart.

"I'm good, Mom. How are you?" I look at her closely. Is that fear in her eyes? Panic? Does she know what happened to us today?

"I think we should go to the grocery store. You want to come?" She smiles at me, but the look is so forced it's a grimace, and it worries me more than honest feeling from her.

"Sure."

We drive to the little market, the old one Costco's almost driven out of business. It clings on by its proximity to downtown. Tourists wander in to buy ice and drinks for days out on the lake, and in late June their fireworks stand will do brisk business.

Mom doesn't say much in the car. When we get out and walk to the doors of the store, I take her hand, like we always did when I was little.

"We had a good day today, the storm at the end aside."

I try hard to sound middle of the road: not too giddy, not too bored.

"Who'd you hang out with?"

Mom sounds totally plastic. I wonder if she's taken something. A few doctors ago, one of them prescribed something for her that put her into robot mode. It might have been Klonopin, but whatever it was, it didn't react well with Mom's body chemistry, and I lost her to a dazed state of mechanical response. It was scary. I'd rather have her all wound-up than disappear into a fog of medication.

"Win and Fiona and Phoebe. Lulu made Orion win her a big panda. It was really funny." I chuckle about that. It really *was* funny.

Mom stops me before I can go in the store. "I don't want you to do trips like that. There's just so many things that can go wrong. I saw where a girl fell off a tram during a windstorm at a park once."

I grit my teeth. This is why I didn't tell her about the Ferris wheel. "Mom, it's done. I'm fine, and we had fun."

She stands there, looks up at the sky and back at me. "I don't know about Win. You seem really smitten."

"Maybe I am. He's a good guy." I feel like I'm going to cry.

"Just don't get too carried away, Vivi. First love can be misleading. It feels so wonderful, but it can lead you to lots of decisions you might not be ready to make."

"Who said it was love? Who said it was first love? Maybe it's one-hundredth love. I've lived a lot of places, maybe I've had a sailor in every port. You don't necessarily know every little thing." I turn around to go to the car.

"The car's not open."

"Open it, Mom."

She calls after me. "Vivi, come on. I'm just trying to keep you safe."

I face her. "Unlock the car. And quit the 'keeping me safe' thing."

"You don't want me to care about you being safe?"

"I'm almost eighteen. This is about fear or maybe about change. If you could take a deep breath and step outside the old habit of worrying about things we have absolutely no control over, you'd see it."

She unlocks the door to the car. I hear the click of the locks. "You're being really disrespectful. If hanging out with these new friends brings out this side of you, maybe you're done with the new friends. You're not eighteen yet." She turns her back on me and walks into the grocery store.

That's a line she's not drawn in the sand before, but I've never really pushed back before. I've never had anyone like Win before, either.

I need to tell him the whole truth, and soon.

I go back and sit in the car.

Mom does her shopping, comes back to the car, and drives the whole way home in silence. I sit next to her, quiet.

She parks in our driveway and turns to me. "Give me your phone."

"What?" I immediately thank my lucky stars it's protected with my thumbprint. There's nothing bad on there, but I don't want her reading my Snaps or texts.

"You talk to me like a ten year old? Ten year olds don't have phones. I take your phone. That's how that goes." Her tone is cold, but I can tell I really hurt her feelings. She's mad.

I hand it to her.

She starts crying.

I've seen this before. She doesn't punish me very often. I don't talk back hardly at all. When I do, it hurts her feelings terribly. It makes the whole thing kind of awful.

"Mom." I touch the top of her hand, trying to bring her back to the conversation, console her a little.

I almost apologize, but then I catch myself. I just want to enjoy the fact that I had a nice day out with my friends. I didn't do anything wrong, except call her on her nonsensical worrying. I take in a deep breath.

She still cries silently, dabbing at her eyes with a balled-up tissue in her hand.

"Mom."

"What?" She looks at me.

"Listen, I mean it when I say we need to get a hold of this. I'm going to be eighteen. It's going to happen."

"I'll never stop being your mom."

"I *will* move out at some point. I'm not going to be forty and still live with you." I skip mentioning the plan to move out in less than six months. I reach for my phone back.

She hands it to me.

I pull up the contacts and write a number down on the Post-it pad on the console. "I talked to a counselor at school. She gave me the name of someone really good with PTSD."

"What?" Mom's voice goes ice cold again.

I'm not stopping. She can take my phone. I don't care.

This needs to be done.

"PTSD. You've got a good reason to be worried. I don't know if it's because of Northridge, but you've got history, and it's not made up. But we need to stop running."

"Why do you think I moved us here? I want to be done with this as much as you do."

"But you lost it today over a thunderstorm. We can't get away from those. We can't get away from everything. We can't get away from the fact that we could be sitting here, and I could have a huge tumor growing inside of me right now."

Her eyes go wide.

"I don't, Mom. I feel fine, but we don't know. We can't, as much as we try."

She puts her hand out for my phone, but she does also take the Post-it.

"I don't like the new Vivi."

"This is me, Mom. It's not because of friends or moving here. It's just me—I'm not any different."

She gets out of the car and goes inside.

She makes me dinner, pot pies with carrots and apples, but she doesn't speak to me the rest of the night.

Mudslide

On March 22, 2014, forty-three people were killed in a massive mudslide in Oso, Washington. Weeks of heavy rain had saturated the soil, and it gave way on a sunny Saturday, burying the entire neighborhood of Steelhead Haven.

The mudslide that crossed the river was one of many on the same hillside, recorded as early as 1900. The slide left mud and debris as deep as twenty feet in some areas. The Stillaguamish River's channel had been shifting north since as early as 1932, undercutting the hill above it.

The mudslide was the deadliest in US history.

Often mudslides or debris flows are the result of an earthquake, heavy rain following a hurricane, or heavy rainfall in a burn area that has yet to recover from a forest fire.

In some cases, the area impacted is heavily populated and receives an unprecedented amount of rain in a short time, as in the 2011 Rio de Janeiro slides—in a 24-hour period, the area was inundated with more rainfall than what is expected for the entire month.

In the United States, the USGS monitors slopes in real time, using slope movement sensors and rain gauges. There are a dozen areas across the country monitored, with the hopes that an early-warning system for debris flows can be developed.

Areas of high impact in the United States include several areas in Oregon, Washington, California, Colorado, and North Carolina.

CHAPTER TEN
UNEASY RIDER

To say it was a chilly weekend would be the understatement of the century. After our fight Friday night Mom was quiet; I was apologetic. Relations did warm to the point that I was allowed to take my phone to school today. When I was finally able to check it this morning, I realized Win had been trying to get a hold of me all weekend.

He says he has a surprise for me after school today. Waiting 'til then will be an eternity, but it's our last day, and seniors only have a half day. This last quick Monday will be followed by two days of practice and prep for graduation. Wednesday is the big night. My knees tremble—*graduation*. Just saying the word brings a quiver to my voice.

But I feel bold today. I practically strut into the art

room. I know Win will be by to pick me up after, and that we're going on an epic adventure, one that'll go long into the night, or so he promises. I've told Mom there's a graduation meeting after school, and that I'm going to dinner with friends afterward. I don't know if it was my tone, or if she was feeling sorry about our fight, but she didn't protest. I hate, hate that I lied to her, but every day that passes is a day closer to Win going to college, and I'm not going to miss any chance to be with him.

And I want to kiss him again. I take a blissful moment to think of his mouth, his dark eyes sparkling above his white smile, leaning in to feel his breath on my cheek, when Fiona and Phoebe both poke me in the back at the same time.

"Bébé."

"It's the Fi girls. What's up?"

Rushing in front of me, Fiona does the unthinkable and hands Phoebe her phone. "Hold this for a minute."

"Okay, someone's died. I've never seen you voluntarily give up your phone. Ever," I say.

She's too busy to comment on this. "You're about to spill on whatever Win has planned for you. It's a half-day, the last day of school for seniors, and he's wearing a tie. I've never seen him wear clean socks, much less a tie."

I grin. "He is, is he?"

Phoebe can't help herself, and she plunks down at our table. "Are you having sex? Is this some big lead-up to that?"

"And if we were planning that, would I tell the Fi twins about it?"

"Yes, you would. We're your best friends."

I might take issue with the best friend thing, but I let it go. "No, we're not having sex tonight. Please don't spread that rumor around."

"How come?"

"How come? Because I'm going to be in a relationship with someone long term before I do that. And I'm certainly not going to on my first official date with someone."

"IT'S THE FIRST DATE? Are you insane? We've tried our best, Bébé. We got you the pool filled with pillows, and you fell asleep. What've you been doing for the last month? Holy Christmas on a cracker, that's ridiculous." Fiona's beside herself.

Our art teacher, Mrs. Young, tries to come get us on task, but Fiona can only put up a hand in her general direction.

Phoebe backs her up. "Miss, we cannot deal with art. It's the last day, you've got us in class for like twenty-two minutes, and Bébé here is dealing with some high-key drama."

The girls look at our teacher with such disdain that she actually slinks off to deal with two boys at another table.

I look at my phone. There are so, so many reasons I need the bell to ring right now. The twins are a big one, but I'm so nervous. A tie? What's Win up to that he's wearing a tie?

When the bell does finally ring, Fiona and Phoebe both squeal. I fall off my stool as the two of them usher me out of the art room into the arms of Win, as far as they're concerned.

I'm trying to make sure I actually picked up my phone and my books, looking back over my shoulder, when they both finally stop pushing me from behind.

I turn around to see Win standing in front of me.

My heart thrills.

He's wearing a tie, all right, and a nice pair of khakis, and a plaid shirt, and dress shoes. His hair, normally kind of all over the place, has a deep part and must have some product in it.

"You smell good." These are the brilliant first words out of my mouth on the occasion of our first date. If I get my way and we get married (I've already planned this out, and it's ridiculous, but I also have already planned my first apartment and what dishes I would register for at West Elm for my housewarming, and what dog I'll own when I retire and move to Key West, and I've never even really had a boyfriend, so I don't feel like I'm that far out of the regular range of my freakish behavior), I'll hopefully not say something idiotic like this when he first sees me in my dress. It'll be hopefully something amazing like, *"Today begins the journey of the rest of our lives, a road I hope is long."* Not, *"You shaved. Good job. I remembered deodorant."*

I've clearly surprised him, and he smiles. "Thanks. It's the product in my hair. I borrowed it from Toby."

"You borrowed everything from Toby."

"This is why older brothers who care about clothes do come in handy from time to time."

"Nice." I start to worry that I should be doing something other than standing here, gawking at him. But he's truly, honestly, so good-looking. I want to reach out and touch him, connect myself to something so beautiful, as though I could have some of it rub off on me.

I'd never say I was beautiful, but standing next to Win, I can't help but feel pretty. He chose me; he really did. I didn't think it was possible, but here he is, taking me out on the last day of school. Out on a date. He even used that actual word, and in a text, even, which is documented. I could take a screenshot and print it out and have it framed.

"Let me give you a rundown of our evening of adventure," he says as he takes my hand and leads me down the hall. Fiona and Phoebe follow us for a while, until Win turns and gives them a look. Then they stare at the ceiling and pretend to check their phones and scurry off, giggling.

"Fill me in."

He hesitates, and then launches in. "Remember when you said you wanted to see my house? Well, tonight you get to meet my parents."

"At your house? You're not in witness protection after all, then."

"Not at my house. They're meeting us downtown for dinner. Hence, the clothes."

"You dressed up for them, not me."

"I didn't know you'd get all mushy. If I had, I'd have worn a tie every day to school. Girls are so weird about stuff." He tugs on the blue and pink striped tie. "Why is this so irresistibly attractive?"

"On you, it's the novelty. I've never seen one on you. The newness."

"Huh. Okay, fair enough. Anyway, we're meeting Ma and Pa downtown. Then you and I are having coffee, and we're finishing the extravaganza somewhere special that I'm not divulging until later."

"Stuffing ourselves silly all over town. Sounds adventurous."

"Novel, new, but maybe not bungee-jumping level of adventure."

"It's early release. What are we doing for the next three hours?"

"Making butter. Churning it ourselves, so it'll take a while."

"Umm, is it too late to opt out of the date and go back to being acquaintances?"

"Way too late. Too bad for you!"

I smile and give his hand a squeeze. "Okay, then. I'll just suffer through."

"No, we've got something special lined up to celebrate the last day of school."

With that, Win leads me out of the building and to the bus stop.

"We're taking the bus to our date?"

"I didn't miraculously get a car since you said you'd go out with me. I may look like a first-class date, but I still have holes in my socks."

Then I see something turn the corner and make its way to the bus stop.

A horse and carriage.

"Holy Seabiscuit! You did not get that for our date."

Win smiles wide, and he starts to laugh. "Listen, this is not how all of this typically will go down. It's fair to say that if your expectation is that our next date will top this one, it won't. This is it."

Sighing, I smile slyly. "You're lucky there aren't any promposals in your immediate future. You'd have to get shot out of a cannon or something."

I brought up prom. I'm an idiot. But he catches me looking at the sidewalk and takes my hand.

"It's okay, Smooch. You can say the word. Or a version of the word. I'll survive it."

And with that, I step forward and kiss him. I can't help it.

His mouth is warm, and kissing him sends electricity straight up and down my spine. My hair stands up on my neck. Then his hand is there, pulling me closer to him as I open my mouth and kiss him more intensely.

"Your horse is here. Holy crap! A horse, Bébé!" Phoebe jumps up and down.

Win breaks the kiss and pulls me into a hug. "Don't move. If we're still, maybe she'll move on," he whispers.

"She's not a tyrannosaurus rex. She can still see us," I murmur. But I'd be happy to just stand here in his arms.

The horse clip-clops, and the driver clucks to it as it comes up in the bus lane.

"Our ride is here. We've got to go." Win takes my hand and pulls me away from the Fi sisters.

Fiona has her phone up. "I'll put the video on my Snapchat story. Have fun!"

Phoebe waves. "If you get to feed the horse, you have to tell me all about it at graduation, okay?"

"See you soon, girls." I wave back, and I actually have a moment where I think fondly of them.

Win helps me up into the carriage. "They're sitting on either side of you at graduation, you know that, right?"

"What do you mean?"

"Lewis is right between Leador and Lightfoot. You're

destined to be together."

And here I thought on my first day the art teacher was kindly introducing me to two nice girls. She was just plunking me down in my spot in the alpha-order seating chart.

As I sit down, the driver turns around and tips his hat. "Happy last day of school. Enjoy your adventures."

I laugh and take Win's hand. "This is crazy."

We clip-clop down the shady residential streets of downtown Coeur d'Alene, along the lake on the levee by North Idaho College, down to City Park and the band shell. In the deep shade of the tall ponderosa pines, the horse driver pulls the carriage to a stop by the playground.

Win hops out and makes sure I get down in one piece, too.

The driver busies himself watering the horse, and Win pulls out a backpack. "I made you a sandwich. Want it?" He has a brown paper sack with my name on it.

"You're too good to me." I grab a spot at the picnic table in the shade by a big tree.

"We're good for each other." He sits, and we eat. I don't say much, just lean into him and enjoy being.

After a quick sandwich, we wander around the park, and then turn back toward our carriage and the playground.

"Should we swing a bit?"

I look over at the enormous play fort, with a wide row of swings.

"Sounds great. You're in a tie. Will this be a problem?" It's pleasant out, but it is warm.

"I'm trying to please my mom and dad, maybe, but I've already gotten the mileage out of it that I wanted. You liked the tie, so the big impression is over. I get some sweat on it. No biggie." He makes it to the first swing and hops on. "Come on. Let's see who can really get some air."

"You know, of course, that my mom never liked me on the swings. Too many dangers."

"Uh-huh. She's a worrier, that one." I can see him reconsider saying that. "But she's had a good reason. The swings, maybe not so much, but things are bigger than that now."

And then I do the thing: I choose to miss the opportunity to tell Win the truth. He lobs it to me in conversation, a big old fat softball of a chance to say, *"In fact, Win, things aren't bigger. There isn't anyone after me and my mom. It's just the statistical probability of cataclysmic disaster she's terrified by. Nothing to see here."*

But I don't. I say a weak "Uh-huh" and swing like my life depends on it.

Before long, it's time to finish our carriage ride. The driver brings us around to the shady side of the park and bids us goodbye.

"It's time for the family portion of the night," Win says. He holds my hand and swings it back and forth.

"I don't know if you're going to top the horse and carriage."

"This part won't top that. Guaranteed."

"I bet you I'll like your mom and dad more than I like my own mom right now."

"Why?" he asks.

"Palindrome," I say.

"I get that we have a code word, but if it's something long, we have a ten- or fifteen-minute stroll. Long stories need to be aired out once in a while."

"She says I'm too sassy from hanging out with you. And I need to keep my eyes open in my 'first love' situation. I'm kind of not wild about her right now."

I look at him. I don't want to lie to him anymore, but right now, though I could divulge the truth, I don't feel like letting Mom ruin things. I hate the feeling I have when I'm honest about Mom and me—it's nothing like the feeling I have right now.

"Sassy. I like it," he says.

"She most definitely does not." I can't keep the irritation out of my voice.

"Listen, we all have our challenges with parents. After Franny, my dad wouldn't let me out of his sight for seven months. He'd sit me down every weekend and make me watch *Scared Straight* or ancient Afterschool Specials about kids making bad decisions. It was exhausting."

"I only got my phone back for the whole day today because it was a half day and she was working. She knew it wasn't realistic to expect me to go straight home and wait for her in an empty house. I apologized the next morning, but man, the trip to Silverwood rattled her."

"My mom keeps buying me stuff for my dorm and bursting into tears every time she brings it to my room to show me."

We've walked several blocks through downtown by now. As we walk up to Toro Viejo, *the* family Mexican restaurant for Coeur d'Alene, or so says the sign outside,

Win pulls me back for a moment.

"Remember when we first met, and you were afraid for me to meet your mom?"

"Of course."

"Now's the time for me to have my moment. You didn't call takebacks when you first kissed me, did you?"

"Takebacks?"

"You know, like you could take it back later. For instance, if you later met my mom and then wanted to run for the hills. You didn't call takebacks, right?"

"No, I definitely didn't. Some smart person told me I didn't get to choose my mom, so he wouldn't judge me too hard. Maybe I can apply that logic in this situation."

"Seems fair. Dad'll probably talk a lot about Canada. And besides bursting into tears whenever college comes up, remember that my mom also calls me Winnie the Pooh."

I laugh; I can't help it. "Oh, I thought it was just Winnie. Didn't know about the Pooh part. That's pretty adorable."

He nods. "Glad I divulged that to you, so happy about that. And I feel like it's a little less adorable and a little more overbearing or creepy."

"She's not like Norman Bates's mom, right?"

"No, of course not."

"Then you're fine." I think about kissing him again, but the door of the restaurant swings open, and a tall gentleman waves us in with a red napkin in his hand. He's handsome, like Win, but his skin is a deeper, richer color, and Win's not as slim as he is.

"Dad, what're you doing?"

"C'mon in, kids. Your mom and I can see you out

here. She's dying to meet Vivi." He holds the door open.

Win squeezes my hand. "Here we go."

I follow him into the little Mexican restaurant. His dad stands by our table.

"Hi, Dad." Win gives him a hug.

Win's mom reaches out from her seat at the table to get a hug, too. She's a neat, compact little lady, her jet-black hair in a perfect bob, her Talbot's outfit fresh and pressed. "Winnie!"

"How was your trip, Mom?" Win asks. I approach the table slightly behind him, using him as cover.

She stands up. "We can talk about that later. This is Vivi?"

I step forward. "Hi, Mrs. Kemper."

"Please, it's Meko." She shakes my hand and pulls me over to the seat next to hers. "I'd love it if you sat next to me."

Her husband speaks up. "What about me?" His glass of water and napkin are at my new spot.

"You're chopped liver, Gerald," Win says. "Sorry." He sits on the other side of me, and his dad, Gerald, is across from me.

"Okay, let the grilling begin!" Gerald claps his hands together and laughs—one loud, short *ha!* that echoes off the cool plaster walls of the dining room.

I see a lot of Win in him. His manner is easy, and he commands attention, just like the crowd parting in the cafeteria for Win the first day I met him.

"Great. Tell me about Canada," I say. "Were you born there?"

"Clever girl. I was born there, yes. In Calgary." He

puts an arm around his wife. "I met Meko at University of Toronto."

Meko looks at me. "You don't really care about hockey, do you?"

I shrug.

She gives Gerald a pinch. "See? She's not into hockey. Don't launch into the whole rigmarole."

Win takes my hand under the table and smiles at me. "Dad played in the NHL. If you did like hockey, he'd be in hog heaven. But you don't, so he'll just have to wait to corner you at a barbecue in the future and tell you all about it."

"For how long?" I ask.

"No, don't encourage him. Really, once he gets going he'll never stop," Meko teases.

"Eight years. Last team was the Maple Leafs. Then I went back and got my MBA."

Win gives him a look. "Really, you can just share your resume later."

But I keep going. "When did you all move to Coeur d'Alene?"

"Meko took a job here teaching at NIC. Nutrition. Win was in sixth grade. I was ready to work part-time. I'm kind of an old dad."

"You still travel up to Canada a lot? I've always wanted to go there."

"My company has an office in Vancouver and one in Nanaimo. Stevedoring."

"I've actually heard of that," I say. "Loading ships?"

Meko coughs and punches Gerald. "I know all about you already. I want to know about Vivi."

My gut clenches. I haven't been straight with Win, and now I'm going to do the dance of vague answers and avoidance of real talk about my family. "Mom and I just moved here from Issaquah. We've moved around a lot, really. I met Win on the way to the bus stop."

"What's your thing? Your passion?" Gerald leans in, enthusiastic. He seems to be fired up about just being here. I see the light in his eyes, a lot like Win's.

"I don't really know. I'm starting to like spending time outdoors. And spending time with your son, to be honest." I smile right at Meko and Gerald, who sit back a bit, big grins on their faces.

Win squeezes my hand under the table. "Thanks, Smooch."

Gerald gives another hoot, smacks his hand on his knee in glee. "Oh, it's all out on the table now. Not ten minutes in, and we have the nickname, even!"

Meko waves a menu around. "Guys! Let's order and give Vivi a minute to breathe, please."

Win grins at me. And I grin right back.

Win's parents are lovely. I hear all about Winnie as a little boy, and the dinner conversation is lively. Franny doesn't come up, but Meko dotes on Win and brags about him and Toby and their accomplishments. To hear her tell it, Toby's the next Tiger Woods, and Jim Cantore on the Weather Channel better watch his back.

As the waiter clears the plates, Gerald stretches and sits back in his chair. "What are the plans for the rest of the night? You two want to go grab a cup of coffee at Java?"

Win gets up. "We do, but we're going solo, if you don't mind, Dad. Kind of on our first date, you know."

"Wait. You call her Smooch, and it's just the first date? Good lord."

"Honey, give the kids a break." Meko sips her water and waves us on our way. "I hope to see you at graduation, Vivi. It really has been a pleasure."

"You too, both of you. It's been a pleasure meeting you both." I give Meko a hug. Win winds his way around the tables and leads me out of the restaurant.

On the sidewalk, he kisses me. "Well, they love you. Not a surprise."

I punch him playfully on the shoulder. "You never disclose the nickname to the parents. Your dad will give the toast at the wedding and blab it to the whole world."

I suck in a breath. *Where in the world did that just come from? Wedding? What the hell? I'm done for.*

"Wedding?" Win raises an eyebrow.

My palms go sweaty. "Totally kidding. Never even want to get married. Want to graduate from college and work for at least twenty years before I even consider it. Ignore me." I look for a rock to crawl under. *Why do I ruin things when they're going so well?*

He hugs me. "I know you. I know you're not pining for a husband. But it's still stinkin' funny. I'm going to hold that over your head for at least a month."

"You're not freaked out? I'm so sorry. Really, I don't know why I said that. I'm a total feminist."

"You're an independent woman who don't need no man. I'm with you. No worries." He points down the block. "Let's go to Java."

We meander through downtown. It's a warm night, and the town is out, sitting in sidewalk cafes and packing the bars on Sherman Avenue. Families ride bikes, and couples walk their dogs by the resort, its tall copper-roofed towers standing against the blue of the lake.

We get our drinks to go. Win strokes his chin conspiratorially. "I've got a place we're going to eat our dessert. Follow me."

We stroll down to the resort.

"Can we walk around the boardwalk?" I ask. The breeze coming off the water feels light and fresh, and the sun dazzles the surface as it begins to sink in the sky.

Win follows me. We walk in silence for a bit, next to one another, watching families and tourists gawk at the yachts and restored speedboats. The boardwalk encircles the marina, and the lake is spread out before us, a canvas for colors as the sun goes down.

"When do you need to get back tonight?" Win asks.

I chafe at the thought. "Ugh. I told Mom I'd be back by eleven. I should've told her I'd get home when I felt like it. But I don't want to talk about her. I want to enjoy my time here, with you. Be in the moment."

We've walked to the outermost spot of the boardwalk, and the little deck is filled with people taking photos and sitting on the benches.

"We need to wait here for a minute," Win says.

I sit on a bench, and he sits next to me. I lean into his shoulder, and he puts an arm around me.

"You'll still talk to me when you go to UNR?" I ask.

"I will definitely talk to you. And since you'll be there, too, it'd be really awkward if I didn't." He sounds so optimistic, but right now I can't see how I'll get there, get to college.

Time feels like it's flying past, blurred trees on the highway out my car window.

"I don't even know what your favorite color is." I don't know enough about him yet.

"It's blue."

"You like dogs more than cats, obviously."

"Of course. Where's this going?" He looks at me.

"I'm getting to know you, and we've said 'the words', and there's so much about you I don't know."

"What do you know?"

"That you have a heart for all kinds of people. You take care of your friends."

"And?"

"You love being in nature and being connected to what's happening right now. And you're sometimes sad about your sister not being in your life anymore. And you're better at a lot of things than you'll admit. And you think you only have two friends, but all of the senior class looks up to you. You're grounded, you're funny, and you're at peace in your own skin."

"Geez, all of that? I was thinking you might say my second toe is longer than my big toe." He gives me a squeeze.

A boat glides up in front of us. Toby is at the wheel. It's Jack McCann's boat.

He calls to us, "Hey, kids, it's time to go."

Win stands up and pulls me after him. "On to the next phase of first-date-palooza."

"I prefer first-date-fest." I step into the boat behind

him. "Where are we going?"

"More eating." Win sits next to me behind Toby as the boat pulls away from the boardwalk and out into the lake.

We cruise out across the center of the lake, and Toby slows the boat as we come to a small island right off the opposite shore.

"Kidd Island, as requested," Toby says. "I'll be back for you at 10:30."

Win and I get out, and Win pushes the boat off the sand. Toby reverses the engine, gets away from the shallow water, and glides back the way he came.

"What's this place about?" I ask Win.

"I don't really know. It might have had a house on it once. Somebody built a walk around it." He climbs up and over small rocks and gets to a level spot, the shade deepening as the sun goes down.

I follow suit and turn around to look back the way we came. The resort stands tall to the left, and Tubbs Hill is straight across the lake.

"We've got about an hour and a half." Win walks toward a larger tree that casts deeper shade. Though the island is rocky and dry, the tree stands on a little patch of grass. "I think this used to be the backyard for a house, maybe?"

I point at a sprawling rose bush with white roses that nestles against the rocky wall built at the edge of the rise. "Seems like that might have been planted."

"It was probably the middle of nowhere until people built those big houses on the main shore. They'd be looking into your windows if there was a house here still."

He walks a little farther past the big tree with the little

lawn, and we are on the other edge of the island. "That's it, the island tour."

But there's a little splash of color in another patch of shade, just over the rise. I walk toward it as the breeze comes up and chills my skin.

"Oh, you didn't," I say.

"Oh, of course I did," Win says, laughing a little bit. "This is the date that shall never be topped."

The splash of color is a picnic blanket, blue plaid, spread out under the other big tree on the island. There's a little lawn, maybe the front yard to the other backyard, and a patch of concrete, remnants of the foundation for an outbuilding. Someone's swept off the concrete and drawn WK+VL on it.

The picnic blanket faces out on the lake, toward Tubbs Hill and the resort, its lights coming on now in the summer dusk.

"Hang on, I forgot something. Fiona and Phoebe will beat me within an inch of my life. Close your eyes."

I close my eyes and wait.

"Okay." He comes back to me. I can feel his shoulder next to mine.

I open my eyes. The picnic blanket is lined with twinkling lights. "Now *that* is pretty spectacular." I laugh.

"What? Why are you laughing? This is supposed to be pure romance!" Win smiles.

"The pool filled with pillows was fun. This is so pretty, but it's so not something you'd do."

He puts his hands up. "Which is why I employ the Fi squad to make everything just so. Duh!" He picks up the wicker picnic basket. "This is the only thing I had to contribute. They did all of the styling."

"Where'd you get that?"

"My mom. Duh!"

"You've definitely been hanging with the girls too much. 'Duh' isn't usually so prominent in your vocabulary."

"Come, sit next to me. Enjoy the Pinterest-ness of it all." He sits on the blanket and plunks the picnic basket next to him. I sit on the other side of it.

"I feel positively Insta. What's in here?"

Win smiles. "The girls were kind of appalled that I was already going to have fed you Mexican, so I don't know what they put in here."

I pull out our meal. "Air-popped popcorn." I unscrew the lid on a thermos, pull out two china tea cups.

Win smells the thermos. "I think peppermint tea?"

"And grapes." I pull the bunch from the basket, check for other goodies. "Not a cookie or brownie to be found."

Win sits back and pops a grape in his mouth. "The girls are watching our waistlines, maybe?"

"Or they can't cook or bake?"

We sit and watch the lights of Coeur d'Alene, listen to the call of birds, feed each other popcorn and drink tea with our pinkies out.

Win takes my hand, and we climb over the rocks to the edge of the water. He pulls me close, looks deep in my eyes, unblinking. His lips part, just barely, and I bite my lip, looking at his face.

"You're too much."

He leans closer, his eyes on my lips. "I thought I was lovely."

"Right now I find you flat-out gorgeous," I say, and kiss the tiny open spot between his lips. I run my fingers through his messy hair, and he kisses me back.

We stand there, Win and I, finding each other gorgeous, irresistible, and pretty much all around breathtaking, until Toby comes for us. It seems like just moments later, and I sigh as Win and I cozy up under a blanket for the boat ride home.

The boat pulls up even with the marina dock next to Jack's house. "Figured we'd drop off here before we get Jack's boat stowed." Win stands up and makes sure I get to the dock from the boat in one piece. He climbs up on the dock and pulls me close. "We better hustle home before you turn into a pumpkin." He looks over his shoulder at Toby. "I'll be back in a minute."

"Uh-huh." Toby's unimpressed.

We speed-walk to my house and are on the front sidewalk at 10:59.

"Here you are. I'm prompt if nothing else," Win murmurs.

I pull him close to me and kiss him, hard. "That was the best. You're amazing."

He looks over my shoulder at my front door. "I'll regret this, I bet," he says, and he kisses me again, his hands on my shoulder blades, pulling my body close to his.

"Time to come in, Viv." Mom's voice calls from the square of light at the front door. She hasn't even stepped outside to yell at me.

"Okay," I say. I look right in Win's eyes and kiss him one more time. "Nothing to regret here."

Then I sprint inside to face the consequences.

Mom closes the door behind me. I check my phone. 11:01.

"Well?" She looks at me.

"I had a great time. Thanks for asking. And Win was sure to get us back by eleven."

She crosses her arms over her chest. "Anything else?"

"No. Should there be?"

"You said you were having dinner with friends."

"I did. I had dinner with Win. And his mom and dad."

"You were partially honest. But you went somewhere else with him after? Alone? That seemed like a pretty intense goodbye."

"Mom, for crying out loud. You do realize I'm almost eighteen, yes? What happened? You were all over making sure I knew everything about being in charge of my body. You were all 'you're an empowered young woman'. Win is awesome. There's nothing to be afraid of here."

"Are you being safe?" She looks like there are tears in her eyes.

"Really? Okay, yes, I would be if we were doing anything, and also it's none of your business. You taught me well. I swear." I try to slow down and close my mouth before I say anything else. I want to be so mad at her, but I can't see that it's going to do anything but make things worse.

"I should ground you."

"Mom. Come on. Take a minute."

She sits down on the futon. "You still have to obey the rules."

"And here I am at curfew, just like you asked. Mom, I'm graduating. I've got good grades. I'm not into drugs.

I'm a virgin. I mean seriously, I should be really pissed off that you're giving me a hard time for anything. I'm practically, for all intents and purposes, a middle-aged widow. Possibly a nun, but I think they're wilder."

She smiles. Then she laughs, just a little, and she puts her face in her hands. "I just don't know how to handle this."

I see light at the end of the tunnel. "Come on, ask yourself what Marlin would do."

"Let you get kidnapped by a diver and taken to Sydney?"

"Let me go. And we need to get to someone and talk about the fear. I have to tell Win about why I've moved so much, Mom. I think he thinks Dad is chasing us."

"Your dad?"

"Please, talk to the counselor."

"We'll see."

I sit on the futon next to her. "I'm going to have some chamomile tea. You want any?"

She sits back as I get up to put the kettle on. "Am I the one who turned you into a little old lady?"

"Maybe."

She stands up and comes behind me as I get the tea out of the cupboard. "You look like you love him."

I turn around and give her a hug. "I think I do."

She squeezes me tight. "I'm glad. It terrifies me, but I'm happy for you."

I pull back and look her straight in the eyes. "Hang on to that, and don't let the fear overrun it. Make space for a positive outcome."

She nods. "I'll get my book. I'll read while you drink

your tea."

We spend the rest of the evening, until almost one in the morning, sitting together in our little living room, at peace. I wish I could take a picture of it and save it for when Mom can't see past the panic. The next attack could be right around the corner, waiting when the sun comes up.

I wake up the next morning and smell smoke in the air. It's been bone dry, and something has happened overnight—someone set a fire from fireworks, or a transformer blew and started a grass fire. I get up and throw on a shirt, sweatpants, and slippers, sneak outside to see if I can see smoke in the sky anywhere.

This is bad. Mom, she's hanging on, but just barely, trying so hard, and a natural cataclysm right now might upend the cart.

Out on our front lawn, I don't see anything. I walk toward the corner, where Bancroft meets 8th and I can't see any smoke over the lake. There's a haze, but the heat might be causing that, more than anything. I look up the street, in the direction of the library, and then I see it.

The fire danger sign in front of City Hall.

My brain bullets through a scenario before I even realize I'm walking down the street to the sign.

Mom will wake up this morning, ready to go to work, fresh off a night of worrying about me. She'll smell smoke in the air, see the faintest hint of a haze, and commence to worry. She'll get ready for work and leave—drive the car or worse yet, choose to walk to work—going right by the newly erected fire danger sign in front of City Hall.

Which I find myself standing in front of now.

The sign was put up in response to last year's mess of a fire season. There were sixteen fires on Tubbs Hill alone, and the local news made a huge deal out of the heightened awareness the community wanted to prevent a repeat. So they put up a sign just like the one out by the Interagency Fire Center Dispatch in Hayden, the one with Smokey standing on the brown background with a shovel in his hands, the one with the needle on the dial that swings from green (low) to red (extreme).

The needle points to halfway between orange (very high) and red.

"Seriously?" I say aloud.

Mom will see this, first thing this morning, and lose it. Graduation and all the other best-laid plans will come crumbling down.

Not if the sign's on blue.

I consider this. I can just move the needle. I'll put it on blue (moderate) and switch it back after she drives by. I'll tell her I'm out on a run, and I'll fix it.

"Can I help you?" A man in a blue City of Coeur d'Alene T-shirt and Carhartts stands in front of me.

"Umm." I'm not sure what to say. "How hard is it to change that needle?"

He doesn't even look fazed. He walks up to it, pulls a screwdriver out, and releases a screw holding the needle in place. He holds the screw up to me. "Pretty easy."

"Can you do me a huge favor?"

"What?" He looks less than thrilled.

"Is there any way you could change that for about fifteen minutes around 8:45 this morning? From orangeish-red to blue? Then put it back, of course."

"What?"

"It's a weird, long story." I laugh weakly. Win would appreciate my choice of words. "What's your name?"

"Russell." He pulls out his phone and looks down at it.

"Russell, I'd be really, really grateful."

He looks up. "I'm switching out the sprinklers right about then. This a one-time deal?"

"Yes. I promise."

The smoke just needs to clear, and the dust needs to settle from last night's fight, and it'll be all good.

"Fine." He puts the screw back in its place. "Have a good day."

I wish I could hug him, but he's already walking back into the building, and he's a really tough-looking guy, so I won't.

I head home and steal back into my room before I realize I'm still wearing my slippers.

Crisis averted, I slide back under the covers for a little more sleep.

Tsunami

Tsunami is a Japanese word formed from harbor and waves. Tsunamis are possible wherever a large body of water is found. Because of seismic and volcanic activity in the Pacific Ocean, tsunamis happen in that region most frequently.

On December 26, 2004, the world's largest and deadliest tsunami occurred as a result of a 9.1 magnitude earthquake in the Indian Ocean. The Indian Ocean did not have an early warning system, and the tsunami was ocean-wide—a tele-tsunami whose waves traveled across, in this instance, an entire ocean. More than 200,000 people were killed, almost 170,000 in Indonesia alone.

In 2011, a 9.0-magnitude earthquake and massive tsunami struck the northeastern coast of Japan. Despite an early-warning system, upwards of 18,000 people were killed. In some communities, three-story buildings where townspeople had gone to seek safety were destroyed. The tsunami waves also compromised the Fukushima nuclear power plant and caused meltdown and hydrogen explosions. Two hundred and fifty miles of the Japanese coastline dropped by two feet because of the earthquake and resulting tsunami.

Witnesses describe the tide rushing out to sea, beaches and bays emptied of their water, only to have the waves to come roaring back in, carrying debris and cars and black water, scouring trees from their roots and buildings off their foundations.

The most destructive tsunamis tend to occur near subduction zones. There is a seven-hundred-mile-long subduction zone just off the western coast of the United States.

The western coast of the United States is under the watch of NOAA's Pacific Tsunami Warning Center. The warning center certifies and prepares citizens living in tsunami evacuation zones. Communities on the West Coast can opt in to NOAA's Tsunami Ready program, designating evacuation routes and installing evacuation signs, preparing for responses to emergencies and mitigating risk. As of 2017, the program is voluntary, and not all western coastal communities of the United States have opted in.

CHAPTER ELEVEN
THE ART OF LOSING

With less than 48 hours until graduation, all that's left is practice and gown-fitting and senior slide shows and breakfasts. The long march to "adulthood" seems down to its last few staggering steps. Most of the senior class is sick of one another, and the few that aren't, are sickeningly sappy and saccharine about leaving the hallowed halls of Coeur d'Alene High.

I'm in a weird category. It's a good thing Fiona and Phoebe are sitting on either side of me for graduation, because the new trend has been to call out, "I've never even *seen* that girl before. She's graduating?!" at all the various senior functions I attend.

So I have that going for me—I'm the mysterious "Who's That Girl?" of the class of 2017, and not in a Madonna-movie way, either. It brings graduating from high school to a whole new level of Dante's *Inferno*.

But on the other hand, I'm trying to savor the time I have left with Win. He talks a good game, but there'll be visits with his mom to Reno, then freshman orientation, and then he'll be gone. So in that way, I do love this senior year, or mini-senior year, that I've been given.

Yes, I've also applied to UNR, but I haven't told my mom. We have a momentary truce. She's keeping a lid on her panic, and I'm working hard to make sure nothing throws her off her even keel. I have a hard time envisioning me moving to a different state without some kind of support from her. And I haven't heard back from the admissions office, anyway.

I wake up the morning of graduation ridiculously early, as though I need to get ready for school. But Mom's already in the shower when I wander out of my bedroom, and I wonder why. She was careful to ask for the whole day of graduation off as soon as we moved to town.

We don't have family coming to celebrate. We don't have family. But Mom wanted the day to be special.

The water shuts off, and she emerges from the bathroom a few minutes later, hair wrapped up in a towel.

"You're up and at 'em early," I say.

"I made an appointment with that counselor. Thought a big day like this might not be a bad time to prepare to be more mellow." She smiles as she rubs her hair with the towel, blond wisps fluffing with her efforts.

"Mom." I can't say anything more. I just give her a big hug.

"You off to run?" she asks.

I point at the little bag I've packed. "Housesitting for

Nomie and Jack for the next two days also. So going there, then a run, graduation practice, then home, then graduation."

"Big doings for sure. Big doings." She repeats it, and I notice she's worrying a little thread on the seam of the towel in her hair.

"All good stuff, Mom. It's all good," I say it clear and loud so she'll believe it, I hope.

My little bag in hand, I get to Jack's gargantuan place and let myself in. I disarm the silly alarm system (Jack said I could leave it off while I was there except at night, but that he'd have to set it when they left so Nomie wouldn't fret) and go set my bag down in the oversized kitchen. I grab a water bottle and my phone.

It's fun to pretend Jack's house is my house. It's big. It's really, awkwardly big. I wander for a minute, trying to find the guest bedroom Nomie showed me to when she was telling me all the ins and outs of housesitting. I pass two separate powder rooms before I stumble upon the correct guest room. Getting lost in my own house isn't a life goal for me.

My sleeping quarters sorted, I go out for a run.

On the street, the light is bright, and the air is already hot. It's been miserable and dry and much hotter than normal, or so says every native I run into in the store when small talk is in order.

And then I see the slim young man in the black suit with his arms full of roses again.

He stands for a minute in front of the big, white

Colonial house, just like last time. Like last time, I can't really tell if he just appeared here—maybe dropped off? Or if he arrived here and was given the roses, or if he emerged from the house.

It's Toby. It definitely is.

And so I have a dilemma. He's far enough down the street that I could go the other direction, go unnoticed, have a nice Graduation Day morning run, and be done with it—let the mystery of the roses delivered to the base of the angel statue live on as a mystery.

But I don't. I walk down to the postage-stamp beach and pretend to stretch my calves, limbering up for my run, and then I take off.

I think I know where he's going, so I run one block over from him the whole way, sometimes doubling back down the block when I get too far out in front of him.

When he turns on to Government Way, I know I'm right. He's walking to the cemetery again. I use my alternate entrance and book it to my hiding spot behind the enormous ponderosa pine and wait for him to come.

He does, and again he carefully lays the huge bouquets of white roses at the base of the statue.

I look at my phone, afraid to breathe. He's a little later to the cemetery than last time. I watch him walk off, down the white-shell driveway, back out to Government Way.

I sit down, worried for a minute. Did Franny die, and Toby knows it, and this is how he pays his respects? She's met some terrible, untimely death, and he just can't bring himself to tell Win?

Or maybe his mom and dad and Toby know that Franny is gone, but Toby is the only one who can publicly memorialize her, because the whole family is trying to protect Win? Maybe Win takes the anniversary of her disappearance and discovery even harder than he seems to, and this whole thing is an elaborate way to protect a brother who's too tender to be told the truth?

I sit and think about Occam's razor—the simplest explanation is usually the truth, the straightest line between two things. My thoughts are headed in a million different, complicated, tangled directions. These ideas are probably not the truth. I take in a few deep breaths of the pine around me and try to think.

It can't be more than a minute and a half before I hear a car turn into the cemetery.

I hear it because it's loud. The muffler—something is wrong with the muffler, because the car sputters and coughs, and it's really conspicuous.

I don't move from my hiding place.

The car stops. The engine's still running, but I hear the door swing open and then footsteps, running. Heels. A woman in high heels.

I risk a look around the tree trunk.

There's someone in a hoodie and very short jean shorts with the pockets hanging out below the hem, with little white ruffled socks and black Mary Jane high heels. I can see some long, dark hair and sunglasses, but the rest of her face is hidden by the hoodie.

She turns her back to me. She runs to the bouquets of roses, stoops down, scoops them up, and rushes back to her car—a little green hatchback, its hood worn down to the bare steel, all the paint rubbed away. I want to get a better look, but I chicken out. I pull my head back behind the tree.

The door slams, and the faulty car revs up and sputters off, back the way it came, back out the entrance of the cemetery.

"What are you doing here?"

Toby stands in front of me. He must've walked out and circled back around, sneaking up on me as I watched the girl pick up the roses.

"I followed you," I confess. "I saw you leave the roses once before, so I wanted to know what the story was. That was Franny, wasn't it?"

Toby turns and walks away. "Win might be all about you, but you're just a girl who has no idea about anything. Definitely no idea about my sister. You should stay out of it."

"I didn't mean to—"

"You definitely meant to. You followed me from our house."

"Your house?"

Toby laughs. "Oh, that's choice. Win never let you know where he lived?" He turns his back on me again. "Yeah, we live in the enormous white Colonial on Lakeshore."

He starts walking and doesn't stop until he's out of the cemetery, until I can't see him anymore.

I don't stand up. Not for a while.

Then I get up and walk back toward Lakeshore Drive.

I'm not mad, I don't think. As I walk back, I try to process. I feel scared. That's what I feel. Why wouldn't he just tell me where he lives? I try to remember what I said about the house when we first went on a walk down there.

I get more scared because maybe he thinks I'd use him if I knew.

I worry because he's kept something from me, and I've kept something from him. Our "like me" label extends to lying? We're like each other because of our tendency toward omission?

I get to his house. I open the gate to the huge front lawn, cross the wide expanse, and knock on the big black door.

It swings open. It's Win.

"Hi." I'm at a loss for words. Really.

"Hi. You want to come in?"

I shake my head. "I don't know."

"You want to walk on the beach?"

"Yes," I say.

He turns and calls over his shoulder. "I'm going on a walk with Vivi."

I hear Gerald call back. "Tell her hi from me and your mother."

He pulls the door shut. "My folks say hi."

We walk for a minute down the road, and then he takes me by the elbow. "We can cut through here." He crosses the street and pulls a key on a chain from his pocket. He unlocks the gate to the private lawn, the private beach.

"We called you lake hogs," I remember.

"Yeah."

"And I think you said the people who lived in your house must be weird or dysfunctional."

"Yeah. It's not untrue. I told you I was weird. Our story is definitely dysfunctional."

"Win." I look at him.

He locks the little gate behind us. "What?"

"Why didn't you tell me?"

"Why didn't you tell me you followed Toby? That you saw him leave the roses? He texted me."

"I don't know. Is that Franny who picks them up? What's that about?"

He walks over to the white pergola and sits on the stone wall in the little shade it provides. "I didn't want my house to be a big deal for you. I thought you might feel weird about it. I could tell you didn't have a ton of money."

"So? I'm not *Grapes of Wrath* poor. We get by fine."

"I get that now. But it was too late by the time I figured it out." He closes his eyes and takes a deep breath.

"I'm sorry I followed Toby. I just saw a guy with a huge armful of roses, and I was curious. At that point all I knew is that you had a tough patch this time of year."

"What do you mean, at that point?"

Now my throat tightens. "Today was the second time I followed him."

"What? Why didn't you ask me about it the first time?"

"I wasn't a hundred percent sure it was Toby."

He looks at me.

"Okay, I was pretty sure it was Toby, but why did I even follow him in the first place? It was a weird, dumb thing to do. I couldn't tell you about it."

"I wish you'd asked about it. I wish you hadn't followed him. Twice. Mom and Dad don't really know about the roses, so I'd appreciate it if you don't mention it to them."

I bite the inside of my cheek. I can feel my blood pounding in my ears. I've really done it. I can feel him putting distance between us. This is how it feels when you've broken a relationship, I'm sure of it.

"Why would I? I love you, Win. I told you that. I've never told anyone about the roses. Why would I say a word about your secret to someone else?" I focus on his face, and I notice little tiny gray dots appearing in the margins of my vision. I ignore them.

"When Franny went missing, and we thought someone had taken her, Toby and I went to the angel statue and left roses. Every Sunday. Toby always loved that statue, and Mom once told him it was a place where prayers were heard. Toby's a very private, closed-off person, so for him to do a big outward display of emotion was a big deal. Keeping vigil is a big thing for him."

"Isn't a cemetery kind of morbid?"

He sighs. "I think he and I both thought Franny was already gone. So when she turned back up, and then came to me and Toby for money, he insisted on leaving her cash in the roses at the statue. It hurt him badly that she was doing this thing to herself."

"Oh," I say.

My heart beats so hard I can feel it with my arms crossed over my chest.

"It's his bitter irony that he makes her pick up the money there."

"Is she still using?"

"Probably."

I sit down next to him. "I don't have a dad who wants to hurt us." It tumbles out.

He looks at me, surprised. "What?"

"There isn't someone we're running from. I should've cleared that up. I didn't ever really know my dad, and he was never abusive." I struggle to get a full breath.

Win stands up. "For two people who've said they love each other, we've got a lot we aren't honest about."

I don't know what to say. We stand in front of a huge palace of a house. It's his, apparently. And my lies, my lies are too much.

All of this just needs to be over and done with. I can feel my heart racing, and the edges of my vision continue to darken. I know a full-on panic attack is on its way, so I need to speak my piece and get out of here. I need to be real with him. I owe him that.

"My mom and I, we don't run from a person. I wish it were that straightforward. We run from natural disasters."

"Excuse me?"

I'm crying, but I can't hear myself cry, because the panic is crashing down around me. It feels as though I'm in a deep pool of black water, with a waterfall pounding down around me.

"What my mom is afraid of is nothing. She's afraid of the tsunami we can't predict, the earthquake that might happen. The ghost of natural disasters past that will probably happen again. That's all. No real thing. We're crazy, Win. That's why Dad didn't follow us. He's not chasing us. He doesn't want anything to do with us. Who would?"

The words trip over themselves, and I think I'm yelling. I gasp for air and force myself to focus on the tunnel of vision I still have.

We're not going to be together, Win and me. Even if he could see past the crazy, he's going off to school.

"I don't think I can do this. You deserve somebody better than this." I hear it come out of my mouth.

As things in my field of vision dwindle to a hazy gray, I can tell that Win puts his hands on top of his head, like he's winded, like maybe I've knocked the air out of him.

"You've got to be kidding me. C'mon, Vivi, you're not thinking clearly. Stop."

"Why are we doing this?" I feel like I'm going to faint.

"Because we love each other?" His voice sounds strained, and louder than before.

I take a step away, feel for the gravel path down to the lake's edge. "I have to go. I need to…"

I don't even say anything else, I just take huge, hurried steps down to the high water line, getting myself out of his sight and back to Jack's property before I fall apart. I don't faint, but I do throw up. I hide on a lawn chair behind the outdoor bar. I hear Win call for me for a little while, but I can't even get a breath to answer him if I wanted to. I wait for half an hour before I dare go inside. If I puked in Jack's gorgeous house it'd be the capper to the worst-timed panic attack ever.

When I finally can see straight, I pull my phone out and text my mom that I'm fine. I text the Fi twins to cover for me at the last graduation practice.

And I see that Win's texted me. *I wish you'd come back and talk to me. Where are you? Are you okay?*

I text him back. *I'm okay. I can't do this to you.*

You aren't doing anything to me. Vivi, please.

I feel the anxiety, the panic, start again as a numb

sensation in my toes and fingertips. I have to push it back down.

You deserve better. I'm sorry I wasn't honest from the start. I'm turning my phone off.

I turn it off and crawl into the guest bed to sleep.

Graduation sucks. I cry through the whole ceremony. Fiona and Phoebe think it's for all the normal rite-of-passage reasons. Mom's bewildered, at best, but also exhausted. Her therapy appointment went well, but it unearthed a lot of habits and fears she's been trying to ignore, and I can tell she's ready to take a nice nap and forget all of it for a while.

I just want to forget everything that happened this morning and start the day over. I could go on my run, ignore the boy with the enormous bouquets, and go get ready for graduation, where I would get to see my boyfriend because I hadn't screwed it all up.

This train of thought leads me back to Win, and I start crying again.

I can't even properly shake the hand of Trustee So and So as I cross the stage for my diploma. She has to kind of wedge my diploma into my hands between the wads of Kleenex I'm gripping for dear life.

Then Mom takes me to our house for some late-night ice cream before she drops me at Jack's.

"With everything today, I didn't even check the mail box." She grabs the mail and brings it inside as I scoop a lot of ice cream out.

"What's this?" She holds up an envelope for me to see.

It's from UNR. Of course it is.

"I applied to University of Nevada Reno."

"What?" Mom's voice sounds like the bottom of the ocean in Antarctica, it's so cold.

"Open it, Mom. I probably didn't even get in."

She slices it open, unfolds it, reads. She looks up at me. "You got in. You got an aid package, too."

"Huh." My stomach feels like a squished racquetball.

I can tell she's winding up. "When were you going to tell me about this?"

"Right about now, when I found out if I got in or not." I look down at the sizable bowl of ice cream that's beginning to melt into soup.

"Why Reno? What's in Reno?"

"Win's going to go there," I whisper. "He wants to be a storm chaser."

"What?" Mom says loudly. Really loudly.

"I wanted to go because of Win."

She's done. "Go to your room."

"I can't."

"What?" She remembers why. I have to housesit. "Fine. I'll drive you over, but you're grounded."

I think better of asking whether most graduating seniors would get grounded for getting into college with a sizable financial aid package.

The day is a colossal failure as it is, so why push it?

She drops me off at Jack's, and I celebrate my one and only high school graduation by crying myself to sleep.

Good times.

CHAPTER TWELVE
MADMEN

I know I'm dreaming because the leaves don't crunch. Everything is wet, damp, and the mist in the air makes my knuckles ache. My brain knows. It's different all right. The last time it rained in Coeur d'Alene was April 23rd.

It's a relief, the rain. And its patter on the leaves beside the window makes me feel safe. I stand on damp, dark earth, and I feel the wet first on the soles of my feet. I feel it there because there are holes on the bottoms of these black Puma socks.

I also feel the anxiety creep back into my chest. Holes in my socks remind me who else always has soles in his socks, and a cascade of worry flows down all around me. I try to fight and feel the rain again, but soon I wake and smell acrid smoke. There is no moisture anywhere. I am on dry, hot bedsheets, the window has blown open, and there is fire in our valley—snaking around our lake, tightening around our town like a fiery noose.

Someone last night must have thought graduation was a great time for fireworks, and lo and behold, they've started another grass fire. When I check breaking news on my phone, it's already been put out, but the wind off the lake smells of trouble and danger. I don't have the energy for this. And I can't change the sign. I promised Russell, after all. I know when to wave the white flag of surrender.

I make myself a cup of tea in Jack and Nomie's kitchen and take stock.

I cried a lot last night.

My mom is mad at me.

I've ruined all of it with Win.

On the plus side, I have actually finished high school and gained admittance to a college. But that's about it.

I pull on a T-shirt, brush my teeth, and go outside. I've destroyed pretty much everything, but the least I can do is make things right for Win. He's a good person, and I love him, and if I really do, I need to make sure he knows he's played no part in how I messed everything up between us.

I slip on sneakers and walk across the street to his house.

The door opens before I can knock. It's Meko.

"Hi, Mrs. Kemper. Is Win around?"

"Oh, baby, you look so sad. Come here." She pulls me into a big, warm hug. I feel the tears start, and I worry I won't be able to stop. I swallow hard.

"Thanks. I needed that." I manage to look at her.

"Let me get Win. Come in."

"It's okay."

She tilts her head. "That was an order, not an invitation. Ask Win's dad. I'm a very persuasive person."

I walk in behind her and stop in the vast foyer. I stand there as she disappears into the house.

Win comes in from a different direction. "Hi."

I just want to sit down and cry, honestly. Instead, I point to the front door. "Can we go walk?"

"Sure."

We step outside, and Win touches my elbow before I can say anything.

"I know where I want to go," he says. "Follow me."

I nod and we walk up 10th, in the shade of the trees, and past my house on Bancroft. Then we turn and stop in front of City Hall.

I swallow hard.

"So since we've got a lot of secrets we seem to have kept from one another, I thought it would be good if I shared two more with you."

"Okay." I steady my breaths. My hips and my shoulders hurt from trying to keep from falling apart.

"I saw you the Sunday before you came to school the first day, you know."

I try to remember that day. "Doing what?"

"You were unpacking that tiny, beat-up white car."

"Okay."

"And I saw you the day before yesterday, the day before graduation, standing right over there." He points. "Right over there in front of the fire sign. I was out early, checking on your house, getting the dogs a little exercise."

I feel my hands get shaky. I'm probably going to sweat and pass out, right here. Another attack can't happen.

"You were just standing, looking at the sign. But then a groundskeeper came out."

"Russell."

"Fine. Russell. The two of you talked for a while, and then later, when I came by as I was taking the dogs to the dog park, I saw him do something strange."

He knows. I still have to ask. "Yeah, what?"

"He changed the fire danger sign. To Moderate. Then that tiny, beat-up white car went by, he looked at his watch, and he changed it back to High."

I feel the water at the rim of my eyes. "Yeah."

He whistles, a little soft sound. "I know that's your mom's car. That white car's one of the reasons I decided on that Sunday I wasn't driving the rest of this year. I was taking the bus."

"What was the other reason?"

"I could tell I was gonna like you. You looked like someone who might need a friend. You looked like someone I'd like as a friend. Maybe you looked like you wore the same label."

"What is our label, anyway? Besides 'like me'."

His shoulders go up. "I don't know. We're fixers? Protectors?" He laughs. "Maybe it's just the holes in the socks and the spoon for a bracelet."

"You have a car?" I ask.

He looks at me, his lips pressed together for a second. "Smooch, my dad played in the NHL and owns a huge shipping company. You know what my house looks like now. Yes, I have a car."

"What kind?"

"It's a 2010 Nissan Sentra. Stay focused here. I didn't

want to pry about the fire sign. I figured you had your reasons. But I still don't fully understand your secret—yesterday you were so upset. I can't understand why you're pushing me away. Maybe it doesn't matter, but I thought I should tell you what else I knew, since we're trying to clear up a lot of secrets and misunderstandings."

I nod, looking at the ground. "I swear I've been trying to tell you this whole time, since I met you—really trying hard for the last two weeks especially, once I figured out you thought my dad was after us."

It's weird, you know? Shame is weird. It hits while I'm talking, hot and red at the back of my neck, and it flushes my cheeks from the jaw up. I wipe a tear with the back of my sleeve and exhale, the rush of air loud. I look up at him, which is brave for me. I look him right in the eye. But his eyes are soft, relaxed.

"But you don't have to hide it from me now," he says. "So maybe that's a help."

He says it so soft, so gently, the hot embarrassment sort of seeps away. I'm crying more now, and I wish I could just swallow it all down and stop shaking.

"Can I tell you a story?" I ask, hoping beyond hope that he really is here to listen, to understand.

"Sure." He puts his hands in his pockets. Maybe he's nervous, too?

"So, when I was in Issaquah, before we moved, I took Chinese."

He frowns. "What does this have to do with anything?"

"Please, Win." I sound about five years old, my voice pleading and squeaky.

He seems to soften. "Okay, Smooch."

I suck in a shaky breath, wipe my face again on my sleeve. "The instructor came from Beijing. He spoke very little English. He conducted the whole class in Chinese, pretty much, and I was not a good student of the language."

I take another breath. Win doesn't move or speak.

"We're taking the final exam, and I turn it in, and the teacher brings it back to me almost immediately. He points to a sentence I've written in characters, poorly, and asks, 'Is this right?'"

Win seems a little interested. "What was the sentence?"

"'Wo mama bing le.' It means 'my mother is sick.'"

I realize as I say it that this story resonates on a lot more levels than I was planning, and I hope Win doesn't notice that. I plunge ahead before he can turn and walk away.

"I say to him, 'Yes,' thinking I'm saying, 'That sentence is right; that sentence is correct.'"

"Uh-huh."

"He lets me leave class that day, and that night I find out I passed the test, which I was not expecting. But then…" I struggle to breathe, because I can tell I'm going to start crying really hard, but I go on. "Then I realized he'd used the Mandarin word for *true*, not *right*. He was asking if my mom was really sick, and I told him yes, she was. So he passed me instead of letting me flunk the class. I lied to him without even realizing it, and he took pity on me."

Win looks at me skeptically. "But you knew you didn't have an abusive dad, and you knew you'd let me think you had someone in Washington who wanted to hurt you."

I sit down on the ground, feeling the dust settle all over

my legs. I'll be filthy, but I don't care. I can't stand up anymore. It feels like everything is collapsing in on me, and I can't hold myself up, much less everything else.

"I know. I'm so sorry."

Win kneels next to me, so his dark eyes are level with mine. The intensity there is almost scary. He's usually so mellow; to see him fired up unsettles me.

"I would've fought him off for you," he says, his voice like granite. "I had a plan in case he came and tried to get in your house. I started walking the dogs by your house in the middle of the night, just to make sure you were safe."

I don't know where to go if Win won't forgive me. I take his hand. "I'm so sorry. I knew you'd be hurt. I knew your lie was so much smaller than mine."

He looks at the sky, stands up, and walks in a circle, hands on his head. "I didn't want you to give up on us just because my family has money and yours doesn't."

"I didn't want you to give up on me because my mom is crazy."

"Your mom isn't crazy. She's got anxiety." He takes a minute, walks another loop, thinking. "Do you want a little unsolicited observation?"

"Yes?" It really can't get any more honest, I don't think. I've tried to put it all out on the table for him. He always notices everything about me anyway.

"You strike me as kind of a satellite." A small crooked smile tugs at one corner of his mouth.

"Not sure where you're going with this."

"You've had a couple anxiety attacks since you've been here, but did you have more before?"

"I guess." I think back. "Yeah, I did."

"Your mom's fears, her anxiety, you spend time and energy reacting to it, preventing it, protecting her. You're caught in her orbit. You revolve around her, anticipating her reactions to things, trying to be a buffer for her."

I take that in. I take a deep breath, because he's right. I nod.

"What's helped here? Since you've lived here?"

I don't have to think about that. "Being with you. Getting some space from Mom. Being outside, just doing, not thinking."

"Be here now. I've been trying to do that since Franny." He looks at me. "I get it. I get your mom. I get why you're her satellite. There's no shame there. I wish you'd told me."

"I guess I'd rather have an abusive dad than a crazy mom."

"You know how seriously jacked up that is, right?" He puts a hand out to me. I take it, and he pulls me up.

"Lucky for me, my dad's not interested in being involved. Otherwise, boy, he'd be mad when he found out he'd been unjustly accused of being a wife beater."

Win hasn't let go of my hand. "I'm sorry. I'm sorry he's not around for you."

I keep my eyes on his hand. "He tried. I think he really did. But Mom exhausted him. The only thing I got from him was his last name.

He just never came around. He didn't want to leave a good job in California because Mom was afraid of earthquakes. He thought he could help her get past it."

"How long did he live with you and your mom?"

"We left California when I was eight months old."

BECK ANDERSON

"Have you seen him since?" he asks.

As I answer, the roof of my mouth tightens with tears. I swallow them back. "No. No, I haven't. But I don't even know him to miss him." I don't know where to put that feeling.

Win brings me to the bus stop bench, and he sits, motions for me to do the same. When I drop down next to him, he puts an arm around me.

"I'm sorry about that," he says. "Listen, we have stuff. You have your mom. I have my sister. What can we do but love them? We can only love them."

"I hate that Mom makes me move so much."

"I know. But you know what they say: 'a rolling Stone gathers no moss.'"

I want to kiss him for breaking the tension. I elbow him instead. "Not even funny."

"What about a tad ironic?"

"All right, I'll give you that."

He takes both of my hands. "You know what? When Toby came to me and asked about giving Franny the money, at first I was so mad. I was mad she left me. I was mad that she wasn't the sister I expected. I felt like I should be mad at her, wait for her to fix things. I held her responsible, too, for that terrible, terrible fake out, for all of my feelings—fearing the worst, thinking she was already gone, then feeling ashamed at the truth."

"Yeah." I wait for more, wondering if he's figured out how to get our families to fix the messes we've had to live in up to our eyeballs.

"Then I was walking one night, out on Sanders Beach, and for whatever reason, I asked myself what I was

242

supposed to do. Never mind what my mom, or my dad, or Toby, or Franny was supposed to do to fix things. What was *I* supposed to do?"

"What was it?"

"Love Franny. Love her, and forgive her. Don't be nice to her if I don't want to, and don't spend time with her if I don't want to, but forgive her. There's no reason to be mad at her. She's probably not ever going to fix it. If she miraculously does, then great, but I was waiting for her to apologize or fix it before I would forgive her. And all that did was make me furious."

I swallow hard. "So then?"

"So then, I just realized I still wanted to love her, even though nothing was like it was before, not even her. That sucks, and it makes me sad, and I keep remembering how it was when things were good, but I'm the person with the heart that I want to be big. I need to dig deep and love her. And it's not to teach her a lesson. It's to let me move on and not be so mad anymore. That's all. I push myself to love the parts of her that might still be the same, and to love her even though she's all messed up, and even though I know she's not going to fix any of it. Not even close."

"What does that feel like?" I look in his eyes, and I see them glisten with tears, but he looks up at the already-hot sky.

"It's a relief. It feels warm, and it feels like I'm loving someone in spite of their failings. And it's okay. I would want someone to love me that way if I messed up."

"My mom moved us because of the Northridge earthquake. Then she moved because of the tsunami in Japan. Then she freaked out about a mudslide that wasn't far from our house. Then there was an article in a magazine. And a FEMA exercise, and here we are moving again. And I'm not even counting all the little moves, from one house to the next, from a school on one side of town to the other, all in the name of keeping me safe."

Win looks down at the pavement. "How many moves total?"

"A dozen. I'm seventeen, Win. We've moved a dozen times. I've only been in school for thirteen years."

"Well, those moves made you who you are."

"I'm a neurotic basket case."

He touches my hand, turns it over, traces the thumb, where his name was written not long ago. "Those moves brought you to me."

"Win, c'mon."

"Stop."

"What?"

"Stop writing the ending to us. So I go away to school. So what?"

"So your life goes on without me. But speaking of school, I did get in." I feel a little smile on my lips.

"How's your mom feel about that?"

"I'm grounded."

"Figured as much. She wouldn't be mad if you had told her when you applied. But here's the thing. Don't go to UNR."

I'm wounded. "Okay."

He leans in, touches my face with a finger, traces right over the last wet tear to blob down my cheek. "Stop. Listen. Don't go to UNR because you're afraid we'll grow apart. That's acting out of fear. Some smart girl once told me she liked to presume positive intent."

"Make space for a positive outcome. I think I read it in a magazine somewhere."

"So, why don't you study something you like? Somewhere you want to be? I can find you anywhere, visit you anywhere."

"Huh."

"Just think about it. I know you hate how one person you know makes decisions out of fear."

I look at him, and it's just there, right there in front of me: I don't have to hang on to him the way my mom hangs on to me, because he'll come back. He will.

"Winchester Kemper, I swear you are the oldest soul I've ever known." I kiss him, and I think I can actually feel the Earth righting itself.

Which is a relief, because I was about to fall off the edge into the reaches of cold space.

CHAPTER THIRTEEN
NEVER CLOSER

Jack and Nomie are due back tonight, so I clear out and get the house all locked up tight. Win hangs out with me, and I take him to lunch at Hudson's with some of the money Jack left in an envelope for me. Nomie must've nagged him about not forgetting to pay for housesitting, because the front of the envelope has my name in gigantic red letters with two exclamation points, and I think the audience for those points was not me.

Then I decide it's time to go get ungrounded.

When we get to the house, I start to worry.

"This'll be good," Win says. "You have a plan; she's had a little time to process. No worries." He sounds like he's trying to convince us both.

"It'll be fine. See you later unless I'm grounded forever." I kiss him, and he pulls me into a hug.

"Only good things."

I walk up to the front door and go in.

Mom's standing in the front room, and she comes to me and gives me a hug. "I'm sorry. Before we even start, I need to get something for you."

I sit on the futon and worry.

"Stay right here, Vivi." Mom walks straight to her bedroom.

"Mom?" I cross my fingers. I really do. I've done it since I started going to third grade on the bus by myself. I'd cross my fingers, and that was the luck I needed to come home to a mom who was out of bed, smiling, and making macaroni and cheese with the cut-up hot dogs in it, which I would have eaten every day of my nine-year-old life if I could've swung it.

"Okay, come on in here." She doesn't sound mad. She doesn't sound anguished.

I walk into her bedroom. She's sitting on her air mattress with a big, gray, cloth-bound scrapbook on her lap.

"What's up?"

She pats the spot next to her. "I'll show you."

I sit, and she opens the scrapbook for a moment, closes it, runs a hand over the cover. "This isn't a gift. This is something I need to share with you, but then you're going to do me a favor and get rid of it."

I look at her. "Mom, I'm not going to UNR. It's all going to be fine. We can stay here."

She straightens her shoulders and sits up a little taller. "Vivi, you can go or not go to UNR. You should be so proud of your accomplishments." She sighs. "I'm embarrassed at my reaction. Honestly. You got into a good college, and I could only think of the worst-case scenario. Now that just seems ridiculous and heavy-handed. I blew up your graduation night. It was supposed to be good."

I don't mention the stuff I blew up with Win, my part in my crappy grad night disaster.

"So now what?" I ask.

"I think we talk about what you want to do next, and go from there. I like this counselor; I really do. There's work she and I can do. I'm taking as many sessions as she can schedule me for right now."

"I don't know yet—about what I want."

"You've got all summer. Take the time to hang out with Win and think about next steps. Take time."

"So I'm not grounded?"

"No, you're not." She hands me the scrapbook. "But now I really do need two things: first, we should definitely go find some ice cream to make up for the bowl that melted in the sink. Then, when you think the time is right, you to take that out of here. This is a big step in getting healthy for me, and I like the symbolism of you helping me to make the first move."

"Can I look at it?" It's heavy. I don't want to lift the cover now—I'm afraid it would upset her.

"Sure. It's part of my story. I think it's important that you understand more about me."

I think about the past, all the sudden relocations, how hard I've tried to understand for so long.

When I was little, Mom's moods, her protective streak, and especially the moves were mystifying. She would come to me, crying, eyes bloodshot, and suddenly I was packing up my favorite books and blankie, and we'd land somewhere different. As I got older, I started to track down little clues. She'd leave the TV in her bedroom on, all day and night, turned to a news or weather channel. That would be followed by the all-night vigils at my bedside, and, sometimes, we'd move. Or I'd hear about some nearby crime from a kid at school and lo and behold, Mom would be in pieces when I came home. She'd have heard about it and, in the course of a day, have plotted a move across town where I'd be "safe." When the tsunami in Indonesia struck, at Christmastime, I made the definite connection, figured out what was her worst trigger. The day after Christmas, Mom woke me up at dawn and drove me to her friend's house. Then she told me she had to go see a doctor. She stayed in the hospital overnight, but when she came home, she was just as unsettled and scared as before.

And here, in my hands, is the tangible record of all that worry and pain. "What's the counselor say about all of this?"

"It's kind of a relief to hear that other people feel things, react to things the way I do. She makes PTSD seem almost run-of-the-mill, as though it's normal to be so abnormal."

I feel a little protective of her. "You're not abnormal."

"Maybe a better way to say it is that she makes it seem okay to have issues. To struggle. Elise, she makes me feel like it's not an ugly secret."

I can't help but smile, because it feels like we've all been dragging around a boat-load of shame. Mom, me, even Win about his sister. What would things be like if we could all let go?

Maybe this will be our fresh start. For real this time.

I take the next week or so to look through the scrapbook. It's the greatest hits of a master of disaster. Newspaper clippings, articles printed from websites, and notes—longhand journal entries written carefully on quality stationery—detailing tsunamis, mudslides, avalanches, earthquakes.

It still feels private, and I only can take small doses. But each day, after I meet Win and we go hike or take the dogs to the dog park, or paddle board or swim, Mom and I sit on the front stoop or in the front room, and we try to process tiny bits of her story.

Jack might be right—the biggest piece of this might be that Mom has people to talk honestly with now.

Today I watch her pull weeds from the front flowerbed. The sun is hot, but it slants and casts a deep shadow from the roof on to the front yard. Tomorrow is the first day of June, and summer has settled in for the long, hot march to fall.

"Can I ask you about your job?" I broach the next subject like it's a tender bruise.

She sits up. "Teaching?"

"Yeah, being a PE teacher. Why'd you stop that?"

"I'll answer if you tell me more about Win wanting to be a storm chaser."

I wave a hand. "That's not really what he wants. I was kind of mad when I told you that. He wants to be an atmospheric scientist."

She looks up at the blue sky, stretches out her back from hunching over the weeds. "Interesting. Maybe less terrifying than tornado chaser."

"He likes fire science. Maybe just as terrifying?" I smile with all of my teeth, knowing it's probably not the greatest thing. "You first, though."

She pushes all the way back from her haunches and sits in the grass, legs criss-crossed. She sighs. "It was so fun. Kind of exhausting, too, like herding thirty-two nine-year-old cats, some days."

"Why'd you stop then?" I pick at the concrete of the stoop, a little afraid to look right at her. These daily talks are more honest than we've ever been with each other about her fear.

"Well, first the principal walked us through active shooter training. She brought in the police department, taught us about run, hide, fight."

"Oh."

"I didn't sleep for a couple days, but I dealt with it." She takes a deep breath. "And we'd always done earthquake drills. They weren't terrible."

"Yeah?"

"But then everyone started talking tsunamis, and the principal tossed around ideas for evacuation, and I couldn't focus. I was like a spooked animal."

"When was this? Where were we living?" I can't remember her teaching.

"When we first moved to Tacoma. You were too little to remember." She rolls her shoulders front and back. "I think that's all I can do for today." She stands up.

"Weeding or sharing?" I ask.

She chuckles. "Honestly? Probably both."

"You want to hear more about Win's stuff?"

"Also probably done with that for now. But these talks,

they're good, yes?" She brushes off her shorts, pulls her hands out of her gardening gloves.

I hug her. "Yeah, Mom. They're good." I go inside to make lemonade and thank whatever it was that brought us to this place, this honest place. It feels good.

CHAPTER FOURTEEN
ONE WILD & PRECIOUS LIFE

The first day of June, Win knocks on my front door. It's actually wide open, as I'd been sitting out on the front porch, reading. I like the honesty of the view straight into my life.

"Smooch?" he calls.

"I'm ready." I come from the bathroom, pulling a brush through my hair.

"You're still brushing your hair. No, you're not." He stands in the front room, impatient.

"No dogs?"

"Gerald took them to the beach to swim. He's convinced we're going to have a thunderstorm. Tacocat hates storms. They make him puke on the rug."

We get out the door on our way down to the Tubbs Hill trailhead.

"You should be more sympathetic," I tell him. "It's not easy being the dog of a weather lover."

Win takes my hand. It still thrills me, every single time. I can't even describe the electric charge that pinches my heart and squeezes me right between the shoulders.

I look up at the sky, and there are dark clouds building on the horizon, out across the lake.

"I know, I know, don't even say it," he murmurs sweetly.

"It's gonna rain. We shouldn't go on a hike when we know it's gonna rain." I weave my fingers, one in between each of his, let the charge tingle between each knuckle in my hand.

"You said it. Now it'll definitely rain. Way to go."

I drag my feet, tug on his hand. "Let's just go back. C'mon."

Now he's determined. I can see it in the sly side-eye grin he gives me. "Once around. It's quick. We'll stay to the low trail so we don't get zapped by lightning."

I reconsider the tingle I feel between our entwined hands. Maybe it's more than just our chemistry. Maybe it's the oncoming thunderstorm charging the air.

"I don't know about this."

He steps to me and looks me in the eye. "If *you* really want to go back."

I'm being dumb. I'm being my mother's daughter. "No, it's fine. But one rumble, and we book it back to the house."

Win smiles, leans in, and kisses the tip of my nose. "I promise."

We start down the low trail, and the pine needles and

leaves crunch under our feet. The trail is dusty, even in the shade, so out of character for the woods. I remember the dream I had of rain, and wish or wonder if the oncoming storm might be more than dry lightning.

The trail is quiet, and we make our way up a rise, climbing to the middle of the hill, before we can take the fork of the trail that dips down to the water on the far side. The breeze picks up a bit, and I enjoy the cool air. Win ambles next to me, letting go of my hand now and then to inspect a rock or a wildflower.

We chat about the summer. "Mom's still not a hundred percent in love with having my birthday party at your house. Your house intimidates her."

"You mean my mom intimidates her."

"Your mom scares me, sometimes. She's so perfect, and the nicest person, and she knows how to make sushi. But your house, Win, you know, it just..."

"Do we have to have this discussion again? You and I fit in our world. We don't have to fit into anyone else's. Let it go, and let's just hike."

I do, and the rain opens up—huge, fat droplets of water pelting my hair. I watch it drip from Win's bangs to his eyebrows, coat his gorgeous, brown face.

I look up and feel the rain all over my skin. Between the trees, the sky has turned from a faded-blue-jean blue to dark purple-black, and the dark clouds moved across the lake in only a moment.

The mother's daughter in me knows this is bad. But the pure me, the one who just wants to take things in, I can't help but marvel at all of this unleashing itself so quickly. Standing in the middle of it, nature fierce and raw, is kind of amazing. I can see why Win thinks of the Earth as a living creature, prowling under our feet and breathing down our necks.

Then there's a white light and a pop in the next breath, but I haven't taken a breath because what follows is chest-crushing thunder. A crack like an enormous, loud whip splits into a boom I feel inside my stomach. I drop to the ground, and Win is on top of me, his body covering mine.

I cry out, from the shock of it more than anything.

Win shouts above the wind, which is driving rain at us now. "Stay low! We might just have to find an outcropping and get under it!"

He pulls me up, and we plow off trail. Win knows Tubbs Hill well, and it's not huge. There'll be a place we can tuck under, wait out the storm.

I let one thought of my mom in. She's probably undone. Me, out in a thunderstorm, lightning so nearby.

The underbrush scratches at my calves, and Win pulls me down the slope. I keep my head down, eyes on the next places to put my feet, terrified I will trip and fall forward, pushing Win off his feet and getting both of us hurt.

We make it—after what feels like an hour, but was probably ten minutes—to a broad, flat spot, and Win scrambles around, sinking down the ledge past it. The rock juts out from the side of the hill, and sure enough, through the rain and the wind, Win's found us an overhang, a place we can slide in underneath and be safe, out of the rain.

It's not tall enough to even sit up straight. I can pull my feet up and rest my head on my knees, but if I forget and raise my head to look at Win, I'll hit it on the overhang.

He lies flat and pulls me closer as everything flashes white again with a huge, deafening crack-boom simultaneously.

I kiss him then, hard, with an open mouth, and let all the fear take over me. He kisses me back and holds me, lets me bury my face in his shoulder. Then I scream into the fabric, loud as I can, and it feels like the fear leaves.

I'm left with Win holding me, and the wind and the smell of the downpour, and the grime of wet dust, still loose and silty, on my arms.

Win looks at me. "It's better?"

I nod.

And that's when we smell smoke.

I've lived here not very long, but Win's lived here forever. When he looks at me, I know I've never seen the sparkle go out of his eyes this way.

"Viv, that's the forest. That's trees."

I know what he means. Tubbs Hill—the little thought bubble jutting out into the lake on three sides—it's on fire. Lightning has struck the top of the hill, above us somewhere, and it's on fire.

And no one but us would have been so dumb as to be out on the trails.

"We've got to go." He pushes me over on my side, so I can slide back out into the storm.

"Do you even know where we are?" I can't see the lake through the rain and dust and now, smoke.

"We go down, we'll hit the lake." He pulls me by the hand, and we resume our flight down the side of the hill.

I can't figure it out. Will we come out at the bottom of the hill and see the marina? Or will be on the far side of the hill, trapped with a fire on one side of us and the lake on the other?

"Fire boats. The city has boats." Win must be thinking what I'm thinking.

A fire boat will come to get us.

Another flash of light and crack, then a thunderous boom of lightning. I drop to my knees, slide down the slope into Win's back. I can feel something slice into my knee.

"That'll leave a mark."

I know Win can't hear me, but it makes me feel better to say it out loud.

I push up to standing and see I'm bleeding now, but the rain pours down, and the smoke is a thick blanket beginning to settle over us from up on the top of the hill. I reach a hand down to Win.

He takes it, and I pull him up.

I'm not afraid. I am focused in this moment, and there are things to be done, and I'm not afraid. I know exactly what's going on, and I know what I have to do. It seems a lot easier than the whole part where things *could* happen.

The *could* is the worst part. There are so many *coulds*. So many ways for bad things to befall me. That's what Mom was always so afraid of—the what-will-happens, the could-happens, the scary what-might-it-be-likes. And I'm tired, so tired of us being afraid.

I think back to Win in the lake when we paddle boarded and nothing bad happened. When I jumped from the cliff and didn't bash my head in. When we sat on the picnic blanket surrounded by twinkle lights and looked up into the universe and nothing bad happened.

And guess what? Now something bad has happened.

Pretty A+ spectacularly bad, as I see it. Win would agree, if we weren't busy trying to get down the hill as fast as we can. But it happened, it is happening, and the knowing means there are things I can do to react.

The waiting, the wondering, the fearing, that's definitely worse.

This is the worst-case scenario, right here. We're in it, and it's not great, but it is what it is. I think I might finally understand what that means, that thing Jack says. It is what it is—not good, not bad. The universe didn't decide to strike the top of Tubbs Hill right when we were hiking it. It just happened.

There isn't a what-if right now. There's an is. And we're dealing with it.

We're hauling down the hill as fast as we can, bloody and wet and dirty, holding hands and dealing with it.

I cough and choke on the smoke. It's a bit like standing in front of a camp fire when the wind changes and you get a nice, big mouthful of wood smoke. Except there's no stepping out of the way of the campfire.

But then, something does change. I can see in front of me. The wind must have shifted, and I can see blue water. But I can also see bright blue, the bright blue tops of the marina covers. And the glint of copper roof, Jack's house. And men, and fire engines.

We came out on the right side of the trail! We're on the right side of the fire, not stuck between the lake and the fire. We got past it.

Win pulls me to him just as my legs give way beneath me. The smoke, and maybe all the blood gushing down my leg, makes me light-headed, but it feels like the air is sweet and fresh and nine times softer and moister in my lungs.

"Hang in there, Vivi." He lifts me up, and I throw my arms around his neck, let him hold me. Then I reach down inside of me and gut it out, pushing through the smoke and dizziness and confusion.

A firefighter is upon us, and then it doesn't feel like I'm walking at all. He's on one side of me, and Win is on the other, and we charge past the marina, down the road, past Jack's house, and to an ambulance with its back doors swung wide.

A paramedic has me sit on the stiff white sheets of the gurney. She hands me a plastic oxygen mask. I pull Win down next to me, and we sit shoulder to shoulder. The firefighter throws a blanket over the two of us, across our backs, but I still feel a soft rain on my neck. It seems gentle now, not the relentless, wind-driven pounding from out on the trail. There hasn't been thunder again, and besides the squawk of walkie talkies on each firefighter's belt, it seems quieter. No wind.

I sit and breathe.

Win looks right at me. I can tell this is a panic-attack check. He scans my face. "You okay?"

I pull the oxygen mask away. "I'm good. Yes."

I think I might be right. I am good. I am okay, and I suspect I might be done with anxiety attacks. It feels like the what-if panic has blown away, pushed out by dealing in the moment with reality. Now that I've done it, it is what it is.

Cascadia Rising

The Cascadia Subduction Zone lies off the western coast of the United States and runs for 700 miles from Northern California to Vancouver, British Columbia.

A full-margin rupture of the subduction zone would result in a 9.2-magnitude earthquake along a 700-mile stretch of ocean floor. The following tsunami would roll in after approximately fifteen minutes.

In a Pulitzer Prize-winning article about the subduction zone in The New Yorker, author Kathryn Schulz quoted FEMA region director Kevin Murphy: "Our operating assumption is that everything west of Interstate 5 will be toast."

Scientists project the odds of a large-scale, high-magnitude earthquake and subsequent tsunami happening on the Cascadia Subduction Zone within the next fifty years to be roughly one in three.

In Japan, engineers have devised an early-warning and response system that activates when the first high-frequency seismic wave hits. It shuts down regional systems like bullet trains and kicks backup systems into place before the heavy shocks hit.

In Oregon, there is no system in place. There was no seismic building code until 1974. The region, Washington and Oregon, is just now beginning to consider the prevention, mitigation, and responses required to deal with a major natural catastrophe striking an area with six major cities and more than seven million people.

On June 7-10, 2016, more than forty-five federal, tribal, and state agencies participated in Cascadia Rising, an exercise to practice a whole community, coordinated, simulated response to the predicted disaster of a 9.0-magnitude earthquake and its resulting tsunami.

In January 2017, the Cascadia Rising 2016 After-Action Report, a multi-state, joint after-action report on the exercise, identified areas of need for the response to such a disaster. The forty-two-page report details the needs of the region: "a full rupture of the CSZ will result in impacts beyond the response capabilities of the region and will require resources from around the world to effectively respond and recover."

A full-margin rupture, according to the AAR, would result in significant loss of life. In examining preparedness across the region, the exercise revealed that several jurisdictions had no plans for catastrophic disasters and other plans were inadequate.

CHAPTER FIFTEEN
THIS IS JUST TO SAY

I see Mom coming toward me as I sit on the back bumper of the ambulance.

I'm not sure what anguish looks like, but her face, it's contorted in pain, in a whitewash of panic and heartbreak.

"But I'm here," I say out loud. I stand up and take off the oxygen mask, wave an arm out of the blanket around Win and me.

"What is it?" he asks.

I wave again and call out to Mom. "I'm here, Mom, I'm here," I say.

Win nods. He knows what this will be like, and he stands, clasps my hand for a moment, and ducks around the side of the ambulance.

Mom barrels in past two large firefighters, her arms outstretched. Her mouth is open in an O, but no sound comes out.

I step forward and hug her, hug her as tightly as I can. "I'm here. I'm safe. I'm here."

I think what I mean to say is *I'm alive. Your worst-case scenario didn't come true. I'm living proof.*

She stands and holds me, and her body begins to shake. Then the sobs come, and the crying finally surges out of her body, shuddering gasps.

"I know, I know." I try to think, find something stored somewhere in my head, retrieve anything I know about PTSD. What can I do? This isn't a panic attack. This is the after, the reaction. I don't know what we do to fix this.

A paramedic approaches. I hug Mom tightly, and I feel a surge of protectiveness. "She's just really upset. She worries about me a lot," I explain, not letting her go.

The paramedic, an older Hispanic man with a wide, kind face, nods and places a hand softly on Mom's back. "I know, it's so scary." He pats her back a bit and then gently touches her shoulder, leaning in closer to us. "Why don't you and your daughter sit next to each other, here?" He gestures to the ambulance, where I was sitting a minute ago.

Mom takes one step away from me, lets her grip on me loosen. "Yes."

He nods again, slowly, calmly. "That's good. You two sit here as long as you need. Let's put another blanket around both of you."

I marvel at him. This is pretty intense—to Mom, with PTSD, it must feel like everything is happening all over again. But she follows the paramedic's instructions and sits next to me as he drapes a blanket around us. Maybe the work with the counselor has helped.

The paramedic places a little tube of oxygen back under my nose, fitting the extensions into my nostrils. "This'll just give her a little fresh air, let her lungs get a nice boost. Isn't that a good idea?"

He looks at me for a fraction of a second, but he's tending to my mom, mostly.

"Is she hurt? Did she get hurt?" Mom asks in a trembling voice.

He points to my knee, the butterfly bandages tracing a line down the kneecap onto my upper shin. "Nothing a couple stitches won't fix."

Mom looks at my leg and begins to cry, shuddering silently this time. I hold her hand and worry as her shaking seems to get worse. I don't know if she can get herself under control.

The paramedic raises a gloved hand. "Ma'am, do you mind if I check your vitals? Lots of times in these situations we see a parent go into shock, and I sure wouldn't want anyone shock-y on my watch."

She nods, and he holds her hand in his, places two fingers of his other hand at her wrist.

"Can you look me in the eye, ma'am?" he asks.

Again, she silently nods and looks up at him. The tears don't stop streaming from her eyes, but she holds his gaze as he checks her pupils.

She trembles as he takes her hands in his. "Can you take a deep breath for me?"

She does as she's told.

He kneels down in front of both of us. "Here's what I think we should do, and I will let you ladies decide if it makes sense to you."

I feel my heart rev up. "Okay."

"Genevieve here needs stitches, and we'd like to keep her on oxygen for a little while longer, since she had a front-row seat to that overgrown campfire. What would you think if we took you both in the back of the ambulance to the hospital and took care of her? Your mom can ride along, hold your hand."

"Do I have to lie down on a gurney?" I ask. I don't want that. It might end my mom, to see me like that. And I don't want Win to see me like that either.

"Of course not. And I'll ride back here with both of you."

My mom takes a huge, deep breath, swallows hard. "I think that sounds good. I'd also like you to call my counselor, if you can. She could meet us at the hospital."

"Your counselor?"

"I have PTSD, anxiety. I think she could help." She unclenches her left hand and pulls a business card from the sleeve on the back of her phone.

"You know it. We can definitely do that."

I look at this man, this man who's helped my mom out of this spiral. "What's your name?"

"Alex." He smiles and boosts me up into the back of the ambulance, has me sit on the gurney.

"My mom's Samantha," I tell him.

"Well, Samantha and Genevieve, let's go get you taken care of." He gently helps my mom get situated, sitting next to me.

"Wait!" I cry out. "Win!"

Win comes to the door of the ambulance. "You okay?"

His dark eyes are wide.

"I'm okay. Stitches, you know. No biggie." I can't help it; when I see him, I smile. I grin just looking at his face, just relieved to see him, hear him.

He grins back. "Come find me when you're done. They said I could go home."

"Okay," I tell him.

"She'll see you soon," Alex calls as he closes the doors.

I sit back and take Mom's hand, and I hope everything will be as okay as it feels like it's going to be right now.

When we get to the hospital, I get the up and down from a PA, and then she disappears to find a kit to do stitches. There's a lot less waiting in the ER when you arrive by ambulance, I discover. I mentally wince at the bills we'll see because of that, but Alex has been worth the ride.

He chatted the whole time, soft and calm and even, kept Mom talking. She cried nonstop, tears streaming down her face, but she wasn't sobbing, and she stopped shaking. And though she held my hand the whole way, I could still feel my fingers at the end of the short ride, which is a good sign.

Alex comes into our room now with a large lady who has bright red hair.

"Someone's here to see you two." He shakes my mom's hand, gives me a wave. "I'll leave you to it. Good luck, Vivi, and heal that leg." I assure him I will, and he slips out the door.

Mom stands to welcome our new guest. "Elise, thank

you so much for coming."

"Of course, Samantha, of course." Elise strides across the room, almost as calming and assured as Alex, and she takes Mom into her arms and gives her a big hug.

I wasn't expecting that—not exactly. They've only had six appointments since graduation day, but I guess I shouldn't be surprised given all the progress Mom seems to have made.

Elise turns to me. "I'm so glad to see you, Genevieve, safe and okay. How are you feeling?"

I can hear the counselor check-in voice, but I don't mind it. It seems sincere. "I'm fine. It was pretty intense, but it sort of clears the head, to have to get out of the way of a wildfire." I know it sounds crazy, but that's what it was like.

She laughs, a light, gentle chuckle. "Nothing like an emergency to get your attention." She looks at Mom. I can tell she's assessed me and moved on. "She's going to have a bit of a wait before they get that leg stitched up. What do you say we go grab a Coke in the cafeteria?"

Mom frowns. "I don't know. Vivi's not ever had stitches before."

I wave at her. "They won't even get to me before you're back. You two go. If they do come in, I'll text you."

Mom gives me a tight squeeze. "I love you. I'll be right back."

I look her straight in the eyes. "You two go chat."

All three of us know what I'm talking about.

They leave. They're gone for a while, but true to form, the PA doesn't return.

Mom walks in just as the PA comes in, pulling a

rolling cart with sutures and needles and all sorts of unsavory things on it.

"Sorry for the wait. Ready to roll?" The PA smiles, and she raises her eyebrows as she looks at my knee. "I'm betting six stitches. You want to weigh in?"

I laugh. "You're the expert. I'm not betting against the house."

Mom looks petrified. "Can I have a word with my daughter before you start?" She smiles nervously.

The PA shrugs. "Of course. I'll step out and be back in two."

She leaves.

I shake my head. "Mom, I'll never see her again. You never ask for a minute in an ER. It'll be Christmas before she makes it back to see me."

"I need to talk with you, alone." Mom sits on the edge of the bed next to me.

I drop my head, defeated. Here comes a huge lecture, or a plan to move, or a panic-stricken vow to never let me see Win again. "Fine."

She looks at the ceiling. "Elise and I think it would be a good idea if I spend the weekend in the care facility where she works."

"What?"

"It's a safe place for people with PTSD and anxiety. It's a chance for me to have care and be in conversation with someone, someone who can walk me through this."

"I'm so sorry, Mom. I can stay home with you. I won't go out. I can stay in, and we can talk." I feel the wave of guilt pound in my ears.

She puts up a hand, her eyes filling with tears. "Oh,

honey, no. It's not a bad thing. This is a healthy, safe place for me to process. That's all. What happened, it terrifies me, and I won't talk more about it now so it doesn't all come right back to me, but it's not your fault that I have such a strong reaction to it. This has nothing to do with you. Elise and I both think a couple days to come down from the initial shock of the fire, some really intense individual therapy, maybe some yoga and meditation, and I'll be feeling solid."

I look her right in the eye. "You don't have to do this."

"No, I want to, Viv. I've been feeling so much better, *so* much, for the first time in I don't know how long. You know what it took to give you that scrapbook? That was huge. And I don't want to backslide. I can get through this, but I have to do something. I can't just hide in the house or run and hope that my shock at seeing you emerge from a wildfire will go away."

She gives me another huge hug, and we're quiet for a while. She kisses the top of my head.

I look at her. In her eyes, there really is calm. Their blue looks placid.

"You're sure?"

"Yes. I even texted your friends Nomie and Jack. They'll pick you up and take you to their house for the weekend. You'll be well attended."

I smile. When we checked in, I put their names down as our emergency contact. Back in Washington, I used to make people up when I filled out those forms in school. This time, I actually had someone. "Jack won't leave me alone. It might be worse than staying in the hospital."

The PA knocks and comes around the door. "Who said

you were staying? We stitch you up, and you're golden."

"I bet nine stitches. Loser has to buy the other a Grape Fanta from the machine I saw out in the lobby." I squeeze Mom's hand.

"Are you sure you're supposed to have pop?" Jack McCann comes waltzing in the room, Nomie apologizing to someone in the hall caught in his wake.

The PA looks around at the room, suddenly full. "You're popular. Let's get this done. I don't have room for all these friends of yours."

Who knew I would have an entourage.

CHAPTER SIXTEEN
NOTHING LIKE THE SUN

Jack is so loud. For the last twenty minutes of my brief hospital stay, he talks and talks, and I swear I'm prepared to check in to the Refuge with Mom, just to have some peace and quiet.

Nomie drags him out to the waiting room as they discharge me, so Mom can kiss me goodbye. She and Elise are driving straight from the hospital to the facility.

I've already looked it up online, and it just looks like a nice yellow bed and breakfast with a big porch and lots of ferns.

I ride in the back of the McCann's car, leg up and eyes closed. Nomie brought a velour blanket for me, and it could put me to sleep from the sheer coziness. But I eavesdrop, and I hear Jack explain to Nomie that he has people, you know, and knows the folks who run the Refuge, and he'll be damned if they send Vivi's mom one cotton-picking bill if he has anything to say about it, and boy, don't get him started about what they were trying to charge for an ambulance ride and eight puny stitches before he took care of it.

I keep my eyes shut tight, but I can feel tears slip out and down my cheeks. Jack, as loud and irritating as he is, just can't stop being a high school counselor, fixing things. In this case, a high school counselor with a lot of money, but my heart feels stuffed with the love and care of these people, and I don't even know what we did to stumble into this place, where Mom and I finally got lucky and got a fresh start.

"We're home," Nomie coos as Jack parks in the driveway.

Jack shadows me like a nervous hen. I'm not even limping, and when the doctor came in to listen to my lungs and sign off on my discharge, I was given a completely clean bill of health.

"What do you need?" Jack asks. He paces around the kitchen table. I'm sitting at the bar.

"I'm good."

"I can at least make you a sandwich." He picks up a loaf of bread, starts to dig through the fridge for cold cuts.

"I don't really want a sandwich." I look at the clock. It's not late, and mostly I just want to go to bed, but it's not even past seven. "Do you guys think it'd be okay for me to go see Win? I didn't really get to say goodbye before the ambulance hauled me off." My phone died while we were at the hospital, but he did say he was at home.

Nomie comes and gives me a little side hug. "Jack will

even walk you over, won't you, Jack?"

He shows me out the front door. "You women are so bossy. That's fine, but Gerald and Meko are out of town, and I'm no idiot. You'll come back to our house before it's too late."

"What would I get up to?" I ask him as we cross the road to the gigantic white house. "I just narrowly missed severe injury. You think that puts me in the mood for love?"

He rolls his eyes. "You're seventeen. The breeze changes direction and you're in the mood. Catastrophe doesn't stand a chance in the face of adolescent hormones."

"Blecch. I don't want you talking about my hormones, thank you very much. And I'll be home before midnight. I'm a high school graduate."

"Fine." He points to the open door. "Go ask lover boy Winnie about near-death experiences and if they've put a damper on—"

"Nope! Stop talking! No more!" I plug my ears before I'm scared straight.

"I'll take good care of her!" Win swings the door wide and pulls me in before he shuts the door in Jack's face.

We stand in the foyer for a long time, and Win holds me.

"I was—" he starts, but then the words don't come.

"Me too," I whisper. "My mom went to a place for people with PTSD. For a few days. She wants to get better."

"That's good, right?" he asks, stepping back to search my face.

"I think so. It's just different." I lean into him, inhale the smell of clean skin, of Win.

"But it's a good different. No more running, maybe." He rubs my back, in between the shoulder blades.

I look up at him, reach for his face and pull him to me, kissing him. He kisses me back, urgent and needy.

The intensity overwhelms me. I feel Win holding me up, and fatigue sweeps through me.

Win breaks the kiss. "Maybe you do need a sandwich." He laughs.

"What?" I ask lightly, but my head spins a bit.

"Jack. As you were walking over, he texted and said I needed to feed you a sandwich." He picks up his phone from the hall table. "Yeah, he's texted again and said you could still be in shock, and that I better keep my hands off of you."

"I'm fine." I thread my arms around him, but he turns me toward the kitchen.

"No, you and I aren't going to start the bad habit of blowing stuff off. A big thing happened to us today, and your mom is recovering, getting the help she needs. So let's take a cue from her and take care of each other. Starting with a sandwich."

He makes me a pretty epic sandwich. A Monte Cristo, which is decadent and destroys the kitchen.

"I'd always imagined pizza rolls. At my house," I tell him.

"What?" he asks, a smile on his lips.

"It was really important that you know all about me. You know, no more closed door, standing on the porch, hiding all our secrets. So I thought I'd invite you over and have pizza rolls. Like normal people do."

He smiles. "I don't know what normal is. I don't think it exists. And it definitely doesn't involve pizza rolls. Nobody should eat those."

"What? They're good." I can feel exhaustion settling into my eyes, my shoulders. My leg hurts, even though the gash wasn't that bad.

"You look tired." Win always notices. Everything.

"I want to see your room," I say between mouthfuls. He pours me a glass of milk.

"It's a room. And a guy's room." He looks up at the ceiling, as if trying to remember the state he left it in.

I get up from the kitchen table, taking the last of my sandwich and my milk with me. "We've got some long stories we still need to tell each other. Yes, we're in recovery mode, but seize the day and all, right?"

"Fine. The grand tour it is." He leads me up the stairs to the second floor, then climbs to the third.

"Wow, top floor." I can't get over this house. It's enormous. But I keep quiet. Win doesn't seem comfortable making a big deal out of it.

We come to his bedroom door. He swings it wide to reveal a long, open room with hardwood floors and high ceilings, the length of the opposite wall punctuated by floor-to-ceiling dormers. The windows give the room a spectacular view of the lake. The walls are a pale gray, and there's a gray area rug with a low, sleek modern bed and dresser. An architect's work table is in the corner, and a laptop perches on a long pine bench that's also stacked with books. The walls are clean, one picture of a rainy coastline, a couple of concert posters, and a cluster of framed pencil drawings of Tacocat and Racecar.

"So, this is my room."

"This is gorgeous. I would never leave." I turn to notice that the large bed faces the view. It crosses my mind that we're in his room. Near his bed. "Where's Toby?"

"He's in Vancouver for the weekend." He strolls to a window, and I watch as his hands go into his pockets.

Uh-oh. He's nervous. "What's wrong?"

"Smooch, I can tell you right now that I want to spend the rest of the night with you, here, in this room, in that bed. But I just don't think it's right."

I come over and wrap my arms around him. "Win. It's fine. That's not how I want it to happen, anyway."

"What do you mean?"

"You're right. We survived something very intense. It makes me want to throw myself at you. I want to lose myself in you. But I also want to be fully present. Be here. And I'm tired, and still shook up, and worried to death about Mom, who's acting all healthy and practical and taking care of herself, but I keep waiting for her to fall apart."

"I love you; you know that."

"Me, too. And I think you also know I want to be sure."

"About?"

"It doesn't have to be perfect timing, but this isn't even close. So just kiss me senseless."

"More than a smooch, I gather."

"Flatten me."

He turns to face me, takes my face in his hands, kisses me, and gently walks me backward, until my knees hit the bed. I sit and open my mouth to him as he sits close to me. His hand slips to my neck, and he pulls back to look into my eyes. "I love you."

"You take my breath away, Win Kemper. I love you." I kiss him.

And even though I want more, right now, this is all I need. He is enough.

At some point, wrapped in his arms, warm and safe, I must have fallen asleep.

I wake to him gently whistling.

"Hey, we need to go." His breath is soft on my cheek.

"I want to nap."

"That's what you were doing. Now it's almost midnight."

"We finally get a huge chunk of alone time, and I sleep through it? That's tragic."

"I think it's fair to say today was an extraordinary day, and anyone would be ready for a good, long nap."

I roll to my side and up on my elbow, looking in his eyes. "Can I ask you a question?"

"Sure."

"You said when we first met that you were rudderless. But you're so on it. You know your major, you had your college picked out before you were in grade school, as far as I can tell."

"When you say it like that, I sound so boring—"

"Don't change the subject. How is it that you feel you're lost? Without direction? That's not just something you said to match me, was it?"

He looks up at the ceiling, both hands tucked behind his head. "When Franny went missing, I spent so much time trying to anticipate what was coming. Then, after it was all over, the only thing that brought me joy was to be outside, under the sky, in the moment."

"So? There's nothing wrong with that. You saved me with that. Brought me to life." I kiss his fingers, one at a time, for emphasis.

"Well, if you get used to living in the moment—like, always in the moment... I guess I just have gotten out of the habit of thinking ahead. Sometimes I feel like I go where the wind blows me."

He moves a hand out from under his head and pulls me to him, so my head rests on his shoulder.

"Win, you're the wisest person I know. The wind isn't pushing you anywhere; it's whispering to you, hoping it can follow you to your next destination."

"That's a lovely thing to say." He kisses the tip of my nose. "Our next destination is Jack's, before he charges over here and wakes up the whole neighborhood in the process."

He kisses me again, and my hands move all over him, trying to feel every bit of tonight, memorize it down to the marrow of my bones. He finally sits up, stands up, and runs a hand through his messy hair. "Okay, we've got to go or my resolve about what a good idea it is to wait is going to dissolve into thin, midnight, parents-aren't-home air."

I stand up and try to reset, shaking my head for some clarity. "Okay. I'm going to go across the street, take a hot shower, and go to sleep for a thousand years."

He takes two steps to me and sweeps me into his arms

again, kisses me hard on the mouth, pulls my hair off my neck and gently kisses me there, too.

"Quick. I can feel it."

"What?" I nuzzle into him, grinning against his chest.

"Resolve…slipping…away." He takes my hand and looks up at the ceiling, groans, and takes a deep breath.

I straighten my shirt. "Does it look like I've been sleeping?"

He grins. "We just need to stop talking. Everything you say, you leave me a wide, wide-open opportunity to say something terrible."

We leave the scene of the almost-crime.

Next time, though, I don't care what we've just been through. No one has resolve that strong.

The next Monday, Mom makes me breakfast, gives me maybe the millionth hug since she picked me up at Jack's after her three days with Elise at the Refuge, and points to the scrapbook I've left on the kitchen table. I worry for a moment it'll trigger her again and curse myself that I forgot to put it away.

She doesn't seem upset, just curious. "Any ideas on how to dispense of that?"

I tuck the book under my arm. "Maybe I'll go catch up with Win."

"You should." She gets up and walks by me. "We'll get there, Vivi. You're already there, but I promise I'll get there, too."

I hug her and leave, pulling out my phone as I go.

When I open the door, Win stands outside with

Tacocat and Racecar. "We thought we'd come check on you."

"You are all amazing kinds of awesome. Come help me find a quiet place for me to show this to you."

We wander downtown to the pocket park on Sherman. It's already hot, but the sun's angle leaves a deep patch of shade against one of the old brick walls, and it's right next to the little fountain that keeps one corner of the park cool, even though it's tucked between two storefronts.

I open the scrapbook.

"This is my mom. This is why we moved." I push the book over to Win.

He looks through it for a long time. For some of it, I look over his shoulder, but after a while I close my eyes and listen to the trickle of the fountain, its slim stream of water splashing on little pebbles in the basin.

Win brushes my lips with his. "It's okay. I'm done."

I open my eyes. "Well?"

"Did you read through much of it?"

"Some of it. I asked Mom a few questions about it."

He leafs back through it. "Interesting that most of it is statistical analysis, really, and thorough research."

"Is this like what you keep in your notebooks?" I ask.

He shakes his head. "I write poetry."

"What?"

"My weather stuff, my nature stuff, it's poetry. A la 'Lines Above Tintern Abbey.' I love that poem."

"Really? I thought you said you wrote scientific observations." Now I want to see that notebook again.

"Who wants to hang out with a guy who writes nature poetry? I was trying to retain a shred of dignity."

BECK ANDERSON

I look again at my mom's scrapbook of things she fears the most. "Why? Why would she torture herself with a scrapbook? Or research something that terrifies her?"

"It feels like a human compulsion. Kind of like poking the bruise you got on your skateboard. Or maybe she hoped she'd become more immune if she immersed herself in it."

"I'm seventeen years of proof that was a bad idea: the satellite stuck in her mom's anxious, compulsive orbit."

"I have to say, maybe a tiny piece of it comes from the same place my love for atmospheric science comes from."

"Weirdness?" I tease.

Tacocat licks my ankle in support. He and Racecar have found a triangle of wet grass under the benches that are in deep shade, and they aren't interested in moving anytime soon.

"The delusion that we can assert some sort of control. By knowing something, we control it. Which we don't, but you know…" He lets the sentence trail off.

I know where this feeling comes from. "I remember watching her plan evacuation routes from the ice cream shop, the library. She always prepared for the worst, wherever we went."

"But you know what?" Win stands up. "I think I have a good analogy."

"Uh-oh. Okay. Hit me with it." I pretend to slump over, comatose.

"Smooch, you need to give me a little latitude. This is good stuff, I promise."

I sit closer to him and put an arm around his shoulder. "Fire at will."

"Someone asked me once about the cliff jumping. Why

take a chance? Why not just stay at home, inside, where I'm safe?"

"Was that someone my mom? Because it sounds suspiciously like her."

"Here's the thing." He points to the parking meter at the spot in front of us. Some guy in a straw fedora parks there while we're looking, struggling to get his Dodge Charger tucked in close to the curb.

"The thing." I prompt.

"So, when I come downtown, I need to feed the meter. If I don't, it expires."

"Yep."

"But I don't come downtown to stand next to the meter and watch it until the moment it expires so I can put change in it again. I come downtown to go shopping, maybe eat at the Iron Horse, maybe get a paddle in on City Beach."

"Yes, all things I can see you doing except for the shopping part."

"Life is just like that. I can't stand around and wait for the meter to run out so I can try to stall the inevitable. I need to go live, love my life, and if I come back and the meter's run out, well, that's how it goes."

"A ship is safe in harbor, but that's not what ships are for."

He rolls his eyes. "I like my complicated parking meter metaphor better."

"Then by all means, go with that." I kiss him.

I get up to go, but he stops me. "There's one last thing. Did you see this? Your mom wrote this and taped it on the last page for you."

I look at the cream-colored, folded stationery, curious.

"Guess I didn't get to the end like I thought."

He hands me a letter, and I sit back down, unfold it, and read:

My dearest,

I wasn't always the way I am today. There used to be whole days—days that were whole, not sliced up by panic and fear the way my days are now. I could go from waking to night and just live. Without a worrisome thought or a panicked moment—I could live my life. Now, if I'm not paralyzed, I'm driven to action, and fear is what compels me.

Although I want to try, it's probably impossible to explain this to you because you don't have kids yet. I don't want you to have kids yet. Of course not. But this all got particularly bad or out of control when you were born. And that's not to say it's your fault— it's not about you. This is all me, all my brain. But motherhood changes a person. It did me, at least. Maybe you won't understand until you're a mom yourself.

Honey, I'm from Derby, Kansas. Before I had you, before I met your dad, I lived in a place with wide, flat prairie and bright, blue sky.

And tornadoes.

When I was six years old, my mom left me with my nana and papa to play while she went and did laundry at the laundromat. Our washer wasn't working, and she took a Saturday afternoon to try to get us squared away.

That Saturday a tornado roared through my grandparents' backyard. I remember the sky going yellow and my ears popping. My nana was trying to crack the windows to equalize the pressure. I remember wanting to help, pushing on the glass of the window. The tornado sucked the plate of glass right out of the frame and sliced my hands. Nana grabbed me, my hands bleeding from the shards of glass, and we ran to the storm cellar. Papa was at the door to the cellar, waiting for us. When I looked over his shoulder, I saw the tops of the trees across the street twisted off like I'd twist a bottle cap off a Coke.

Papa got the door closed, and what sounded like a freight train rattled and pounded above us. Nana wrapped my hands in torn pieces of Papa's undershirt, and I remember the blood. I was terrified.

I will never forget that feeling. We all came out of it in one piece, but when I ran away to California, one of the things I thought about was getting away from tornadoes.

I didn't know my fear would follow me wherever I went.

The first earthquake I experienced in California sent me running. When Northridge shook the pictures off the walls in the first apartment I had with you and your father, I moved north.

I don't know exactly when it happened. Maybe it was right when I first heard you cry. Maybe it's when you made those tiny little O shapes with your mouth, while you were sleeping. But at some point very early on in your life, I was gripped with a level of terror I'd never felt before. In the middle of being a new mom, wrapped and coiled around the heart of joy, tightly wound around the best feeling in the entire world, was the worst. Suddenly I realized my baby could be gone. That I could drop you. That you could stop breathing. That life can inexplicably, in the moment between waking and sleeping, in the drowsy moment of eyelids blinking and closing, life can be death.

I thought, well, that's fine, just be vigilant. Keep an eye out for trouble. Meet it before it comes to take the one person in the entire world I can't live without. The one person I never knew would take over my entire body, occupy every pore of skin, every strand of hair, could fill me to bursting with joy and wonder. Imagining waking up without you, thinking of all the ways you could leave me—it was unbearable. Unless I was busy. When I was busy, it didn't feel so bad. And busy keeping you safe was the best busy of all. Near you, vigilant, but doing things to give me control. Child locks on all the cabinet doors. Foam on the corners of the coffee table. Gates at bottoms and tops of stairs. Toilet cleaner locked away. Blinds taken down, replaced by soft drapes with no strings. Choking hazards made my eyes water. I pictured grapes lodging in your throat, so I took Red Cross classes and learned the Heimlich. I stripped your crib of toys. I put you in complicated baby tents that would not suffocate you but kept you warm (but not too warm) while you slept.

I read every article, every Good Housekeeping

story about the mom who lost her child, checked off the boxes of disasters I could keep at bay, accidents I could fight off with preparation and safe homes and planning and foresight.

But then the tsunamis came. One far away, in a tropical land I couldn't imagine, and then closer, another one that caused tsunami sirens to wail here, one that devastated Japanese towns, towns that looked like places I lived. I hadn't prepared myself. I didn't know tsunamis would happen. They knocked the wind out of me.

I tried to be reasonable. I looked up the facts on USGS. A scientific, reasonable source. But when I read about the Cascadian Subduction Zone, I was done. There was no coming back from reading reasonable estimates that everything west of I-5 could be destroyed, perhaps in the next forty years. It happened in 1700. There were people in its path. The tsunami that traveled ten hours to Japan then made the recent Japanese devastation seem like child's play.

These were facts, reasonable facts, about terror I'd tried not to be able to conceive, not even imagine.

But my subconscious, it had a good idea what it might be like. The ocean began to rise up in my nightmares, slap the glass in the windows of second-story houses, come toward me, gray-green and massive, and I would be in the path of such power and horror. I would wake up with tears on my face, and I knew we had to move—away from such an unknowable, unpredictable terror. It felt real. It felt like I knew what it would be like, and it was devastating.

Nightmares aren't real. I kept telling myself that. But there were videos. People who had been swept away by the floodwaters in Japan. The waters came ceaselessly, above the sound of tsunami sirens, and people watched the wall bear down on them. Those people had lived my nightmares. I couldn't babyproof a tsunami zone or a fault line.

I tried to be normal. I tried to live and ignore it. But how could I, when all the information about the worst thing I could imagine was right there, right at my fingertips, provided by knowledgeable, reasonable scientists? I had to run away with you.

So I followed my own tsunami evacuation route, left the unsuspecting neighbors and friends we'd made, and moved inland, to higher ground. And I could feel the fear lodged above my belly button soften more each mile inland I drove.

When I was with your father, he tried to help me. We tried yoga. Meditation, running, swimming (take the fear out of the water). He brought me to a doctor. I was willing to take a pill, swallow the terror and the loss of control, until he told me I would have to talk about it, too. I couldn't talk about this. I tried to describe it to your dad, but he never really understood. He didn't feel the fear the same way I did, and after a while I stopped trying to explain. I needed to focus on what was most important.

See, Viv, the thing is, before—before you—I could manage the anxiety, because the worst that could happen was that I would die, and some nights, wrapped up in a blanket and wondering when the earthquake or tornado or tsunami would come, dying didn't seem so terrible. When the worst thing that could happen was I would die and all of it would be over. That didn't seem so awful.

But then you were born, and Vivi, I realized the worst thing that could ever happen to me would be to lose you. If you died. And the terror blossomed into a foul, night-blooming, pestilent flower. Once there was a small, helpless person involved, someone who depended on me to keep her safe, that's when this got really bad.

And I'm sorry for that. I don't know how to let go. I wish I did. But I don't know. I definitely promise to work through all of this with the counselor. I'm going to try talking again, because this time, someone really wants to listen. And I think Elise can help.

I want you to know that I love you so much, and I just look at you and thank God you are here and you are healthy. I thank God for you.

And then I start worrying about all the things that could take you away from me. Like I always do. It's messy and out-of-control, but that's my truth. Thank you for letting me share it with you.

I sit back, stunned.

Win stands and pulls me up from the bench. "Let's get rid of this thing."

"Yeah." But I fold the letter and put it in the back pocket of my shorts. I want to keep it.

Walking the dogs down Sherman, I rack my brain for an apt way to bury the literal object of Mom's fear.

"Maybe this means I've broken loose from her orbit, too," I think aloud.

"You're a pretty strong celestial body." Win smiles.

"No, that's terrible. That's more a terrible pick-up line than appropriate metaphor."

But it gives me an idea.

"Let's go this way." I take him toward the library.

"What are we going to do with it? Shelve it in the wrong Dewey Decimal section?" he asks.

"City Hall, Win. C'mon." I turn the corner and can't believe my luck.

Russell is down on the ground, up to his shoulder in a hole in the lawn, working on the sprinklers.

Win just looks at me.

"Um, Russell?" I ask. My voice sounds tiny.

He turns his head, his arm still in the hole. "Yeah?"

"You remember me?"

He sits up now, points at my feet. "You do own a pair of shoes." He wipes the sweat from his face and stands. His body is gigantic, tree-trunk-like.

Win whispers. "He's even bigger than Orion."

"Are you in charge of a chipper truck, by chance?" I smile wide, pleading.

He rolls his eyes. "You are the weirdest girl. This one time only?"

I hold up the scrapbook. "Just for this."

"And no more weird requests?" He checks his phone.

"I promise."

Win interjects. "If you're almost on lunch, we'd take

you to Hudson's in thanks."

Russell tilts his head, considering Win's offer. "Yeah. Give me twenty minutes to finish this. You'll have to leave the book with me—we're not chipping anything until next Wednesday."

"Happy to."

We run the dogs home to Win's, then come back to sit on the bus bench and wait for Russell to finish. When he does, we turn the scrapbook over to him, take him to Hudson's, and eat lunch with the city groundskeeper. Russell tells us about the dog-grooming business he runs on the side as he eats three burgers with a fried egg on each. And a Diet Coke.

As one does.

Win and I part ways at Bancroft, and I go home.

"Mom?" I call. The house is quiet. I need to try to break the habit of immediately worrying.

"Out back!" she yells.

I come out to find her attempting to hang a hammock between the hooks of a big green hammock stand. "Where'd that come from?"

"I found it at the thrift store. Consider it an early birthday present." She looks at my empty hands, no scrapbook in sight. "You got rid of it?"

"It took a few Hudson hamburgers and a chipper truck, but it's done."

I come grab the other end of the hammock, and we get it strung up on the hooks.

She sits on the hammock. "I'm not brave enough to lie

down in it yet. I don't trust my construction skills that much. Come sit."

I sit next to her, and we sway. It's nice, and she seems relaxed.

"I read the letter," I offer.

"Good. I was worried you wouldn't notice it." She keeps her eyes down.

"Win's the details guy. He found it and gave it to me to read. Can I ask you about one thing?"

She puts her arm around me. "Sure, honey."

"How come Dad didn't try to keep in touch? With me?" I struggle to keep my voice even. It's ancient history, really. No reason to get upset.

"He did try; he really did. When you were very little and he decided to stay in California, I was really angry with him. And he was mad that I wasn't trying harder to get well. I don't know, Vivi, but the whole process was long, and I think he just eventually lost track of us."

"Pretty lame excuse for not knowing your daughter, though."

"It's my fault for letting that happen," she says.

I lean back and let the sway of the hammock settle me. "Maybe I'll reach out."

"You should." She sits up. "I wonder if I can get out of this thing."

I push myself up and out of the hammock to offer her a hand. She takes it, and when she's standing, I hold on to her hand a moment longer. "The tornado. You still have scars from that?"

She pulls her hand from mine and turns it over. There, along the curve where her palm joins her thumb, is a silver scar. "Most of them healed a long time ago. That one's stubborn."

"Huh. Funny." I trace my heartline, touch the scar on hers.

She gives me a good, long hug, and I think about scars and worries and healing.

And I go to find Win.

CHAPTER SEVENTEEN
SONG OF MYSELF

"What is the point of these things?" Jack yells. "I can't see my hand in front of me. How am I supposed to see the eclipse?" He wears a pair of eclipse glasses, hands out to feel for the picnic table in front of him.

It's August 21st. Eclipse day. Jack is yelling. Natural phenomenon or no, he's still the center of the action.

Summer has been amazing. It was full of Win, of course. But I did get a job, though not at the library. I'm working part-time downtown at an insurance office, as an assistant—to the partner in charge of catastrophe modeling, of all things. I haven't told Mom that part. Probably won't. From the office windows we have a view of Tubbs Hill, and it's hard to see any evidence of the fire on the first of June.

Win and I thought about going out to Acapulco to get a good view of the eclipse, but Jack McCann would have none of it. We won't get eclipse totality here in Coeur d'Alene, but Jack made sure there was a plan for an epic party down by the Fort Sherman playground, and NIC is hosting Art in the Park. Full eclipse or no, today will be a good day.

Win is here, and that makes my day good. Classes start for him next Monday at UNR.

I've decided to stay in Coeur d'Alene and go to NIC. My favorite thing is art, and they have a great department, and I want to make myself happy, so that's what I'm doing.

I didn't get the same kind of aid package as UNR offered me, but Jack and Nomie have graciously offered to put me up at their house.

Because Mom? Mom's moved again. It's okay, though. She's stayed in counseling without fail since graduation, and she's making good gains—enough gains to move somewhere and get a PE job, teaching students with special needs. She's down in Boise, an eight-hour (seven if she's not in the car) drive from Coeur d'Alene.

And I will be on my own.

I'm excited. Win and I spent a huge chunk of the summer paddle boarding, and I'm learning to mountain bike, both things I want to keep doing on my own, until he can come back and visit.

Win taps me on the shoulder. "You're a million miles away."

"I'm going to miss you." I put my arms around him.

"You work this whole artist angle, get your muse on, and then come find me. I know where to find you in the meantime."

He gives me a meaningful smile just as Lulu walks up,

carrying a huge stack of eclipse glasses.

"Where'd you get those?" Win asks. "We all have ours."

Orion points over to the basketball courts. "She caught some guy gouging people for them."

"He's charging twenty bucks a pair! They were free on the internet." She's indignant.

"She told him I was going to bring the rest of my motorcycle gang down and pound him if he didn't let her pass them out for free." Orion looks proud and exasperated at the same time.

Lulu leans in and kisses him on the cheek, just for a nanosecond.

Win laughs. "Did I just see that?"

Orion shoots him a death stare.

"See what?" I say, winking at Lulu.

"Please don't." She frowns at me.

"Sorry." I take a step behind Win for protection.

"Lulu!" Win gives her a hug. "Take a break from being you for a second. I'm going to miss you."

She hugs him back. "Fine. Orion and I are going to go hand these out on the playground."

"There they go, the Robin Hoods of eclipse glasses," Win says.

"People! I have an important question." Jack approaches, beginning the conversation from ten paces too far away, as usual.

"Ask away." Win checks his phone. "We've still got some time before the big moment.

"Who said I was asking you, Winnie?"

I put an arm around Win. "Why do you get to call him

Winnie, anyway?"

A huge grin spreads over Jack's face. "Oh, you don't know?"

"No," I say, and Win covers my ears.

Jack points at him. "I'm his godfather. I named him. After my favorite deer rifle."

I wiggle out of Win's arms. "What? That's why you're Winchester?"

Jack smiles. "He still hasn't forgiven me, either."

"I swear, Jack, why Gerald thought he could trust you to pick a name for me, I'll never know." Win puts his arm around my waist.

I speak up. "You had a question for me, Jack?"

He turns around and yells, of course. "Nomie, you can come over!" I see his wife turn her head and nod to him.

He smiles and comes next to me. "Do you know if dogs have to wear the eclipse glasses too?"

Nomie steps through the crowd, a golden retriever puppy in her arms. "Jack's already spoiling her rotten." She hands me the puppy.

"Are you talking about Vivi or the dog?" Win asks.

"Are you kidding me?" I look at Jack and back at Win. "You got a dog?"

Jack shrugs. "I have a built-in dog walker and dog sitter. Why not?"

"What's her name?" I ask.

"Don't believe she has one," Jack says, and Nomie nods again.

I can't believe it. "Could I name her?"

Win's eyes narrow. "Yeah, she'll do a much better job."

Jack looks at his watch. "Eighteen years. You'd think he'd be done with the complaining." He looks at me. "Yes, you're welcome to name her."

Nomie rubs the puppy's ears. "Any ideas?"

I smile. I know exactly what I'm going to name her. "Kayak."

Win kisses me. "You are perfect, Smooch, you know that?"

Jack snorts. "You two." He puts on his eclipse glasses.

Win leans close, whispers in my ear. "I expect to hear about it if Jack drives you crazy."

"Of course."

"Okay, enough small talk." Win pops on the eclipse glasses.

I follow suit and look to the sky. "You know, this is exactly the kind of thing that should freak my mom out to no end."

"The sun's not going to go out," Win assures me.

"Eclipse glasses are an astronomer's answer to the mom's nag of 'You're too close to the TV—you'll go blind.'" I squeeze his hand, and we watch the moon cover the sun.

We stand quiet. The sky gets dark, and the birds still, nodding off in the trees, lulled to a mid-morning nap. The air cools, and I shiver.

"Look, look at the shadow of the tree," Win tells me.

I look down, and there, in the silhouette of each leaf, is a little crescent moon, thousands of them.

"Any little gap between leaves is a pinhole camera," Win whispers, as a hush has fallen over the park.

I close my eyes and let the quiet sink in. Then I feel

Win kiss me.

"Leave it to you to close your eyes during the only eclipse of our lifetime."

I put my arms around him. "We've got a long time together. I'll catch the next one." And I kiss him again.

Acknowledgments

Each time a book of mine is done (total miracle any of them get done, by the way), the village that supports me and cheers me on grows a little larger. Always first on the list is my husband, Marcus. I am so lucky and love being married to you.

And of course, to my sons, who are eternally patient and light up my life.

To all my family near and far, I love you.

To Jessica Royer Ocken, best editor ever. Thanks for shaping this beast.

To my school team (we rock) and my writing group (we also rock).

To Lindsey, thanks for making the inside of this so pretty.

To Caroline, you are a creative genius. My cover is gorgeous.

To Angie, thanks for being my PA—let's do it again!

To Angy and Midian, my favorite readers ever.

To Jennifer, Jennifer, and Nancee, you all are the best fellow authors a girl could have.

About the Author

Beck Anderson writes about love and its power to heal and grow people past their many imperfections. She is a firm believer in the phrase "mistakes are for learning" and uses it frequently to guide her in writing life and real life.

Beck writes novels and screenplays, works full-time as an educator, mothers two boys, loves her husband, and makes time to walk the foothills of Boise, Idaho, with her pup Stefano, the suavest Chihuahua north of the border.

Learn more at www.authorbeck.com

Also by Beck Anderson

The Jeweler
The Fix You Series
Fix You
Trouble Me
Use Somebody